CHRIST'S TRIUMPHANT APPEARANCE

Bruce Davidson

CHRIST'S TRIUMPHANT APPEARANCE

Copyright © 2022 Bruce Davidson

All rights reserved. No part of this book may be used or reproduced by any means (graphically, electronically or mechanically), including photocopying, recording, taping or by any information storage retrieval system without written permission of the publisher.

ISBN – 9798416131227

Library of Congress Control Number: 2022903020

Printed in the United States of America

First Edition (2022)

CHRIST'S TRIUMPHANT APPEARANCE

*This story is dedicated to the memory of
Jacqueline Bouvier Kennedy,
The most gracious lady who ever lived.*

THE DAVIDSON CENTER IN JERUSALEM, ISRAEL

Christ's Triumphant Appearance

TABLE OF CONTENTS
CHAPTERS TO THE STORY
"CHRIST'S TRIUMPHANT APPEARANCE"

Introduction	7
Chapter One Pray for the Peace of Jerusalem (Psalm 122:6)	12
Chapter Two For Whom the Bell Tolls	18
Chapter Three The Seventy Weeks of Years Prophecy	32
Chapter Four The Battle of Gog and Magog	59
Chapter Five I Would Be True	74
Chapter Six The Prophetic Path of No Return	114
Chapter Seven The Marriage of David and Bathsheba	132
Chapter Eight The False Messiah	140
Chapter Nine The Battle of Armageddon	157
Chapter Ten The President of The United States' Address to the Nations of the World	183

Christ's Triumphant Appearance

TABLE OF CONTENTS

Chapter Eleven Pray For Our Troops	192
Chapter Twelve I've Been to the Mountaintop	210
Chapter Thirteen The Restoration of The Throne of David	230
Chapter Fourteen The Ark of the Covenant Remains Significant	243
About The Author	247
The Star of David	249

INTRODUCTION

Song of Solomon 2:1
"I am the Rose of Sharon."
Bathsheba, The Queen of Israel

    War has plagued the Earth from the very time our planet plummeted into a fallen state. Mankind has adequately demonstrated that we have much more of a propensity for destruction and war rather than a longing for peace. The initial primitive weapons that man once employed have escalated into the modern-day nuclear weapons that we all wake up to every single day. The armament industry is the largest industry in the world. And the unmerciful effects of war have ravaged innocent men, women, and children for centuries. Wars, great and small, are still springing up all over the world in the name of religion and politics. None of the factors or elements of change, whether they be militarily, political, spiritual, industrial, philosophical, economic, demographic, or otherwise, can be excluded in considering the impetus of where we are today, compared with the past that has brought us to this place.

Christ's Triumphant Appearance

International Affairs today are raging out of control. Geneva Conventions (Conferences in Geneva, Switzerland), the United Nations, negotiations, diplomatic efforts, and all the various agreements are failing to bring about lasting peace. There appears to be no ultimate unity in our world, at least in the mind of an idealistic person. And the fact that there is no ultimate unity in the world more than implies and even confirms that there also exists no ultimate peace as well. The luxury of genuine peace appears to be somehow eluding us and slipping right through our fingers. And when it gets right down to it, in all reality, none of us see eye to eye with each other. Everyone seems to have their own perspective of life.

Crossfire, outright hatred, and madness have emerged from our varied religious communities. Jews, Muslims, and Christians have different and conflicting views concerning Jerusalem. While well-intending Jewish, Islam, and Christian society circles all around the world have attempted to bring about harmony, this desired hope of peace has not been achieved, and therefore, never really has been fully realized, understood, or appreciated in all of our lives. The turmoil and chaos continue.

We do not need any more wars that lead to yet more wars. War, as a last resort, should preserve and protect the sacredness of obtaining ultimate peace for all people concerned once and for all.

Seeking peace in a world that thrives on strife and disorder is equivalent to looking for a needle in a haystack. At the very least, where everlasting peace is concerned, we are not capable of seeing the forest for the trees. Lasting peace appears to be more and more evasive, elusive, and unattainable to mankind. And the sand flowing through the hourglass constantly serves to remind us that we are running out of time.

The Hebrew Bible (Tanakh; equivalent to the Old Testament) speaks (prophesies) of a day when peace will, ultimately, come to those who covet that sort of connection. It will be a day when genuine peace is so abundant that the end result will be freedom in its truest form.

"Christ's Triumphant Appearance" depicts the paradox and struggle between war and peace. Jerusalem, Israel is a city atypical of that paradox. Despite the many prayers that have been lifted to God throughout time for peace to come to Jerusalem, the truth of the matter is that more wars have been waged over the City of Jerusalem than any other city on our planet. There are very solid reasons why this fact is what it is.

Jerusalem has been and will always continue to be the center stage for all international affairs around the entire world.

Should everlasting peace come to stay in the City of Jerusalem, that is, the City of David, then, peace will, indeed, bring rest to all the nations around the world.

"The weapons of war must be abolished before they abolish us," the 35th President of the United States, John F. Kennedy, heeded.

To not have any solution to bring peace about will, ultimately, mean the annihilation and extinction of all of mankind. No chance of attaining peace is the exact same thing as having no hope. Yet the truth of the matter is: When war is no longer waged in Jerusalem, then, there will be no more wars ever waged again in the entire world. The moment when peace is secured in Jerusalem for good, everyone will be safe.

As conventional approaches to world peace by Presidents, Secretaries of State, Ambassadors and Heads of State have all miserably failed, perhaps, a closer inspection of biblical prophecy on the topic of achieving peace should be considered. The chief objective of mankind should be to bring unity among all the nations of the world. The end-result of world peace can only bring joy and freedom to the human race. This would allow us all to explore more constructive and creative pursuits, collectively and individually.

It should be noted that I am not a theologian, neither am I a scholar. And I, certainly, am not an expository preacher. I am a writer desiring to convey an uplifting story, and "Christ's Triumphant Appearance" is that story. It is a tale of hope. There have been many narratives told with a plot intended to promote peace for our world. This account is a rendering of how, based on a biblical foundation, world peace may be acquired. The Bible provides a very clear syllabus for this story. I merely filled in pertinent details based completely upon that outline.

Christ's Triumphant Appearance

And I should point out that all of the biblical references (verses) found in this innovation are derived from both the King James Version and the New King James Version of the Holy Bible. The reader needs to be aware that each and every Bible verse employed in this story is, intentionally, positioned where the verse is designed to be in the book, as opposed to being arranged in some sort of random or haphazard manner. And every single verse included in the narrative of this account, from the beginning to the end, speaks loud and clear for themselves. Hebrews 4:12 in the New Testament affirms that: "The Word of God is quick, and powerful, and sharper than any two-edged Sword." It would not be prudent to discount, discard, or discredit this reality. The impact and power of God's Word can either work for you, or it will work against you. Granted, there are parts of the book where I allow the Word of God to speak for itself.

It will be the manifestation of the Millennial Temple, built by the Israeli Messiah on the Temple Mount in Jerusalem, Israel, that will bring all wars in the world to a grinding halt forever. The very trademark of the Millennial Temple will, indeed, be everlasting peace. Selah. The Millennial Temple is the main theme of this story, and rightly so. Only the presence of the Millennial Temple will bring absolute rhyme and reason to our world.

It was Henry Kissinger, a former United States Secretary of State, who once said: "No foreign policy, no matter how ingenious, has any chance of success if it is born in the minds of a few and carried in the hearts of none." Congressman Jo Bonner, a very prominent, distinguished United States Congressman, took that concept a step further, when he stated: "While attaining a lasting, permanent peace in Israel has been elusive to many of our world's greatest minds, perhaps the best way to make this goal a reality is to speak more to the heart than to the head."

Jerusalem, Israel is crying out for everlasting peace, the very same kind of peace that we all crave to have deep in our souls and spirits, that is, a liberating peace. In regard to the eschatological significance of the Millennial Temple, the longing for the coveted peace that will inevitably accompany this particular Temple is the inescapable theme of "Christ's Triumphant Appearance."

Christ's Triumphant Appearance

There is a unique wonder to the Promised Land of Israel, and the City of Jerusalem embodies all the intrigue of the entire State of Israel. Once anyone has been to Jerusalem, they will never forget her beauty. The history, the culture, the timeless splendor of the marketplaces, watching the sun go down over the walls of Jerusalem, the Temple Mount, the Western Wall (the Wailing Wall), children of all different backgrounds playing in the schoolyards, people of various belief attempting to enhance their personal journeys in life. The beauty of Jerusalem, once you have embraced her Spirit, will never leave you. Jerusalem carries with her all the essence and meaning of Israel.

No one loved the City of David, Jerusalem, more than Jesus Christ. Jesus, in high drama, yearned for peace to abide in Jerusalem.

"O, Jerusalem! Jerusalem! The city that kills the prophets, and stones them who are sent unto you. How often I would have gathered your children together, even as a hen gathers her chickens under her wings, but you would not!" (Jesus Christ, Matthew 23:37)

The outcome of our future will vividly reveal, one way or the other, whether the world was fortunate enough to realize and grasp in time where the only genuine source of peace may be found.

Bruce Davidson

CHAPTER ONE

PRAY FOR THE PEACE OF JERUSALEM
PSALM 122:6

1020 B.C.

It was the early beginning of Israel as a nation. Much too soon to be concerned about the Restoration of the Throne of David, because the Throne of David had not even been established yet. But, one day, the drastic need for restoration would come.

David, the future second king of Israel, was too young at the time to be a warrior in the army of Israel, but that did not stop him from daring to defy the Philistine champion, Goliath. The Philistines had amassed their forces for war and assembled in Judah. Goliath came out of the Philistine camp. His height was nine-feet, nine-inches tall. And he challenged the army of Israel for forty days to send out one man to do battle with him in a win-all, lose-all fight. Every soldier in the army of Israel was absolutely terrified of Goliath. But David, who left the flock of sheep that was in his care, responded by saying, "Is there not a cause?" Just a brief time prior, Samuel, the Hebrew Prophet, had anointed David to succeed Saul as king of Israel.

Christ's Triumphant Appearance

And David was appalled and insulted by the giant Philistine's arrogance, as he mocked the God of Israel. David's indignation to the entire situation was only outdone by his brave reaction to it.

And David said to Saul, the first king of Israel, "Let no one lose heart on account of this Philistine. Your servant will go and fight him." So, Saul said to David, "Go, and the Lord be with you."

And as David approached the Philistine giant with his slingshot in hand as a weapon, Goliath said, "Come to me, and I will give your flesh unto the fowls of the air and to the beasts of the field." When David heard this threat, he did not hesitate to retort, "You come to me with a sword, and with a spear, and with a shield, but I come to you in the name of the Lord of hosts, the God of the armies of Israel, whom you have defied. This day the Lord will deliver you into my hand, that all the Earth may know that there is a God in Israel. And all this assembly shall know that the Lord does not save with the sword and spear. For the battle is the Lord's, and he will give you into our hands."

Then, Goliath arose to meet David. And David immediately advanced toward the giant and the Philistine Army. David put a stone in his slingshot.

Then, he did precisely twirl and sling it, only to hit Goliath right in the forehead, causing him to fall dead face first to the Earth.

So, David having prevailed over the giant Philistine, took Goliath's sword. And the men of Israel and Judah arose, shouting with the joy of victory, and pursued the army of the Philistines. In other words, it took the courage of a young, Jewish shepherd boy to wipe out the disgrace of the entire Israeli army. And from that very day on, David was anointed as an Israeli warrior.

When David and the army of Israel returned to Jerusalem after defeating Goliath and the Philistine army, the women came out from all the cities of Israel, singing and dancing with joy, and playing musical instruments. The women sang out loud, as they played, with the lyrics, "Saul has slain his thousands, and David his tens of thousands."

And Saul responded with tremendous anger in regard to David, saying to his confidants, "They have credited David with slaying tens of thousands in battle, but only credited me with thousands. What more could be left than for David to attain the kingdom of Israel?"

Saul had heard of an occasion when Samuel, the Israeli prophet, had anointed a young man to take his place as king of Israel. And after just witnessing David's performance in battle defeating Goliath, it was a very safe assumption that David was that very man he suspected. Saul became envious beyond control, and he kept an eye on David from that day forward. In fact, the very next day, Saul threw a javelin at David, with the full intent of killing him. But David behaved himself wisely in all his ways. David fled and escaped into the night. David refused to raise his hand against Saul, whom he considered to be "God's anointed king," despite the fact that Saul had completely lost favor with the God of Israel. The bottom line remained that David was a total threat to Saul's absolute power.

Now, Jonathan, King Saul's son, loved David as he loved his own soul. Jonathan assisted David in fleeing from the wrath of his father, the king. And Jonathan grieved for David's safety, and said to David, "Go in peace, forasmuch as we have both sworn in the name of the Lord, saying, 'The Lord be between you and myself, and between my descendants and your descendants forever.'" In other words, Jonathan made a Covenant with the House of David that throughout all generations, David and Jonathan's descendants would always be miraculously associated with each other, even up to a day in the future when David and Jonathan would be, literally, restored to each other in an era that would be referred to as "the last days." As a matter of fact, another acclaimed future Hebrew Prophet by the name of Zechariah would later confirm this Covenant and refer to the David and Jonathan of the end time as "the Two Anointed Ones, who stand by the Lord of the whole Earth." Zechariah would also refer to David and Jonathan as "the Two Olive Trees" and "the Two Olive Branches." And in the very same breath of the fourth chapter of the Book of Zechariah, referring to these two latter day heroes, Zechariah quotes the verse, "'Not by might, not by power, but by my Spirit,' says the Lord," directly in regard to the building of the Israeli Temple in a modern-day setting. According to pertinent prophecies of the Hebrew Bible, David and Jonathan will reappear in the theater of the last days. These two dynamic, charismatic champions are destined to be used mightily in conjunction with the combined power of Moses and Elijah, graphically foretold in the eleventh chapter of the Book of Revelation. The might and power of God's Spirit upon the Restored David and Jonathan of the last days will be availed to them for the express purpose of making it possible for the Millennial Temple to be built in the end time, just as much as King Solomon and Zerubbabel of the Hebrew Bible were chosen to clear the way for the building of the first and second Israeli Temples. The third Temple, that is, Solomon's Temple Rebuilt, will be built by the hands of men. Yet, as it is mentioned in Zechariah 6:12,13, the fourth Israeli Temple, the Millennial Temple, will be built by the Israeli Messiah alone. This event will secure eternal protection for Israel and everlasting peace to the entire world. This promise was given by the Lord to all our ancestors, who died waiting for the fulfillment of this event. And our ancestors, during the interval between dying with the hope of the Messiah's appearance to the day that the Millennial Temple finally stands, are being protected and cared for exclusively by the God of Israel. They will abide in Paradise (Abraham's bosom; Luke 16:22; Luke 23:42, 43; Revelation 2:7) until this wonderous development takes place.

Christ's Triumphant Appearance

1010 B.C.

And there came a day when King Saul died in battle at the hands of the Philistines, and all the Tribes and Elders of Israel came to David and anointed him king over Israel at the age of thirty. And David went on to conquer the Jebusites, who were the current inhabitants of Jerusalem at that time. So, David seized the City of Jerusalem for Israel's sake. David overcame the stronghold upon Zion, and Jerusalem became known as the City of David.

It would be at the beginning of his forty-year reign that King David would purchase a piece of land in Jerusalem on Mount Moriah, which would later be referred to as the Temple Mount. This was the very first decree of King David, that is, to see his vision of building a permanent abiding place on Earth for the God of Israel becoming a reality. After David bought the land, he built an altar there. He built this altar unto the Lord on the very same spot where Abraham, the father of the Jews, had once built an altar. David stood before the piece of land envisioning the Ark of the Covenant being carried into the newly built Temple by the priests of the Israeli Tribe of Levi. The Ark of the Covenant would, at last, have a final resting place. And the God of Israel would have an official place to meet with his people.

As King David was caught up in the rapturous moment of his thoughts in seeing his vision come to pass, with a heavy heart, he lifted up his voice to his God, and said, "Lord, remember David, and all his afflictions. How he swore unto the Lord and vowed unto the Mighty God of Jacob. Surely, I will not come into the comfort of my house, nor go up into my bed, or give sleep to my eyes, or slumber to my eyelids, until I have found a place for the Lord, a Habitation for the Mighty God of Israel." (Psalm 132:1-5)

And from that moment on, David perceived, with no doubt, that the Lord had established him king over Israel, and that the God of Israel had exalted his kingdom for the sake of the people of Israel, because God honored David's pledge and desire to build the Temple.

David had an understanding of both the short-range and long-range goals of the Israeli Temple. Even in regard to the last days, David knew that, afterward, the children of Israel would return, and seek the Lord, their God,

Christ's Triumphant Appearance

and also the end-time David, Israel's king in a modern future, as prophesied in Hosea 3:5. The David who was written of in the Hebrew Bible, where his life is graphically illustrated, was fully aware that Israel's ultimate salvation, protection, rest and peace would not come in that particular era depicted in the Scriptures (The Old Testament and The New Testament). He knew there would come a time in the distant future when people worldwide would fear the Lord and his goodness in the latter days. And in David's mind's eye, aside from all the advanced technology that would have developed by that eschatological period of time, he could vividly glimpse, discern, comprehend, and grasp exactly what kind of effect that shaping events would have upon the entire human race alive during those days.

About three centuries after King David's reign on Earth in the B.C. Period, an Israeli Prophet by the name of Jeremiah would come along to sum it all up best, when he penned the words of Jeremiah 23:20: "The anger of the Lord shall not return, until he has executed and until he has performed the thoughts of his heart. In the latter days, you shall consider it perfectly.

Christ's Triumphant Appearance

CHAPTER TWO

YAD VASHEM HOLOCAUST MUSEUM
ON MOUNT HERZI, THE MOUNT OF REMEMBRANCE
IN JERUSALEM, ISRAEL

FOR WHOM THE BELL TOLLS
John Donne

"Every man's death diminishes me, for I am involved in mankind. Therefore, send not for whom the bell tolls. It tolls for thee." (John Donne)

"And I will put my breath into you, and you shall live again. And I will place you in your own land." (The God of Israel; Ezekiel 37:14)

970 B.C.

Now, David of the Hebrew Bible was old and stricken in years. And the days of David were coming near that he should pass away. David admonished his son, Solomon, with his wife, Bathsheba, by his side, saying, "It is my time to go the way of all the Earth. Therefore, I want you to be strong, and show yourself to be a man. All my life, for Israel's sake, the Lord has designated me to be a man of war, conquering the enemies of our country. I have prepared with all my might to build the House that my God desires. I have invested out of my own abundance of gold and silver and given all that I have to ensure that the Temple of God, indeed, be built. The Lord's House must be so magnificent that the fame and glory of it will spread throughout the nations of the Earth. But I have shed much blood in protection of Israel and Jerusalem. And war has distracted me from my most important cause of building the Temple. The Lord told me, 'Behold, a son shall be born to you, who shall be a man of rest. And I will give him rest from all his enemies round about. For his name shall be Solomon, and I will give peace and quietness unto Israel in his days. He shall build a House for my name. And I will establish the throne of his kingdom over Israel forever, as there shall never fail a man to sit on the Throne of David.' So, now, my son, the Lord be with you, and prosper you, as you build the House of the Lord, your God, as he has said of you. Only the Lord can give you wisdom and understanding and give you authority concerning Israel. The Lord, your God, is with you and will give you rest on every side. And because the God of Israel has chosen to make me a man of war, he has given the inhabitants of the land into my hand. And the land is subdued before the Lord, and before his people. Now, set your heart and soul to seek the Lord your God. Arise, therefore, and build the Sanctuary to bring the Ark of the Covenant, and the holy vessels to be used for the Lord's service by the priests, into the House that is to be built to the name of the God of Israel."

And King David took his son, Solomon, by the hand, and with his last ounce of breath, prayed a heartfelt prayer, saying, "Blessed be the Lord God of Israel forever. Yours, O, Lord, is the greatness, and the power, and the glory, and the victory, and the majesty. For all that is in the Heaven and Earth is yours. The kingdom is yours, O, Lord, and we exalt you as head above all. Both riches and honor come from you, and you reign over all. In your hand is power and might. It is your hand that makes people great and gives strength to all. But who am I, and what is my people, that we should be blessed in such a glorious manner? For all things come from you, O, Lord. And of all these things you have given to us, we have chosen to give back to you. O, Lord, with all of this bounty that we have received from you, we have chosen to prepare to build you a House unto your name. Everything comes from your hand, and all belongs to you. O, Lord, God of Abraham, Isaac, and of Jacob, our fathers, keep this forever in the hearts of your people, Israel. And give unto Solomon, my dear son, a perfect heart to build the Temple for which I have made provision."

And when King David concluded his prayer, the eyes of David, Bathsheba, and Solomon were full of tears. David's wife, Bathsheba, also stricken in years, was crying uncontrollably. And the moment they shared together on the day David died spread like wildfire throughout the land of Israel, and the people all shared their sincere love and devotion for their departed king.

And so it was, after he had blessed Solomon, his son, to be king over Israel, David had gone the way of all flesh. David died at the age of seventy, after reigning as the king of Israel for forty years, full of days, with riches and honor. Then, Solomon reined in his father's place. Solomon sat on the throne as king. And the God of Israel magnified Solomon exceedingly in the sight of all Israel and bestowed upon him such royal majesty as had not been provided to any king before or after him in Israel.

959 B.C.

And it came to pass that King Solomon successfully finished the building of the Temple of the God of Israel in 959 B.C., sparing no expense. Of course, the glorious Temple was the crowning achievement of King Solomon's reign. The magnificent Sanctuary was referred to as Solomon's Temple, and rightly so. The Temple quickly became one of the great international astonishments of the world. Even the Queen of Sheba would develop an insatiable curiosity to meet Solomon, desire to learn of his wisdom, and have a yearning to visit the new Temple. King Solomon commanded all the gold and silver treasures, that were dedicated by his father, King David, to be brought into the newly built House of the Lord. Then, Solomon assembled the Elders of Israel, all the Heads of the Twelve Tribes of Israel, and the Chief of the Fathers of the Children of Israel, that they would bring the Ark of the Covenant into the Temple located in the City of David, Jerusalem, which is Zion. All the Elders of Israel came, and the priests took up the Ark. All the priests of the Tribe of Levi, the most important tribe in Israel, with the High Priest out in front, led the Ark of the Covenant into Solomon's Temple. And the Ark was carefully placed into the Most Holy Room of the Temple, the Holy of Holies. The wings of the Cherubim spread out over the Ark, with its contents inside, which included the golden pot containing Manna, Aaron's rod, and tablets of stone bearing the Ten Commandments received by Moses on Mount Sinai. When the priests came out of the Holy Place, a cloud filled the House of God. And because of the intensity of power radiating from the cloud, the priests were unable to minister. The Shekinah Glory of God had filled the Temple to such a degree that the ministers could not even stand up, due to the power displayed and dispersed by Yahweh, the Eternal One.

"Put the holy Ark of the Covenant in the House that Solomon, the son of David, king of Israel, did build." (The God of Israel; II Chronicles 35:3)

It was at that exact moment that King Solomon dedicated the Temple to God and blessed all the congregation of Israel and spoke, saying, "Lord, I have surely built you a House to dwell in, a settled place for you to abide in forever. Blessed be the Lord God of Israel, who spoke unto my father, David, saying, 'Since the day that I brought forth my people out of Egypt, I chose David to be over my people, Israel.' And it was in the heart of my father to build a House for the name of the Lord God of Israel. Nevertheless, the Lord told my father that it would be his son, Solomon, who would be designated to build the Temple in the name of the Lord. And today, the Lord has performed the word that he spoke. And the Lord has also elevated me to the level of my father, to sit upon the Throne of Israel, as the Lord promised. And, as of today, I have built a House to the glory of the name of the Lord God of Israel. And I have prepared a place for the Ark of the Covenant, which the Lord instructed our fathers to make, when he brought our people out of the wilderness, and into the land of Israel." Solomon stood before the altar of the Lord in the presence of all the congregation of Israel, and reached toward Heaven, saying, "Lord God of Israel, there is no God like you, in Heaven above, or on Earth beneath, who kept such a Covenant with your servant, David, in fulfilling your promise today in the sight of your people to build a House unto your name, that there should not fail a man to sit on the Throne of Israel. And now, O, God of Israel, let your word, I pray, be verified, which you have spoken unto David, my father. But will God, indeed, dwell on the Earth? Behold, the Heaven and Heaven of Heavens cannot contain you. How much less this House that I have built? Blessed be the Lord, who has given rest unto his people, Israel, according to all that he promised. There has not failed one word of all his good promise, which he has promised."

Christ's Triumphant Appearance

And, so, when King Solomon made an end of praying unto the Lord, he arose from kneeling before the altar. He stood before the congregation of Israel, and said with a loud voice, "The Lord, our God, be with us, as he was with our fathers. Let him not leave us, nor forsake us, that the Lord may incline our hearts unto him. And let the words I have spoken to the God of Israel today be well received by the Lord, our God, so that he may maintain the cause of his servant, Solomon, and the cause of his people, Israel, at all times, as the matter shall require. That all the people of Earth may know that the Lord God of Israel is God. And, that there is none other."

And the dedication continued with animal sacrifices being offered on the altar by the priests of the Israeli Tribe of Levi at the newly built Solomon's Temple in Jerusalem. The Coming Israeli Messiah will advocate and approve of sacrifices being offered after he has built the Millennial Temple in the latter days. Some may disagree that there will be sacrificing of animals in the Millennial Temple, but God sees all animal sacrificing as pointing to the ultimate sacrifice made by the Israeli Messiah. Tragically, Solomon's Temple was demolished by the Babylonians in 586 A.D.

The second Israeli Temple was destroyed by the Romans in 70 A.D. But the importance of animal sacrifices would be of no less significance when the Temple would be built on some unknown future date. The infringement of not being able to sacrifice animals, among other denied observances of Judaism related to a Temple-less reality since 70 A.D., has been a dilemma for the Israelis ever since the Temple was destroyed. This only left the Western Wall (Wailing Wall) intact, an extremely significant note.

In 586 B.C., Nebuchadnezzar, the king of Babylon, and his army carried the Jews into captivity, upon destroying Solomon's Temple and the City of Jerusalem, the single most fought over city in history. The hardship that the Babylonians inflicted upon the Jews was unbearable.

In 538 B.C., by way of a decree from Cyrus the Great, the current king of Persia, the Jews returned to the land of Israel from Babylonian exile. Then, in 445 B.C., in the twentieth year of his reign, King Artaxerxes of Persia issued an edit, commanding that the Israelis be allowed to rebuild Jerusalem. It is at this exact point in history, when the Jews began rebuilding Jerusalem, that the Seventy Weeks of Years Prophecy by the Prophet Daniel

Christ's Triumphant Appearance

begins in the Hebrew Bible (Daniel 9:24-27). This prophecy would prove to be one of the most pertinent of prophecies concerning the rejection of the Israeli Messiah. It is quite poetic that the Seventy Weeks of Years begins with the rebuilding of Jerusalem, Israel.

SOLOMON'S TEMPLE
959 B.C. {BUILT} TO 586 A.D. {DESTROYED}
THE SEVENTY WEEKS OF YEARS – DANIEL 9:24-27

THE SECOND ISRAELI TEMPLE BUILT BY ZERUBBABEL

Christ's Triumphant Appearance

"'In that day,' says the Lord of hosts, 'I will take you, O, Zerubbabel, my servant, and make you a signet. For I have chosen you.'" (Haggai 2:23)

Zerubbabel, a Governor of the Province of Judah and a descendant of David, was hand-picked by the God of Israel to build the second Temple.

The Seventy Weeks of Years, mentioned in Daniel 9:24, is equal to 490 years total, and broken down into THREE SEGMENTS OF TIME: SEGMENT 1) 49 years, equivalent to the 7 Weeks of Years of Daniel 9:25, to rebuild the City of Jerusalem, which is completed in 396 B.C. This rebuilding of Jerusalem had begun in 445 B.C. There had been a long delay before there were no hindrances to restore Jerusalem. SEGMENT 2) 434 years, equivalent to the 62 Weeks of Years of Daniel 9:26, marks the beginning of the very year when Jerusalem has successfully been restored and leading up to when the Israeli Messiah is "cut off," that is, rejected in 33 A.D. SEGMENT 3) This leaves 7 years remaining, equivalent to the 1 Week of Years reflected in Daniel 9:27, which is reserved and carried over to a time in the future, and has been earmarked for the Seven Year Tribulation. The main event that will identify the Seven Year Tribulation is the Abomination of Desolation (Daniel 9:27; Matthew 24:15, 16), that is, when the false messiah, in the last days, desecrates the Rebuilt Temple, which is the third Israeli Temple, and blasphemes the God of Israel.

In regard to the Seventy Weeks of Years concept, it is amazing how exact and precise that the calculations are, based on confirmed, documented historical dates It is also no less amazing how the three blocks of time are consecutively chronicled in the verses Daniel 9:25 for the 7 Weeks of Years (49 years), Daniel 9:26 for the 62 Weeks of Years (434 years), and Daniel 9:27 for the 1 Week of Years (7 years), totaling Seventy Weeks of Years (490 years). The last week of years represents the Seven Year Tribulation. And as a direct result of the Abomination of Desolation, the defiling of the God of Israel's Temple by an impostor with absolutely no conscience, a horrific transformation (metamorphosis) will follow, and the last days Israeli Temple, known as Solomon's Temple Rebuilt, will become dramatically reduced in status when it changes into the Tribulation Temple of the Seven Year Tribulation, where the epitome of evil rules and reigns.

Christ's Triumphant Appearance

31 A.D.

Jesus found it quite necessary to go through the city of Sychar in Samaria with his disciples, near to a parcel of ground that Jacob had given to his son, Joseph. Jesus came to Jacob's well, and being wearied from his journey, he sat on the well to rest. A woman from Samaria came to Jacob's well to draw water, and Jesus said unto the woman, "Give me to drink." And the woman responded by saying, "How is it that you, being a Jew, are asking for a drink of water from me, considering that I am a woman of Samaria? Because the Jews don't have anything to do with Samaritans." Jesus answered and said unto her, "If you knew the gift of God, and who it is that is asking you for a drink of water, you would ask of me, and I would have given you living water." (John 7:37, 38) The woman responded, "Sir, you have nothing to draw the water with, and the well is deep. Where do you have this living water? Are you greater than our father, Jacob, who gave us this well?" Jesus answered and said unto her, "Whosoever drinks of the water of this well shall thirst again. But whosoever drinks the water that I shall give him shall never thirst. The water that I shall give him shall be in him a well springing up into everlasting life." The woman's eyes lit up with anticipation, and she said, "Sir, give me this water, that I thirst not, and so that I will neither have a need to come here to draw water. I perceive that you are a prophet." And Jesus said unto her, "Woman, the hour is coming, and now is, when the true worshippers shall worship the Father in Spirit and in Truth. For the Father seeks such to worship him. God is a Spirit. And they that worship him must worship him in Spirit and in Truth."

And with a very inquisitive look on her face, the woman said to Jesus, "I know that the Messiah will come, who is called Christ. When he has come, he will tell us all things." Jesus responded by saying to her, "I, who speak unto thee, am he."

And upon Jesus saying this to her, the woman of Samaria dropped the pot that she used to carry water and went throughout all the city telling people that she had encountered Christ. Many of the Samaritans of that city came unto Jesus based on what the woman told them. And Jesus stayed with them for two days, and spoke with them, and they said to the woman, "We have heard for ourselves, and know that this is, indeed, the Christ, the Savior of the world." Afterwards, Jesus went to Galilee.

Christ's Triumphant Appearance

JESUS AND THE WOMAN AT JACOB'S WELL

JESUS CHRIST IN THE GARDEN OF GETHSEMANE
JOHN 17:1-26

Christ's Triumphant Appearance

"Father, I will that they also, whom you have given me, be with me where I am. That they may behold my glory, which you have given me. For you loved me before the foundation of the world." (Jesus Christ praying in the Garden of Gethsemane; John 17:24)

The Roman soldiers were totally brutal as they nailed Christ to the wooden cross and suspended him upright from the Earth between two malefactors, with a long row of convicted criminals also crucified on both sides. Jesus was falsely accused, and now, an innocent man was to suffer a horrible death, having been sentenced to capital punishment along with the worst of lawbreakers. The scene was terrifying. The Roman soldiers, guilty of crucifying Christ, were casting lots to win the seamless, purple robe of Jesus, which was worth a fortune.

It was nine o'clock in the morning. The undeserved evil inflicted upon Jesus that day was reflected in the pitch-black sky. Many women in the crowd beneath Christ's Cross, including Jesus' mother, Mary, and Mary Magdalene, were crying beyond repair. As the Hebrew prophet, Daniel, had predicted in Daniel 9:26, "The Messiah shall be cut off," designating the rejection of Jesus, the Israeli Messiah, with a sign above his head inscribed, "JESUS THE NAZARENE, THE KING OF THE JEWS." At one point, Jesus lifted his head, and said, "Father, forgive them for they know not what they do." Then, around three o'clock in the afternoon, after so much suffering, Jesus proclaimed, "It is finished. Father, into your hands I commend my spirit."

"And when Jesus had cried again with a loud voice and yielded his spirit, there was a great earthquake. And behold, the veil partitioning the Holy of Holies in the Temple tore in half from top to bottom, and the Earth shook. And the graves of many saints were opened, and they arose, and went into Jerusalem, appearing unto many people. When a Roman centurion close by, and many who were with him, saw that Jesus had taken his last breath, witnessed the intensity of the earthquake, and the entire ordeal, they were all in great fear, saying, 'Truly, this man was the Son of God.'"
(Matthew 27:50-54)

Christ's Triumphant Appearance

JOHN 15:13

MATTHEW 27:50-56　　　MARK 15:37-40

"TRULY THIS MAN WAS THE SON OF GOD."

Christ's Triumphant Appearance

JESUS AND MARY MAGDALENE

And when the Sabbath had passed after Jesus' death, Mary Magdalene was bringing some sweet spices to anoint Christ. It was early on a Sunday morning, at the rising of the sun. But when she arrived at Jesus' sepulcher, the stone had been rolled away from the door. And Mary stood outside the door of the sepulcher weeping. And as she sobbed, she saw two angels in white, one stationed where Jesus' head had laid, and the other guarded where Jesus' feet had been positioned. And the angels asked her, "Woman, why do you weep?" Mary answered, "Because they have taken away my Lord, and I do not know where to find him." And Mary turned around and saw Jesus standing there. But she did not recognize him at first due to all the tears in her eyes. Jesus asked Mary, "Woman, why do you weep? Whom do you seek?" And Mary said, "Please tell me where they have taken my Lord!"

Jesus replied, "Mary!" And Mary said unto Jesus, with fire in her eyes, "Master!"

Christ's Triumphant Appearance

70 A.D.

The siege of Jerusalem by the Romans, during the Great Jewish Revolt, resulted in the destruction of the second Temple that had been built under the leadership of Zerubbabel. The Roman army, led by the future Emperor Titus, with Tiberius Julius Alexander as his second-in-command, besieged and conquered the City of Jerusalem. 1.1 million civilians died in Jerusalem as a result of the violence and famine. Many of the casualties were observant Jews from around the world who had travelled to Jerusalem to celebrate the Jewish holiday, Passover. The siege lasted for four months, ending with Jerusalem utterly annihilated, and the Second Temple being burned to the ground, with the exception of the Western Wall.

THE DESTRUCTION OF THE SECOND TEMPLE
IN 70 A.D.

"And Jesus went out of the Temple, that is, the second Israeli Temple, and one of His followers said to Him, 'Master, see what manner of stones and what buildings are here!' And Jesus responded and said to him, 'See these great buildings here? There shall not be left one stone upon another, that shall not be thrown down.'" (Jesus, speaking eschatologically, was referring to Solomon's Temple Rebuilt, that is, the Tribulation Temple of the Seven Year Tribulation, being absolutely wiped out. When the second Temple was destroyed by the Romans in 70 A.D., the Western Wall continued to stand, clearly indicating that every stone of the Temple had not

Christ's Triumphant Appearance

been thrown down, contradicting Jesus' prophecy. Jesus was referring to every stone of the futuristic Tribulation Temple being thrown down). And Jesus sat upon the Mount of Olives opposite the Temple, and said, 'Take heed lest any man deceive you. For many shall come in my name, saying, 'I am Christ.' Nation shall rise against nation, and kingdom against kingdom. And there shall be earthquakes in various places, and there shall be famines and troubles. These are the beginnings of sorrows. For they shall deliver you up to councils. And in the synagogues, you shall be beaten. You shall be brought before rulers and kings for my sake, and for a testimony against them. But when they shall lead you, and deliver you up, take no thought beforehand what you shall speak, neither premeditate. But whatsoever shall be given to you in that hour, that shall you speak. For it is not you that speak, but the Holy Spirit. Now, in that day, the brother shall betray the brother to death, and the father the son. And children shall rise up against their parents and shall cause them to be put to death. A man's foes shall be they of his own household. And you shall be hated of all men for my name's sake. And when you shall see the Abomination of Desolation, spoken of by Daniel, the Prophet, then, let them that are in Judaea flee to the mountains. For in those days there shall be affliction, such as what was not from the beginning of the Creation, which God created unto this time. And except the Lord shorten those days, no one shall be saved. Take heed. Behold, I have foretold you all things. For, in those days, immediately after that Tribulation, the sun shall be darkened, and the moon shall not give her light. And the stars of Heaven shall fall, and the powers that are in Heaven shall be shaken. AND THEN, THEY SHALL SEE THE SON OF GOD COMING IN THE CLOUDS WITH GREAT POWER AND GLORY. And then, he shall send his angels and shall gather together his elect from the four winds, from the uttermost part of the Earth to the uttermost part of Heaven, which is the First Resurrection ... BUT OF THAT DAY AND THAT HOUR NO MAN KNOWS. NO, NOT EVEN THE ANGELS IN HEAVEN, BUT MY FATHER ONLY. The Day of the Lord shall come like a thief in the night, in which the Heavens shall pass away with a great noise, and the elements shall melt with fervent heat (as a nuclear blast). The Earth also and the works therein shall be burned up (making way for a new Heaven and a new Earth). Blessed and holy is the person who has part in the First Resurrection.'" (Jesus Christ, the Israeli Messiah; Matthew 10:36; Mark 13:1-3, 5, 6, 8, 9, 11-14, 19, 20, 23-27; II Peter 3:10; Revelation 20:6)

CHAPTER THREE
THE SEVENTY WEEKS OF YEARS PROPHECY

"And while I was praying, the archangel, Gabriel, whom I had seen in a vision at the beginning, flew swiftly in my direction to touch me. And he informed me and talked with me, saying, 'O, Daniel, I have now come to give you skill and understanding. You are greatly beloved. Therefore, understand the matter and consider the vision.'" (Daniel 9:21-23)

Of all the prophesies predicting Christ's initial mission on Earth, the Seventy Weeks of Years prophecy is the most complex. And Jesus fulfilled this prophecy in top form.

The first Israeli Temple (Solomon's Temple) was built in the 10th century B.C. in 959 B.C. The destruction of Solomon's Temple (the original earthly Temple) and Jerusalem came at the hand of Nebuchadnezzar, the king of

Babylon, and his army, WITH THE ARK OF THE COVENANT DISAPPEARING FROM HISTORY AT THIS VERY POINT. The Jews, in turn, were led away from their homeland, being carried into captivity (exiled; uprooted from Israel) by the Babylonians. In 538 B.C., Cyrus the Great's edit set the Jews free. The Persian king had conquered the Babylonians one year prior, which opened the door for the God of Israeli's people to return home.

The Lord God of Israel has used Daniel, the Hebrew Prophet, to reveal the mysteries of Jeremiah's prophesy of the 70 years (Seventy Weeks of Years; Jeremiah 25:12, 13; Jeremiah 29:10, 11; Daniel 9:24-27), as Daniel and Jeremiah were contemporaries.

The archangel, Gabriel, spoke to Daniel, the Prophet, when he made the record of the 70 Weeks of Years in the Book of Daniel (Daniel 8:15-26; Daniel 9:16, 17; Daniel 9:16-27). Gabriel said that this prophetic clock of the Seventy Weeks of Years would start at the exact time when the Jews would begin the rebuilding of Jerusalem, after they returned from exile in Babylon.

"O, Lord, according to all your righteousness, I beg of you, let your anger and your fury be turned away from your City of Jerusalem, the holy mountain. Because of our sins, and for the iniquities of our fathers, Jerusalem and your people have become a reproach to all that surround us. Now, therefore, O, Lord, our God, hear the prayer of your servant, and his supplications, and cause your face to shine upon your Sanctuary (Temple). And while I was speaking, and praying, and confessing my sin and the sin of my people, Israel, and presenting my supplication before the Lord, my God, for the holy mountain, the angel, Gabriel, whom I had seen in a vision at the beginning, flew swiftly in my direction and touched me about the time of the evening oblation. And Gabriel informed me, and talked with me, and said, 'O, Daniel, I am now come forth to give you skill and understanding.'" (Daniel, the Hebrew Prophet; Daniel 9:16, 17, 20-22)

Cyrus the Great, the king of Persia, issued his decree in 538 B.C., allowing the Jewish exiles to return to Jerusalem. (Ezra 1:1-3; Ezra 2:1; Isaiah 44:24-28; Isaiah 45:1) But there was a delay in the work of reconstructing the City of Jerusalem due to the Samaritans.

Christ's Triumphant Appearance

The Samaritans, who had become the dominant inhabitants in Jerusalem while the Israeli refugees were in exile, sought to frustrate the Jews purpose of rebuilding the City of Jerusalem. The second Temple may have already been in place, but the overall reconstruction of Jerusalem was being intentionally hindered. The hold up on progress concerning Jerusalem went on for years and years. The Samaritans continually opposed the rebuilding of the City of Jerusalem.

"Then, the Samaritans weakened the hands of the Jews, and troubled them in building, to frustrate their purpose. And the Samaritans wrote letters to the Persian leaders falsely accusing the Jews who inhabited Judah and Jerusalem. And as a result, even Persian kings were assuring their companions who dwelled in Samaria that a command would be given to not allow the rebuilding of Jerusalem. Hence, no work would be accomplished in reconstructing the Temple either." (Ezra 4:4, 5, 17, 21, 24)

"And the Samaritan official spoke before his brethren and the army of Samaria with great indignation, mocking the Jews who were desiring to rebuild Jerusalem, and furiously scoffed, 'What are these feeble Jews doing? Will they fortify themselves? Will they sacrifice? Will they complete the work in a day? Will they revive stones out of the heaps of rubbish, stones that are burned?'" (Nehemiah 4:1, 2)

The raising up of the 2nd Temple, at the direction of Zerubbabel and under leadership of the prophets Zechariah, Malachi, and Haggai, is chronicled in both the Book of Ezra and the Book of Nehemiah in the Hebrew Bible (the seventh chapter of Ezra; Nehemiah 2:1-11, 17, 18, 20). Zerubbabel had completed the Temple before the Seventy Weeks of Years prophecy began. The second Temple was built in the midst of a city that was still 100% in shambles. The completion of the Temple occurred during the reign of the Persian king, Darius (Ezra 6:16, 17), who lived from 550-486 B.C. Gabriel's 70 Weeks of Years prophesy was in regard the when the rebuilding of Jerusalem itself, not the Temple. The total timeframe of reconstructing Jerusalem from the ashes up, which took a total of exactly 49 years, equivalent to 7 Weeks of Years. The first 7 Weeks of Years represent the first of three segments of the Seventy Weeks of Years. Artaxerxes, also a king of Persia, came to power in 465 B.C. It was, specifically, in 445 B.C., twenty years after he became king of Persia, when

Christ's Triumphant Appearance

King Artaxerxes motivated his own empire to mobilize and accommodate the Jews in the rebuilding of Jerusalem. The city was still in total ruins. Not only did the citizens of Persia approve of Jerusalem being rebuilt, but they also assisted in financing the project. This process is graphically documented in the Books of Ezra and Nehemiah in the Hebrew Bible. King Artaxerxes was regarded in history as a very compassionate man. It is at this very point in time, that is, in 445 B.C. when the reconstruction of Jerusalem commenced, and also marked the beginning of the Seventy of Weeks of Years. The first Segment (49 Years) of the entire Seventy Weeks of Years (490 Years) represent the number of years it took to completely rebuild Jerusalem, which had been in total shambles and ruin.

"And it came to pass in the month of Nisan, in the twentieth year of Artaxerxes (445 B.C.), the king, I took up wine, and gave it the king. Artaxerxes observed that I was unhappy in his presence, and inquired of me, 'Why is your countenance sad?' And I said to the king, 'Why should I be happy, when Jerusalem lies in waste, and the gates thereof are consumed with fire?' Then, the king asked me, 'What request would you make of me?' And I said unto the king, 'That you would send me into Judah, unto the City of David, that I may build it.' And the king said unto me, with the queen sitting beside him, 'How long shall your journey be?' Moreover, I said unto the king, 'If it please the king, let letters be given to the Governors of Judah. And a letter unto Asaph, that he may be given timber to make the beams for the gates of the palace which pertains to the House of God (the Temple), and for the wall of the City of Jerusalem.' And the king granted me my request, according to the good hand of my God upon me. Then, I came to the Governors of Judah, and gave them the king's letters. I was esteemed as a man concerned for the welfare of the children of Israel. So, I came into Jerusalem. Then, I told them of King Artaxerxes' words that he had spoken unto me. And they said, 'Let us rise up and build.' So, they strengthened their hands for this good work. Then, I answered them, 'The God of Heaven, he will prosper us. Therefore, we, his servants, will arise and build." (Nehemiah 2:1-9, 11, 18, 20)

Nehemiah was grieved that Jerusalem's walls were still in rubble almost one-hundred years after King Cyrus had allowed the Israelis to return to Israel from Babylon. King Artaxerxes' decree to rebuild Jerusalem in 445 B.C. kicked off Daniel's Seventy Weeks of Years Prophecy, and at that very

Christ's Triumphant Appearance

moment, set the prophetic clock ticking down to the time when the Jewish Messiah would be utterly forsaken ("cut off") by mankind in 33 A.D. (Daniel 9:26)

The first unit of 49 years (that is, Seven Weeks of Years; 7 Weeks of Years x 7 days in a week = 49 years) of the Seventy Weeks of Years (70 Weeks of Years x 7 days in a week = 490 years) covers the time it took to completely rebuild Jerusalem. But it wasn't until 445 B.C., with King Artaxerxes commanding that Jerusalem be restored, when all hindrances would be eliminated and all obstacles were removed to allow this endeavor to take place. So, 490 years (which is equivalent to the entire Seventy Weeks of Years) minus 49 years leaves 441 years (or 63 Weeks of Years, that is, Seventy Weeks of Years minus Seven Weeks of Years).

It would be the next 434 years (62 Weeks of Years x 7 days a week = 434 years) after Jerusalem had been rebuilt that would take the timetable right up to the day when the Messiah was "cut off" (rejected) in 33 A.D., as prophesied in Daniel 9:26. This would leave One Week of Years remaining, equivalent to 7 years (1 Week of Years x 7 days in a week = 7 years). This seven year period has been designed (earmarked) to be carried over to a future time (eschatological period designated by the God of Israel) that will be referred to as the Seven Year Tribulation of the last days.

At the very latter part of the 62 Weeks of Years, the Jews would utterly reject the notion of the Israeli Messiah, Jesus Christ, being a suffering servant (Isaiah 53:1-12; Daniel 9:26; Hebrews 9;28; II Corinthians 5:21: "The Messiah, the Anointed One, shall be cut off."). The Jews, during this period, were expecting a political deliverer who would rescue them out of the tyranny of the old Roman Empire. This rejection of the Israeli Messiah took place in 33 A.D. Hence, threescore and two weeks (62 Weeks of Years, that is, 434 years; Daniel 9:26) after Jerusalem is back to her proper state, the Messiah was cut off (rejected).

In 70 A.D., thirty-seven years after Christ was crucified and rose from the dead, Jerusalem and the second Temple were set on fire by the Romans. The Temple was destroyed, with the exception of the Western Wall, which means that Christ's prophecy of "every stone of the Temple being thrown down" (Matthew 24:1, 2) did not apply to this event. Jesus was, actually, referring to the great day of his coming, when the Tribulation Temple would be absolutely obliterated toward the end of the Battle of Armageddon. Also, it needs to be stressed that the destruction of the second Temple in 70 A.D. was not the Abomination of Desolation as many believe, because the false messiah has not appeared yet. But he is fully expected to burst forth into the world just prior to the Seven Year Tribulation, close to the time when the third Israeli Temple is about to be built. THE SEVEN YEAR TRIBULATION WILL MARK THE LAST WEEK OF YEARS (SEVEN YEARS) OF THE SEVENTY WEEKS OF YEARS (The Seventieth Week of the Seventy Weeks of Years; Daniel 9:27; "one week"). This is when the Abomination of Desolation will take place via the blasphemy of the false messiah (Daniel 7:25).

No chapter in the Hebrew Bible depicts and predicts the Israeli Messiah (Jesus Christ) to be a suffering servant more than the fifty-third chapter of the Book of Isaiah. The Messiah is predicted to be "despised and rejected of men." He is described as "a man of sorrows, and acquainted with grief," and a man who "has surely borne our griefs and carried our sorrows." The fifty-third chapter of Isaiah goes on to say: "He was wounded for our transgressions. He was bruised for our iniquities. All we like sheep have gone astray. We have turned everyone to his own way. And the God of Israel has laid on him the iniquity of us all. He will be brought as a Lamb to the slaughter. He was 'cut off' from the land of the living. He will pour his soul out unto death." (Isaiah 53:3-6, 11, 12; Daniel 9:26)

"For God has made Jesus (the Israeli Messiah) to be sin for us, who knew no sin, that the righteousness of God may be made manifest in us through Christ." (II Corinthians 5:21)

"No man takes my life from me, but I willingly lay it down of myself. I have power to lay it down, and I have power to take it again." (Jesus Christ; John 10:18)

"Greater love has no man than this, that a man lay down his life for his friends." (Jesus Christ; John 15:13)

Christ's Triumphant Appearance

"But is, now, made manifest by the appearing of our Savior, Jesus Christ, who has abolished death, and has brought immortality to the light through the Gospel." (II Timothy 1:10)

The edict of King Artaxerxes of Persia in 445 B.C. allowed the Jews to begin the restoration of Jerusalem. This set forth the only timeline that fits concerning the Seventy Weeks of Years, rather than adhering to the theory that Cyrus the Great's decree of 538 B.C., which permitted the Jews to return to Jerusalem, marks the beginning of the Seventy Weeks of Years. This theory falls very short of getting even close to the day when the Jewish Messiah was "cut off."

But it is a documented fact in history that Artaxerxes became the king of Persia in 465 B.C. It was in the king's twentieth year (according to Nehemiah 2:1, as recorded in the Hebrew Bible) of his reign over Persia (in 445 B.C.) when he would issue an edit to Nehemiah that allowed the Israelites to restore the City of Jerusalem. It took 49 years (7 Weeks of Years) to rebuild Jerusalem within that timeframe. Then, after another 434 years (62 Weeks of Years multiplied by 7 days per week equaling 434 years), the Israeli Messiah, Jesus Christ, would be "cut off" (Daniel 9:26), that is to say, rejected by the world as Messiah. The Jews, at this point in history, were fully expecting the Israeli Messiah to rescue them from the oppressive tyranny of the Romans. Seven Weeks of Years plus Sixty Two Weeks of Years equals Sixty Nine Weeks of Years (69 Weeks of Years is equivalent to 483 years; 49 years + 434 years = 483 years). SO, FROM THE POINT WHEN THE RESTORATION OF JERUSALEM BEGAN IN 445 B.C. TO WHEN THE ISRAELI MESSIAH IS REJECTED (49 years + 434 years = 483 years), 483 YEARS HAVE ELASPED.

THEREFORE, 69 WEEKS OF YEARS (OR 483 YEARS) HAVE GONE BY SINCE THE REBUILDING OF JERUSALEM BEGAN TO WHEN JESUS WAS "CUT OFF," LEAVING ONE WEEK OF YEARS (7 YEARS) REMAINING, WHICH HAS BEEN RESERVED (HELD OVER) BY THE GOD OF ISRAEL FOR THE SEVEN YEAR TRIBULATION, WHICH WILL TAKE PLACE IN THE LAST DAYS. THEREFORE, 69 WEEKS OF YEARS PLUS 1 WEEK OF YEARS EQUALS EXACTLY 70 WEEKS OF YEARS, THAT IS, 483 YEARS PLUS 7 YEARS EQUALS 490 YEARS TOTAL.

Christ's Triumphant Appearance

Desolating Abomination ("shiqqutzim meshomem" in Hebrew) in the Book of Daniel refers to the Abomination of Desolation, one of the most significant events of the end time. (Daniel 9:27) The false messiah's desecration of the Holy of Holies within the Tribulation Temple will be a supreme, ultimate effort on his part to blaspheme Almighty God, and prevent the building of the Millennial Temple.

"Seventy Weeks (of Years) are determined upon the people and upon the holy city (Jerusalem), to finish the transgression, and make an end of sins, and to make reconciliation for iniquity, and to bring in everlasting righteousness, and to seal upon the vision and prophecy, and to anoint the Most Holy (The Israeli Messiah, Jesus Christ). Know, therefore, and understand that from the going forth of the commandment to restore and to build Jerusalem unto the Messiah, the Prince, shall be Seven Weeks (49 YEARS; THE REBUILDING OF THE ENTIRE CITY OF JERUSALEM TAKES 7 WEEKS OF YEARS). The street shall be rebuilt again, even in troublous times. And after threescore and two weeks (62 WEEKS OF YEARS; 434 YEARS) shall the Messiah be cut off, and the people of the prince (of darkness; Satan) shall destroy the City (Jerusalem) and the Sanctuary (the Temple). SO, AT THE VERY END OF 62 WEEKS OF YEARS, THAT IS, 434 YEARS AFTER THE FIRST 49 YEARS OF THE SEVENTY WEEKS OF YEARS (490 YEARS), THE JEWISH MESSIAH IS UTTERLY REJECTED {"THE MESSIAH SHALL BE CUT OFF" --- Daniel 9:26} IN 33 A.D. And he (the false messiah) shall confirm the covenant (negotiate a pseudo pact with Israel) with many for one week (One Week of Years, that is, Seven Years; The Seven Year Tribulation). And in the midst of the week, he shall cause the oblation to cease (puts a halt to the service of the Israeli priests), and for the overspreading of Abominations he shall make it Desolate (The Abomination of Desolation, which takes place during the Great Tribulation/Jacob's Trouble), even until the consummation, and that determined shall be poured upon the desolate (Satan's strategy backfires on him)." (Daniel 9:24-27)

TO SUMMARIZE, AFTER THE REBUILDING OF JERUSALEM, WHICH TAKES 7 WEEKS OF YEARS, EQUIVALENT TO 49 YEARS), YET ANOTHER 62 WEEKS OF YEARS COMES INTO PLAY, LEADING RIGHT UP TO THE ISRAELI MESSIAH BEING "CUT OFF". AT THIS POINT, 69 WEEKS OF YEARS HAVE ELAPSED, LEAVING

ONE WEEK OF YEARS (7 YEARS) OF THE 70 WEEKS OF YEARS REMAINING. ON YAHWEH'S TIMETABLE, THESE REMAINING 7 YEARS ARE BEING HELD OVER (SET APART) TO ACCOMMODATE THE SEVEN YEAR TRIBULATION OF THE LAST DAYS. (Daniel 9:24-27)

Therefore, Daniel's 70 Weeks (of Years) is a period totaling 490 years (70 years x 7 days a week = 490 years). The 490 years are divided into three segments of time, according to Daniel, the Prophet: 1) 7 Weeks of Years (49 years; Daniel 9:25), which earmarks the time it took to rebuild Jerusalem. 2) 62 Weeks of Years (434 years; Daniel 9:25, 26), which accounts for the period of time immediately after Jerusalem is restored to the day when Christ is rejected by the world. These first two segments of time (49 years + 434 years) come to a total of 483 years, which is the same as 69 Weeks of Years. That would leave One Week of Years (7 years) remaining (Daniel 9:27). This third and final segment of time, of course, represents the Seven Year Tribulation, which takes place in the end time.

Cyrus, the king of Persia, after defeating the Babylonians in 539 B.C., freed the Jews, ending their captivity in Babylon in 538 B.C. But once again, it was the edit of Artaxerxes (The king of Persia) in 445 B.C that allowed the Jews to rebuild Jerusalem (Nehemiah 2:1-9, 17, 18, 20). It was from this point in 445 B.C. that it took the Jews 49 years (7 Weeks of Years) to reconstruct Jerusalem. The period of time between the completion of Jerusalem's restoration and the year when the Israeli Messiah is "cut off" (Daniel 9:26) was 434 years (62 Weeks of Years). The destruction of Jerusalem by the Romans (under Titus, the Roman General) took place in 70 A.D., shortly after Christ lost his life at the hands of both the Jews and the Romans. The last week of years (7 years) represents the Seven Year Tribulation, when the Abomination of Desolation will occur, as predicted also by Jesus Christ himself (Matthew 24:15, 16) and Daniel, the Prophet (Daniel 9:27).

So, the total timeframe concerning the prophecy of the 70 Weeks of Years (490 years) from the time when reconstruction of Jerusalem was initiated in 445 B.C. to the year when the Israeli Messiah was not accepted comes to a sum total of 483 years (69 Weeks of Years; 434 years + 49 years = 483 years; 483 years divided by 7 days in a week = 69 Weeks of Years).

Christ's Triumphant Appearance

That leaves seven years (One Week of Years) remaining. These seven years have been reserved and postponed for the futuristic, eschatological period of time, well known as, the Seven Year Tribulation.

There is an interval between the end of the 69th week and the beginning of the 70th week. This postponement of the Restoration of the Throne of David (The Millennial Age; Isaiah 9:6, 7) was announced to Daniel by the angel, Gabriel, in regard to Jeremiah's 70 Weeks of Years prophesy (Jeremiah 25:10-14; Jeremiah 29:10, 11). The final week of years remaining has been delayed. This week is slotted for the Seven Year Tribulation that is to take place in the last days. The literal actuality of the restoration of Israel (politically and spiritually) will occur in future events which will culminate at the end of the Seven Year Tribulation. (Isaiah 9:6, 7)

The beginning of the 70th week of the Seventy Weeks of Years marks the start of the Seven Year Tribulation. Daniel's prophetic timetable is accurate.

ALL MATHEMATICAL CALCULATIONS CONCERNING THE SEVENTY WEEKS OF YEARS IN THE BOOK OF JEREMIAH (JEREMIAH 25:11, 12; JEREMIAH 29: 10, 11; JEREMIAH 30:7) AND THE BOOK OF DANIEL (DANIEL 9:24-27) IN THE HEBREW BIBLE ARE CONFIRMED AND BASED UPON ESTABLISHED HISTORICAL FACTS AND DATES. THIS INFORMATION IS ALSO REFLECTED ON THE INTERNET, IN LIBRARY BOOKS, AND HISTORY TEXTBOOKS.

It goes without saying that the consecutive order that the ninth chapter of the Book of Daniel lays out, listing the three separate segments of time of the Seventy Weeks of Years in verses 25-27, is absolutely astounding.

Daniel 9:25 mentions the first segment of time of the Seventy Weeks of Years, which is 7 Weeks of Years, equivalent to 49 years. This timeframe began in 445 B.C. and marks the beginning of the rebuilding of Jerusalem that took 49 years to accomplish.

Daniel 9:26 mentions the second segment of time of the Seventy Weeks of Years, which is 62 Weeks of Years, equivalent to 434 years. This timeframe began, immediately, after Jerusalem was rebuilt and ends the moment when Jesus Christ was not received by the world (John 3:18, 19) as the Jewish Messiah. This verse uses the words, "cut off," to indicate the genuine Israeli Messiah has been unjustifiably cut down, to the extent of losing his life.

Daniel 9:27 mentions the third segment of time of the Seventy Weeks of Years which is the remaining One Week of Years, that is, 7 years, that will be reserved for a period sometime in our future, and popularly referred to as the Seven Year Tribulation. This verse not only mentions that the Great Tribulation (Jacob's Trouble; Jeremiah 30:7; Revelation 7:13, 14), beginning in the middle of the Seven Year Tribulation ("the midst of the week") and lasting to the end of the Battle of Armageddon, but it also makes reference to the Abomination of Desolation. The blasphemous event of the Abomination of Desolation will be perpetrated in the Tribulation Temple by the false messiah during the Great Tribulation, which represents the last 3 ½ years of the Seven Year Tribulation. Jesus Christ himself foretold of this event in Matthew 24:15, mentioning and quoting Daniel, the Prophet.

"When you, therefore, shall see the Abomination of Desolation, spoken of by Daniel, the Prophet (Daniel 9:24-27), stand in the Holy Place (whosoever reads, let him understand). Then, let them which be in Judaea flee into the mountains." (Matthew 24:15, 16)

"Alas! How awful that great day will be! For none will be like it! It is even the time of Jacob's Trouble." (Jeremiah 30:7; The Great Tribulation; The final 3 ½ years of the Seven Year Tribulation; 1,260 days --- Also spoken of in Revelation 11:3).

"And I will give power unto my Two Witnesses, and they shall prophesy a thousand two hundred and threescore days." (Revelation 11:3; 1,260 days; equivalent to 3 ½ years; The Great Tribulation; Jacob's Trouble; The Last Half of the Seven Year Tribulation)

"And he (the false messiah) shall confirm the (bogus) covenant with many for One Week (7 years; The Seventieth Week of the Seventy Weeks of Years; The Seven Year Tribulation). And in the midst of the week (mid-way through the Seven Year Tribulation, marking the beginning of the

Great Tribulation), he shall cause the sacrifice and oblation to cease (that is, stop the service of priests of the Tribe of Levi), and for the overspreading of abominations, he shall make it desolate (the Abomination of Desolation; Daniel 7:25; Daniel 9:24-27)

"These are they which came out of the Great Tribulation."
(Revelation 7:14)

The Bible indicates that a world leader, the false messiah, will arise, promising lasting peace in the Middle East. He will act as a diplomat to get Israel's enemies to sign a bogus seven year peace treaty with the Jews (Daniel 9:27). The Bible predicts this treaty between Israel and this powerful world leader (the false messiah) will falsely secure peace and prosperity for the nation and people of Israel. This peace will be short-lived, and will only last for three-and-one-half years (the first half of the Seven Year Tribulation). At that point, this evil world leader will break his covenant with Israel in a dramatic fashion. He will, then, go on to violently persecute the people of Israel for the next three-and-a-half years (the Great Tribulation; Jacob's Trouble; Jeremiah 30:7; Revelation 11:3; the last half of the Seven Year Tribulation). The Great Tribulation is also, obviously, predicted in the Book of Daniel (Daniel 9:27), where Daniel, the Prophet, states: "in the midst of the week" (that is, in the middle of the Seven Year Tribulation), the despicable act of the Abomination of Desolation will commence (be instituted), with no shame whatsoever shown by the false messiah.

"AND IN THE MIDST OF THE WEEK (Halfway into the Seven Year Tribulation; The beginning of the Great Tribulation), the false messiah shall cause the sacrifice and oblation (something presented or offered to God) to cease, and for the overspreading of abominations, he shall make it desolate, even until the consummation, and that determined shall be poured upon the desolation." (Daniel 9:27)

One major clause in the treaty between Israel, the false messiah and Israel's enemies will be that the priesthood of the Tribe of Levi be reinstated. This will not be an option to the Jews, and the false messiah will be well aware of that fact. The false messiah will know that it is imperative to make this short-lived promise to the priests of the Tribe of Levi and all the Israelis. The major types of animal offerings and the significant details of the Tribe of Levi's sacrificial performance (and so forth) are listed in the Book of Leviticus. Aaron, Moses' brother, and his descendants were chosen to be God's priesthood. The vital function of the priests (especially the High Priest) in the Temple (or the Israeli Tabernacle utilized in wilderness between Egypt and the Promised Land of Israel) is central to Judaism. Participation on the part of the Jewish people in a Temple service includes the playing of music and singing. The Tribe of Levi is considered to be the most important tribe among the Twelve Tribes of Israel, responsible for the spiritual leadership of the Jews.

Many Israelis would not dare make a move in their personal lives without the daily guidance of the priests of Israel, considered to be directly appointed and hand-picked by Yahweh himself.

Some may say that animal sacrificing became obsolete when the Israeli Messiah (The Lamb of God; John 1:29; Jesus Christ is regarded as the supreme sacrifice) was "cut off" (rejected; became a sacrifice for the sins of mankind; Daniel 9:26), but that simply is incorrect. The Restoration of the Temple of the future (in the eschatological age) to the Israelis means that the performances of the priests of the Tribe of Levi will be FULLY reinstated. So, for the false messiah to blaspheme, desecrate, and defile anything so sacred to Jews as the priesthood of the Tribe of Levi, the Temple, the Holy of Holies, the Ark of the Covenant, and anything to do with the performance of offering sacrifices to God is a mockery beyond belief. It will be an absolutely unimaginable act. Regarding the last days, it is predicted quite clearly in the Holy Bible that the false messiah will, eventually, perpetrate this atrocity (Daniel 7:25; Daniel 9:27; II Thessalonians 2:1-10). This ultimate wrongdoing is referred to by Daniel, the Hebrew Prophet, and Jesus Christ, the Israeli Messiah, as the Abomination of Desolation (Daniel 9:24-27; Jeremiah 30:7; Matthew 24:15, 16). It will take place in the Great Tribulation, which is the period covering the last half of the Seven Year Tribulation.

Jeremiah, the Prophet, called the Great Tribulation, "the time of Jacob's Trouble." (Jeremiah 30:7; "Jacob's Trouble"). It will be at this juncture that the Gentiles will especially be used by the God of Israel to rescue many Israelis, in the midst of very precarious international events.

Christ's Triumphant Appearance

"Arise, shine, for the light is come, and the glory of the Lord God of Israel is risen upon you. And the Gentiles shall come to your light, and kings to the brightness of your rising. Lift up your eyes round about and see. They all gathered themselves together. Then, you shall see, and flow together, because the abundance of the sea shall be converted unto you, and the forces of the Gentiles shall come unto you." (Isaiah 60:1, 3-6; The Gentiles will come to the aid of the Israelis in the last days)

"Thus says the Lord God, 'Behold, I will lift up my hand to the Gentiles, and set my standard to the people (Israel)." (Isaiah 49:22)

"For thus says the Lord, 'That after seventy years (Seventy Weeks of Years) be accomplished at Babylon, I will visit you, and perform my good word toward you, in causing you to return to this place. For I know the thoughts that I think toward you' says the Lord, 'thoughts of peace, and not of evil, to give you an expected end.'" (Jeremiah 29:10, 11)

It is an unmistakable fact, according to the Book of Ezra, that the Second Temple was already built by the time Daniel's prophesy of Daniel 9:24-27, conveyed to him by the angel, Gabriel (Daniel 9:21-23), began its fulfillment in 445 B.C. The Temple was completed in the sixth year of King Darius' reign and dedicated joyfully by the Jews in 516 B.C. (Ezra 6:14-16). Daniel lived from 621-539, so he did not even see the Temple built. Both Cyrus and Darius issued decrees for the Temple to be built in Jerusalem. (Ezra 1-5; Ezra 6:1-3, 7, 8). King Artaxerxes of Persia issued a very lengthy degree (Ezra 7:1-28), through the persuasion Nehemiah (Nehemiah 2:1-18), that the City of Jerusalem with her walls be completely restored and the Temple beautified (Ezra 8:1, 30; Ezra 9:9; Ezra 10:1, 7; Nehemiah 12:27, 30, 37, 43, 45). 490 years is the length of time of Gabriel's prophecy to Daniel (Seventy weeks of years have been determined – Daniel 9:24). This prophecy was based on the decree of a Persian king. Nehemiah entreated King Artaxerxes in the twentieth year of his reign which was 445 B.C. (Ezra 2:1). Gabriel told Daniel in Daniel 9:25 to "know, therefore, and understand the commandment (decree) to restore and build Jerusalem (which was still in a state of absolute ruins) unto the Messiah, the Prince (Jesus Christ). It would be the powerful, protracted decree of the compassionate King Artaxerxes, who highly esteemed the God of Israel, that would fit the timeframe for the 69 weeks of years leading up to the rejection of the Israeli Messiah ("cut off" – Daniel 9:26), with the 70th week of years carried over to the future event of the Seven Year Tribulation, marked by the Great Tribulation (Jacob's Trouble) to take place "in the midst of the week (Daniel 9:27). Ezra lived from 480-440 B.C. Nehemiah lived from 473-403 B.C. They both lived to see the initiation of the decree that was prophesied to Daniel by Gabriel, the angel. There is little wonder why there is more speculation concerning the Seventy Weeks of Years Prophesy over any other prophecy in the Bible, So many common thread factors are associated with this prophesy, right down to the Gospel of Jesus Christ.

The year 445 B.C. marked the beginning of the fulfillment of Gabriel's prediction that Jerusalem's restoration would not be hindered (by the Samaritans).

"And the Elders of the Jews built, and they prospered through the prophesying of the Prophets, Haggai and Zachariah. And they built and finished it, according to the commandment of Cyrus, and Darius, Artaxerxes, the kings of Persia." (Ezra 6:14)

The Tribulation of the last days would not be coming for centuries. The false messiah has not made himself known just yet. Not to mention that there were many prophecies of the Hebrew Bible that needed to be fulfilled for the all the world events to fall into alignment. One of the major prophecies that was necessary to come to pass first was the restoration of the State of Israel, which took place in 1948. Up until 1948, before Israel reunited as a nation, the Israelis were dispersed and scattered around the world (Diaspora; Displacement) in total disarray since the first hostile siege of Jerusalem in 586 B.C. by the Babylonians.

The Ark of the Covenant and the Restored Solomon, certainly, both play a big part in the distribution of this power that is to be disbursed around the world in the last days to the Twelve Tribes of Israel. The Restored Solomon will be used by Yahweh to rebuild Solomon's Temple (Israel's 3rd Temple on Earth), that is, the Temple destined to become the Tribulation Temple, which will serve as the command base for the false Israeli messiah during the Great Tribulation.

Christ's Triumphant Appearance

The Israelis are ready to rebuild Solomon's Temple (the third Israeli Temple) of the last days. Solomon's Temple Rebuilt in the world will render hope that the Millennial Temple is the next Temple in sight to stand in the third Temple's place.

In the first three-and-a-half years of the Seven Year Tribulation (1,260 days; Revelation 11:3), which will inevitably come, Israel will endure the deception of a pseudo-peace created by the false messiah by way of manipulation. But after that period, the place of God's divine presence in the Holy of Holies is usurped, defiled, and desecrated by the false messiah, who declares himself to be God Almighty in the midst of the Most Holy Place (this utmost desecration is referred to as the Abomination of Desolation; Daniel 7:25; Daniel 9:24-27). The false messiah's covenant with Israel will become null and void, resulting in the calm once enjoyed to cease and desist. The Jews and all of their allies will be horribly persecuted beyond measure.

The rejection of the false messiah by all the Israelis will follow, and thus mark the beginning of the Great Tribulation (the last three-and-a-half years of the Seven Year Tribulation), which is referred to as "the time of Jacob's Trouble" found in Jeremiah 30:6, 7. Despite the false messiah exalting himself above Yahweh and taking God's seat in the Temple, the Jews are promised in the Bible to be rescued from this onslaught (Isaiah 9:12-16; Daniel 7:25; Daniel 12:1-3); Matthew 24:27, 30, 31; Revelation 11:3-15; Revelation 19:11-16). The Jewish Messiah (The Anointed One, Jesus Christ) will come to redeem and rescue his people (Zechariah 14:4; Matthew 24:27, 30, 31).

So, to make it all quite clear, because this point requires emphasis: Due to the Restored Solomon's presence in the world, and the promise (guarantee) that the Lord God of Israel would establish Solomon's kingdom forever, Solomon's Temple (Yahweh's third Israeli Temple built on Earth/The Tribulation Temple) will, indeed, be rebuilt in the last days. The false messiah will have the audacity to set foot in the Most Holy Place of the Temple (The Holy of Holies), normally where only the High Priest of Yahweh is allowed to move into annually on behalf of the Israelis on the Day of Yom Kippur, that is, the Day of Atonement. At this point, the false messiah will arrogantly proceed to exalt himself above Almighty God, appealing to the sinful natures all those who accept his invitation to join him. The end result will be that the Rebuilt Temple of Solomon is defiled and desecrated. This blasphemous act sparks the Great Tribulation (the last 3 and ½ years of the Seven Year Tribulation; 1,260 days = 3 ½ years – Revelation 11:3), commonly referred to as "Jacob's Trouble." The pseudo (bogus) pact of peace between the Israelis and the false messiah is broken, and the Israelis realize that they have been deceived, duped, bamboozled, and betrayed. The false messiah's entrance into the Holy of Holies of the Rebuilt Temple of Solomon fulfills Daniel's prophecy of the Abomination of Desolation (Daniel 7:25; Daniel 9:24-27).

And, eventually, the fate of the last days Temple of Solomon will be utter destruction and annihilation. Solomon's Temple Rebuilt is leveled as a direct result of the wrath of the Almighty God of Israel and his disapproval of the false messiah's deviant actions. The Tribulation Temple will be pulverized as a result of the false messiah challenging the Lord God of Israel in the most unimaginable way possible, that is, the Abomination of Desolation.

The Bible describes the Jerusalem Temple as "Beit Adonai" or "Beth ha-Elohim," which in Hebrew means: The House of God. This denotes the Temple as a place where God dwells. The Temple (which succeeded the Tabernacle that was used temporarily by the Israelites in the wilderness after being in bondage in Egypt) is a connotation that expresses the earliest Hebrew term of representing God's permanent abode. God desires to have a place to dwell on Earth. "Mishkan" in Hebrew means: The Tabernacle or The Dwelling Place. Also, the Biblical Hebrew term for the Temple is "Beit HaMikdash" which means: The Sanctified House. Only the Temple in Jerusalem is referred to by this name. And "Mikdash" in Hebrew means: The Sanctuary, the House of Holiness or the Holy Place.

God's plan for the Temple was first revealed to Moses at the foot of Mount Sinai. Out of the thunders of Mount Sinai, the God of Israel revealed his glorious plan by which the Tabernacle of God would be constructed (Exodus chapters 25-30; Exodus chapters 35-40). The connection between the Tabernacle and the first and second Temples found in the Hebrew Bible (the Old Testament) is unmistakable. They served as God's dwelling place.

Christ's Triumphant Appearance

"Let them construct a Sanctuary for me that I may dwell among them." (The Lord God of Israel to Moses; Exodus 25:8)

Although the Tabernacle was the initial, make-shift fulfillment of this plan, in due time, it was superseded by the more permanent structure of the Temple. The Tabernacle was a portable, collapsible Temple (tent) that the Israelites could dismantle and transport in the wilderness (in between Egypt and Canaan Land; Numbers 7:1-9). When assembled, the Tabernacle was intended to be a place of worship for the Twelve Tribes of Israel during the period that preceded their arrival to the Promised Land. After Joshua's conquest of Canaan in 1250 B.C., the Tabernacle was brought to Shiloh. The children of Israel also carried the Ark of the Covenant during their 40 years wandering in the desert. Then, King David, a man after God's own heart (I Samuel 13:14), was hard pressed to build A PERMANENT SANCTUARY FOR THE LORD, that is, the 1st Israeli Temple. Joshua had conquered the enemies of the Israelites that were attempting to keep them out of the Promised Land (Joshua 6:27). This paved the way for David to, eventually, become the king of Israel. It insured that Solomon's Temple would be built. Solomon's Temple in Jerusalem (The first Israeli Temple) came after the Tabernacle as the fixed dwelling place of Yahweh on Earth. Subsequently, when the Tabernacle became obsolete, the God of Israel would now abide in a permanent dwelling place (place of abode) under Heaven, that is, the Temple.

Although Yahweh once walked with man in the Garden of Eden, the fall of mankind into sin now distanced a holy God from an unholy humanity. Man could no longer go to God. It would be up to God to find a way for man to return to him. The command of the Lord "to build a Sanctuary for me" (to Moses; Exodus 25:8) represented a pivotal point in both the history of Israel and all the nations of Earth (the entire human race). Man's exile from God was now to be ended, and the Sanctuary (Temple) is meant to be God's strategy to bring about Israel's restoration.

The first historical promise of the Temple occurs in the Song of Moses: "Thou wilt bring them and plant them in the mountain of your inheritance, (The Temple Mount) the place, O, Lord, which you have made for your dwelling, the Sanctuary, O, Lord, which your hands have established." (Exodus 15:17)

In The Hebrew Bible, King Solomon, in his dedicatory prayer of the Temple after it was built, stated that God could not be contained on Earth by any structure (I Kings 8:26, 27; Acts 7:47-49). This made it clear that God, who is omnipresent (present in all places at the same time), could not be localized on Earth. Any Temple built to the glory of the God of Israel stands as the visible station of his manifested presence. This obvious divine actualization perceived readily by the senses including sight ("the cloud filled the House of God" --- I Kings 8:10; Shekinah, the glory of Yahweh, comes from the Hebrew verb "shakan," which means "to dwell") is the concentration of God's presence and peace that has been and will continue to abide on the Temple Mount.

The Lord God of Israel cannot be confined to an earthly Temple. King Solomon's focus and awareness is on God's immensity and omnipresence. Solomon is quick to point that out to the Jews who are present at the dedication of the Temple. The God of Israel is everywhere at one time.

God's presence fills every atom and molecule that he has made in the universe. The Lord cannot be limited, reduced, or compromised by space or time.

"And now, O, God of Israel, let your word, I pray, be verified, which you have spoken to your servant, David, my father. But will God, indeed, dwell on the Earth? Behold, the Heaven and Heaven of Heavens cannot contain you. How much less this House that I have built?" (King Solomon; Dedication of the first Temple in Jerusalem, Israel; I Kings 8:26, 27)

"But King Solomon did build a House. Howbeit, the Most High God dwells not in temples made with hands, as the prophet has said. 'Heaven is my Throne, and Earth is my footstool. What House will you build me?' says the Lord. 'Or what is the place of my rest?'" (Acts 7:47-49)

The proper Habitation for God, capable of containing him in all of his infinity, is in the heavenly Temple. The earthly Temple cannot completely contain God.

The Temple is the ultimate religious symbol of Judaism. The Israelis cannot, by any means, reach their proper spiritual status without the Temple

Christ's Triumphant Appearance

being built and present on the Temple Mount in Jerusalem, Israel. The Temple is the supreme statement of Israeli sovereignty. There is a new level of spiritual attainment achieved through the building of the Temple. The Israelis cannot, in any way, experience God's Covenant totally without the presence of the Temple. Ultimately, the Temple shines as a beacon to the entire world, radiating eternal hope from Jerusalem, Israel.

The mission of the Temple means individual, social, national and even international transformation. On the national level, the Temple revives Israel and the federation of the Twelve Tribes of Israel. The Twelve Tribes of Israel include every single Child of God who has ever lived. The Remnant represents all genuine followers of Christ who have lived throughout all time. Many souls died longing for the salvation and freedom that they knew only the Israeli Messiah could one day bring them.

And after King Solomon dedicated the first Israeli Temple, Solomon's Temple, God promised Solomon that there would always remain a king on the Throne of Israel throughout all time. For each and every generation, the God of Israel would designate a king of the line of David and from the Tribe of Judah. The evil kings of Israel mentioned in the Hebrew Bible were not hand-picked by God. For any given period of time, the Lord knew the genuinely special man who he had his hand upon.

"I will establish the Throne of your kingdom upon Israel forever, as I promised to David, your father, saying, 'There shall not fail you a man upon the Throne of Israel." (King Solomon; I Kings 2:4; I Kings 8:25; I Kings 9:5; Jeremiah 33:14-17)

It should be noted that all of the allies of the State of Israel (worldwide) are, indeed, honorary Israelis. For all those who belong to Jesus Christ are the seed of Abraham (our forefather; Galatians 3:29) and a friend of God (James 2:23). All honorary Israelis are heirs to the promises of the Israeli Messiah, especially in regard to the new Covenant. You are always under the watchful eyes of Yahweh. The Israeli Messiah will protect you, guide you, and provide for you. He will never leave you or forsake you. (Deuteronomy 14:2; Matthew 28:18-20; Hebrews 13:5)

"For if you are Christ's, then, you are Abraham's seed, and heirs according to his promise." (Galatians 3:29)

The Temple depicted in Ezekiel chapters 40-48 is a detailed description of the Millennial Temple that will be prevalent during the Israeli Messiah's Millennial Reign (1,000 Year Reign), eschatologically (futuristically) speaking. The specifications of the Millennial Temple in chapters 40-48 of the Book of Ezekiel are most precise, and Jesus Christ will be the supreme architect of this glorious structure. (Zechariah 6:12, 13)

The heavenly Temple is a pattern (The Hebrew word, "tabnit" which also means: the blueprint; copy; same design; model; a shadow; replica; architect's plan; original archetype) for the building of the earthly Temple.

The heavenly Temple will be the shining example of the Millennial Temple of the restored Jerusalem, as the heavenly Temple is the eternal Temple.

"Immediately, I was carried away in the Spirit, and behold, there was a Throne set in Heaven, and one who sat on the Throne." (Revelation 4:2)

"The Lord has established his Throne in Heaven, and his kingdom rules over all." (Psalm 103:19)

"And the Temple of God was opened in Heaven, and there was seen in the Temple the Ark of the Covenant. And there was lightning, and rumbling, and thunder, and an earthquake, and severe hail." (Revelation 11:19)

The Temple had been built to house the Ark of the Covenant, which serves as a repository of the Tablets of the Law (The Ten Commandments; Exodus 20:1-24; Exodus 31:16-18; Exodus 32:15, 16). The placement of God's Sanctuary on the Temple Mount (Mount Moriah) in Jerusalem is confirmation of the Lord's Covenant to Abraham being fulfilled, and proof of God's promise to make spiritual provision there (Genesis 22:14). It is also confirmation of the God of Israel's Covenant to David and Solomon that they were chosen to make it possible for the 1st House of God to be built on Earth.

Christ's Triumphant Appearance

Moses had received the Ten Commandments directly from Yahweh upon Mount Sinai (Mount Horeb; Exodus 20:1-24; Exodus 31:16-18; Exodus 32:15, 16). The Ten Commandments were placed inside the Ark of the Covenant, and the Ark rested in the Holy of Holies within the Temple of God.

God alone would pick the person (King Solomon) who would build the Temple for him. King Solomon, of the Hebrew Bible, was a man of peace. While Solomon's father, King David, was a man of war, King Solomon found rest from all his enemies during his reign as king of Israel (I Kings 3:5-15; I Kings 5:1-12; I Kings 8:17-22). This freedom from the distraction of war allowed Solomon the luxury of building the very 1st Israeli Temple unto the God of Israel.

The first Sanctuary for Israel was the Tabernacle, which could be pitched like a tent. The Tabernacle could be collapsed and transported by the Israelis as they journeyed through the wilderness and into the Promised Land, after the Jews had escaped from Egypt, which, at that time, was under Pharaoh's tyranny. For 480 years (from Moses to Solomon), the Tabernacle served Israel as a temporary Sanctuary. Then, Solomon's Temple built on the Temple Mount in Jerusalem, Israel served as YAHWEH'S PERMANENT SANCTUARY. When David conquered Jerusalem (Zion), he not only made the City of Jerusalem the capital of Israel, he also made Jerusalem the site for the permanent Sanctuary (The Temple). David was chosen by God, and David chose Jerusalem (The City of David). But the first Temple was destroyed in 586 B.C. by the Babylonians. The rebuilding of Jerusalem directly resulted from the power of the angel, Gabriel, and his prophesy that nothing would stop Jerusalem from being perfectly rebuilt.
(Daniel 9:21-27)

From the point when the Jews began to rebuild Jerusalem around 445 B.C. to the very day when the Israel Messiah, Jesus Christ, is misunderstood, misconstrued, and rejected comes to an exact total of 483 years (69 Weeks of Years) that have elapsed.

In 70 A.D., the Romans destroyed the 2nd Temple, leaving only the Western Wall (The Wailing Wall) standing. In Matthew 24:1, 2, Jesus predicted that every single last stone of the Temple would one day be thrown down. But he, most obviously, could not have been referring to the destruction of the second Temple in 70 A.D., because the Western Wall remains, hence, not all the stones were thrown down. The only logical conclusion to come to is that Jesus was making an eschatological prediction and referring to the Tribulation Temple of the last days, which the God of Israel will utterly destroy and obliterate due to the Abomination of Desolation (Daniel 9:27). The Abomination of Desolation was predicted by Jesus Christ in Matthew 24:15, 16. Hence, every last stone of the 3rd Israeli Temple shall be thrown down, as Christ accurately predicted. And Jesus also will be participating in the obliteration of the Tribulation Temple, demolishing it toward the end of Armageddon with the brightness of his coming. (Matthew 24:1, 2, 15, 16, 21, 27, 29, 30; II Thessalonians 2:8)

The interior of the Temple was divided into two sections: 1) The Holy Place ("Hekal" in Hebrew) and 2) The Most Holy Place (The Holy of Holies; "Qodesh Qodashim" in Hebrew), and these two areas were separated from one another by a curtain, that is, a veil ("paroket" in Hebrew). The exterior that surrounded the Temple was referred to as the Outer Court.

Christ's Triumphant Appearance

The Holy of Holies (The Most Holy Place; The inner part of the Temple, within the veil, where only the Israeli High Priest may enter once a year on Yom Kippur, the Day of Atonement, to atone for the sins of Israel) is unmistakably identified with God's presence. And the Ark of the Covenant is the most outstanding feature of the Holy of Holies. The Israeli High Priest, who orients himself towards the earthly Holy of Holies is, at the same time in a parallel fashion, orienting himself towards the Holy of Holies in the heavenly Temple.

Within the Holy Place were housed three objects: 1) The Golden Table for the showbread, 2) The Golden Seven-branched Candelabrum ("Menorah" in Hebrew), and 3) The Golden Altar of Incense.

And within the Most Holy Place (The Holy of Holies) was the Ark of the Covenant. The Ark contained three valuable, cherished, historical Israeli keepsakes: 1) The Golden Pot of Manna 2) Aaron's Rod 3) The Tablets of the Covenant (The Ten Commandments; Exodus 20:1-24; Exodus 31:16-18; Exodus 32:15, 16). The Ark rested on a bedrock platform that protruded within the Holy of Holies, called in Jewish tradition the "Foundation Stone" ("Even haShetiyyah" in Hebrew). While both the High Priest and his priests officiated in the Outer Court (outside of the Temple) and the Holy Place, only the High Priest was permitted to go within the Most Holy Place (The Holy of Holies) to perform the annual act of atonement on the holy Day of Atonement ("Yom Kippur" in Hebrew) on behalf of all the people of Israel.

The phrase "within the Temple" refers to the Most Holy Place (also called the Holy of Holies; "Kodesh Kodashim" in Hebrew), that is, the place in the Temple where the Ark of the Covenant rests. The Ark of the Covenant is the most sacred treasure of the Israelis. In Solomon's Temple of the Hebrew Bible, the High Priest was allowed by Yahweh to enter the Most Holy Place one day each year to atone for the sins of Israel. The Most Holy Place was a small room that contained the Ark of the Covenant. The Ark had a gold covered chest which protected the original stone tablets upon which the Ten Commandments (Exodus 20:1-24; Exodus 31:16-18; Exodus 32:15, 16) were written, a jar of manna, and Aaron's staff. The top of the chest served as the atonement cover (the altar) upon which the blood of sacrificial animals would be sprinkled by the High Priest on the Day of Atonement (Yom Kippur). The Most Holy Place, upon the Temple Mount,

Christ's Triumphant Appearance

was the most sacred and hallowed spot on Earth to the Israelis (Leviticus 16:1-34). A curtain (veil; "parochet" in Hebrew) separated the Most Holy Place from the rest of the interior of the Temple. The Priesthood of the Levites (The Priestly Tribe of Israel; The Tribe of Levi) will be restored in the last days. The Levites will perform ordinances in the Millennial Temple of the end time. This service of the Levites will be completely advocated by Jesus Christ, the Israeli Messiah. All actions of the priests in and around the Millennial Temple will testify and point to the fact that Jesus is the supreme sacrifice and our Great High Priest.

The priesthood and service of the Levites, in relation to the Ark of the Covenant, will not be restored in the Tribulation Temple, because Yahweh will not, under any circumstances, allow the Ark to be present in the Temple during the cataclysmic event of the Abomination of Desolation, the clear indication that the Great Tribulation has begun.

The prophets of the Hebrew Bible saw the Restoration of the Throne of David as the completion (fruition) of God's promises to Israel (Isaiah 9:6, 7; Ezekiel 36:26-28; Ezekiel 37:14; Ezekiel 39:29; Jeremiah 31:33; Joel 2:25-29). At the appointed time, God will send his heavenly Messiah, Jesus Christ (Daniel 7:13, 14), who will usher in the period of restoration of all things, namely, the Restoration of the Throne of David (Isaiah 9:6, 7), on the last day. Restoration henges on the building of the Temple in our modern day.

The Coming of the Lord Jesus Christ will usher in a Paradise of blessing greatly surpassing the Paradise that was lost by Adam and Eve.

In Genesis 3:24, the Cherubim that God posted at the east entrance to the Garden of Eden are guarding access to the Tree of Life, which is located in the middle of the garden. Any Israeli who has read this in the Book of Genesis will not be able to help but think of the two correlating Cherubim that overshadow the mercy seat on the Ark of the Covenant.

"And the Lord God of Israel drove the man and the woman out. And he placed Cherubim at the east gate of the Garden of Eden, and a flaming sword which turned in every direction, to guard the way to the Tree of Life." (Genesis 3:24)

Christ's Triumphant Appearance

But the day will enviably come when the pendulum swings the other way, and Paradise is regained. I venture to speculate that even Juan Pounce de Leon will be allowed to witness the Fountain of Youth and have an understanding of just why he couldn't find it sooner.

"Indeed, the Lord will comfort Zion. He will comfort all her waste places. And the wilderness he will make like Eden, and her desert like the Garden of the Lord." (Isaiah 51:3)

"And they will say, 'This desolate land has become like the Garden of Eden. And the wasted, desolate, and ruined cities are fortified and inhabited." (Ezekiel 36:35)

When God's presence (Shekinah) has one day been restored to his Sanctuary on Earth, the world will witness that the divine purpose of Yahweh has been brought full circle, with mankind restored to a worldwide Garden of Eden and unending fellowship with the Creator. It will be a very good thing.

"At that time, they shall call Jerusalem, 'The Throne of the Lord.' And all nations shall be gathered unto it, to the name of the Lord, to Jerusalem." (Jeremiah 3:17, 18)

Today, Israelis recite three times daily the words, in prayer to the God of Israel: "May it be your will that the Temple be speedily rebuilt in our own time." Many of these prayers are expressed by the Jews at the Western Wall, that is, the Wailing Wall. The Western Wall is all that remains of the destroyed second Temple.

The discovery that the first two Temples were both destroyed on the very same day of the year (The Ninth of Av; Tisha B' Av in Hebrew) is proof to Israeli rabbis that even the destruction of the Temples had been part of God's predetermined plan, rather than a historical coincidence. The lesson and conclusion that emerged is that Yahweh was just as much in control of the destruction of the Temples as he had been in control of their construction. So shall it be concerning the absolute and total destruction (obliteration) of the Tribulation Temple at the end of the Seven Year Tribulation. God has already given us a sneak preview that Israel's third

Temple will be annihilated to make way for the Millennial Temple, that is, the 4th Israeli Temple. It will be very interesting to note whether or not the Tribulation Temple happens to meet its fate of destruction on the Ninth of Av. But whether or not the Tribulation Temple is leveled on the Ninth of Av, we can all still be quite certain that it was the God of Israel who called the shot.

The crisis of "post-Temple-less Judaism" is, indeed, a reality, and the loss of the Temple brought about a threat to the continued national sovereignty of Israel. Not having a Temple is a threat to the very existence of Israel.

"Be merciful, O, Lord our God, in your great mercy towards Israel, your people, and towards Jerusalem, your city, and towards Zion, the abiding place of your glory, and towards the Temple, your Habitation, and towards the kingdom of the House of David, and your righteous anointed one (The Israeli Messiah, Jesus Christ). Blessed are you, O, Lord, God of David, the builder of Jerusalem." (Jewish Prayer of Daily Ritual; Shemoneh Esreh, Benediction 14)

Christ's Triumphant Appearance

CHAPTER FOUR

THE BATTLE OF GOG AND MAGOG

On September 11th, 2001, 19 Muslim Radicals (Extremists), on a suicide mission, hijacked four American commercial passenger planes and intentionally flew two of them into the World Trade Center Twin Towers, in New York City (New York, New York; USA), resulting in the 9/11 disaster. Over three-thousand Americans lost their lives as the terrorists successfully targeted the Twin Towers, the Pentagon, and yet, unsuccessfully carried out their objective of hitting the White House. The two hijacked planes positioned on a trajectory to crash into the North and South Towers of the World Trade Center complex in Lower Manhattan were American Airlines Flight 11 and United Airlines Flight 175, respectively. Both flights had departed from Logan International Airport in Boston, Massachusetts bound for Los Angeles International Airport. The two planes were both Boeing 767's. Within an hour-and-forty-two minutes after the impact of the two planes hitting the buildings, both 110-story towers collapsed, killing 2,799 and injuring more than 6,000 others. In the meantime, the hijackers on board American Airlines Flight 77 deliberately crashed the plane they were piloting into the Pentagon in Arlington County, Virginia, killing all 64 people on board, as well as 125 people at the Pentagon. American Airlines Flight 77 was scheduled to travel from Dules International Airport near Washington D.C. to Los Angeles International Airport. American Airlines Flight 77 was a Boeing 757-223. United Airlines Flight 93 was a domestic scheduled morning passenger flight that was hijacked by terrorists on board, also as part of the September 11th attacks. United Airlines Flight 93 had departed from Newark International Airport in New Jersey bound for San Francisco International Airport in California. The hijackers of United Airlines Flight 93, a Boeing 757, fully intended by the terrorists onboard to make a direct hit on the White House as a target, but it crashed into a field in Somerset County, Pennsylvania, during an attempt by the passengers and crew to regain control of the cockpit. 44 people were killed when the plane hit the ground. The devastation of these horrendous assaults sparked an international war on terrorism.

On September 20th, 2001, just days after 9/11 (September 11th, 2001), President George W. Bush, the 43rd President of the United States, announced the new American policy toward terrorist groups: "From this day forward, any nation that continues to harbor terrorists or support terrorism will be regarded by the United States as a hostile regime."

In November of 2001, Osama bin Laden (who eventually was killed by United States Special Forces in Operation Neptune Spear on May 2nd, 2011 in Pakistan) along with the terrorist group, Al-Qaeda, took credit for the 9/11 terrorist attack. The rationale of their despicable deeds can be traced directly to bin Laden and Al-Qaeda's hatred of democracy, capitalism, free enterprise, the United States, and Israel.

There has been a significant increase in the number of terrorist attacks and major threats since 9/11 (The Travesty of September 11th, 2001).

Christ's Triumphant Appearance

The continuous attacks directed toward Israel show a deep embedded hatred that cannot possibly be resolved through diplomatic protocol. The only way that Israelis will survive and, ultimately, have unprecedented, non-stop victory will be through the power of military force. Unfortunately, war (that is, the war to end all wars) appears to be the only answer to achieving peace, in the midst of a spiritual battle, reflecting the parallel of actual events, in which we are all engaged.

Radical Islam is a religion of fanatics, terrorists, and warmongers, with beliefs and prejudices that are deeply entrenched. For Radical Muslims, any religion other than Islam is strictly forbidden. Islamic concepts of justice and revenge are enforced by way of twisted holy wars (holy jihads). Radical Muslims are running rampant on campaigns of murder, mayhem, and mass destruction, all in the name of Allah. WHILE THERE ARE MANY PEACE-LOVING MUSLIMS ALL OVER THE WORLD WHO DO NOT ADVOCATE VIOLENCE OF ANY FORM, the attitude of Radical Muslims is to spread Islam by the sword, which is justified by the Koran. And the ultimate desire of Radical Muslims is to kill the (so-called) infidels who reject this dangerous brand of Islam.

Of great concern today are potentially hostile governments, such as Iran and North Korea, expressing defiant actions. Countries aggressive in pursuing nuclear programs specifically against Israel include: Egypt, Saudi Arabia, Morocco, Syria, and Algeria, with plans in the making of both Tunisia and the United Arab Emirates, to name a few.

The potential of nuclear war remains an ever-present reality. It is only a matter of time until the nuclear threat we are facing is beyond human control in the Middle East. The world of the 21st century is mired in the quicksand (quagmire) of secularism, superstition, relativism, and mysticism. All of these components are designed to induce fear, and the result will always be rampant spiritual confusion.

People, who advocate unrealistic solutions, are now calling for a new world order (militarily, economically and spiritually) that is every bit prophesied in biblical scripture (The Holy Bible comprising the Old Testament and the New Testament) and is serving as a distinct warning of the signs of the end of time. The false messiah, who is imminent and near to arriving on the scene, will be the undisputed leader of that empire.

Globalists are now insisting that national governments should surrender their sovereignty to a one world government. Such a government would operate through a world headquarters, a world state, a world court, a world military, a world church, and a world economy.

The world economy is already upon us now. No developed nation of any kind can survive today without networking with the global economy.

The new world order will also include a new world religion that insists of everyone total uniformity to the cause of evil. Worldwide religious unity has already been endorsed by the World Council of Churches.

The irreconcilable differences between the Israelis and the Arabs go all the way back to the days of the Hebrew Bible (the Old Testament), even since the days of Abraham. No amount of education, psychology, social welfare, negotiating, or government planning can eradicate this irresolvable hatred. The tearing down of barriers between the religions and races of the world may only be resolved through the power of Jesus Christ.

There is a deep resentment in the hearts of the Arab people toward the United States, for America has continued their support and loyalty to the State of Israel.

The Radical Muslims believe that only they are accurate in their viewpoints. All Israelis, Christians, and advocates of any religion other than Islam are to be considered as infidels (worthy of death).

This global unity of evil will be void of any ethics, normally associated with free market enterprise, democracy, and freedom. There will be very little God-consciousness left in the world.

A global economy is now in place. It is only a matter of time until the whole world is as one economic unit waiting to be taken over by a sinister power.

Christ's Triumphant Appearance

Global economic interdependence (a world economy) will eventually lead to a global political system (a world government) that will dominate national sovereignty of all the individual countries on Earth.

All resistance to the world system will be crushed by a massive worldwide persecution harshly and militantly imposed by the false messiah. Men, women, and children who choose to resist this new one world order will be slaughtered in the name of the world state.

The God of Israel desires to create perfection in the world via the Restoration of the Throne of David, (Isaiah 9:6, 7; Joel 2:25-32; Matthew 24:27; II Thessalonians 2:8), and the Battle of Gog and Magog is a part of the plan to bring it about.

"Why does the small David, armed only with a small rock again and again, need to fight against giants?" (I Samuel 17: 44-52)

The truth of the matter is that the War of Gog and Magog is upon us at this very moment. (Ezekiel 38:1-3) It is interesting to notice that as soon as Israel becomes an exceeding great army (Ezekiel 37:10), the Battle of Gog and Magog begins.

Despite its many wonderful benefits, modern technology is also responsible for the development of weapons of mass destruction, which threaten the very existence of life on the planet of Earth. Nuclear bombs (Weapons of Mass Destruction; WMD) no longer have to be launched by intercontinental missiles. Nuclear bombs can be packed in suitcases or dropped from pilot-less drones.

The dangerous technology of today far exceeds the maturity of man. In many ways, both Albert Einstein and J. Robert Oppenheimer considered themselves the couriers of death in the atomic age, considering the roles they played in bringing nuclear weapons in the world.

Intensified kinds of wars, famines, and plagues (pandemics), based on Biblical prophecy, began their fulfillment in the first part of the twentieth century, escalating to the ultimate fulfillment of other prophecies to take place in the future.

Christ's Triumphant Appearance

While there have been many earthquakes, tsunamis (super tidal waves), volcanic eruptions, tornadoes, hurricanes, climate change issues, extreme weather conditions causing famine, and other various natural disasters (acts of God) all through history, the frequency of these earthquakes and other severe weather phenomena, and the amount of destruction they cause have increased tremendously since the early part of the twentieth century. Even as climate change has caused global warming, there also seems to be an ever-growing number of human conflicts around the world.

Just like Judaism and Christianity, Islam has its own version of the Messianic appearance, that is, the emerging of the twelfth Imam of Islam (Muhammad al-Mahdi), who will burst in dramatic force upon world events. In a November 16th, 2005 speech in Tehran, Iran President Mahmoud Ahmadinejad (2005-2013) said that the main mission of his government is "to pave the path for the appearance of the twelfth Imam of Islam."

"Nation will rise up against nation, and kingdom against kingdom." (Jesus Christ; Matthew 24:7)

Among the nations known to support terrorists are Russia, China, Syria, and Venezuela. Russia has signed a one-billion dollar deal to sell missiles and other nuclear weaponry to Iran. Many Iranian nuclear scientists have been trained by senior Russian scientists. Russian nuclear scientists can easily be hired in the world market. In addition, Russia has agreed to sell missiles to the Syrian government. Russia is involved in building nuclear power stations for other nations. Russia is currently working on projects in China, India, and Iran, with further nuclear development in Turkey and Morocco.

Russia plays a key role in the last days. Russia is in support of Muslim nations and allies of Islam who help terrorist groups. Russia has unleashed a flood of uranium ore and tons of plutonium on the black-market. The West's attempt to prevent the spread of nuclear weapons has failed, and a dangerous new era has begun.

In October of 2004, China, the most populous nation in the world, signed an accord with Iran worth 70 to 100 billion dollars. This marked the beginning of the two counties as major trade powers. With such deeply connected economic ties to Iran, China has been resistant to agree to strong United Nations sanctions. The result will be China increasing favoritism with a nation (Iran) that has a clear desire to destroy both the United States and Israel.

Attacking Syria would be like attacking Russia, especially since Russia has thousands of military advisors, strategists, and special forces in Syria. In order to stamp out terrorism, America will have no choice but to deal with Syria at some point. Syria is home to more terrorist organizations than any other Islamic state in the world.

Democracy, to the Radical Muslims, is a prohibited system of government that contradicts Islamic values and embodies heretical religion. Democracy, to Islam, is the rule of paganism dictated by the United States Constitution, and not in accordance to the laws of Allah.

The Koran (Quran; Muslim book written by the prophet, Muhammad) never mentions the City of Jerusalem. But more recent Muslim apocalyptic literature pictures Jerusalem as the new Islamic capital in the last days. Within this context, Radical Muslims are sparking a renewed jihadist effort to reclaim the City of Jerusalem from the citizens of Israel.

The Middle East continues to be a boiling cauldron of tension, conflict, terrorism, and war. The situation in the Middle East has brought us to the brink of a conflagration that will easily engulf the entire world. The threat of nuclear and chemical weapons in the hands of nations with irresponsible, rogue governments is greater than it ever has been before.

The Exclusive Nuclear Weapons Club use to have only five members: The United States, Britain, France, China, and Russia. Today, the number of nations possessing or attempting to possess nuclear weapons is escalating dangerously. The current nuclear arsenal, collectively, of all nations possessing nuclear weapons has the potential of wiping out all of civilization, as we know it today, many, many times over. We are all facing the reality of a nuclear holocaust. The red nuclear button could possibly be pushed impulsively, as a result of an accident, miscalculation, or madness, catapulting us all into oblivion.

We are all witnessing a quantum leap toward the fulfillment of the Biblical prophecies of the last days. The final climatic acts predicted will bring this human drama that mankind has endured to a final conclusion. Current events could not be more ideally in place (positioned) for the fulfillment of these last remaining Biblical prophecies concerning the latter days. We are being swept down the corridor of time to an inevitable date with destiny. The book of recorded time has been turned to the final chapter of human history.

Nothing marks today's moment in history more strikingly than the acceleration of change. As stated in the Book of Daniel concerning the end time: Many shall run to and fro, and knowledge shall be increased."

In this intense battle against spiritual oppression, the struggle for world dominion is, ultimately, between the power of the Israeli Messiah, Jesus Christ, and the forces of Satan.

Most of the Berlin Wall was tore down on November 9th, 1989. While the fall of the Soviet Union on December 25th, 1991 did much for the advancement of freedom, Radical Muslims attempted to undermine that freedom by taking control of the former Soviet-controlled republics. Six out of fourteen of these republics are, now, under Islamic influence: Turkmenistan, Kyrgyzstan, Tajikistan, Azerbaijan, Kazakhstan, and Uzbekistan.

The conflict of Ezekiel chapters 38 and 39 will drastically alter the world, as we know it. The Battle of Gog and Magog is known by a number of different names including the North-Eastern Invasion, the Russian-Islamic Invasion, or the Gog and Magog Invasion. The stage has, obviously, been set for the climax of this war for some time now. And Almighty God will give indelible evidence of his existence during the closing stages of this battle, when he supernaturally rescues Israel at the last minute from certain annihilation. The entire world will clearly see, in an unmistakable demonstration of his power, that God is who he claims to be. The whole world will witness that Yahweh (The Eternal One) is on the side of Israel, on an unconditional basis. God has not forgotten Israel, and he never will forget Israel.

"And there they shall bury Gog (the leader of Magog/Rosh/Russia), and all his multitude. And I shall be glorified. For I have poured out my Spirit upon the House of Israel." (Ezekiel 39:11, 13, 29)

According to prophecy, it is after the Jews return to Israel from the Diaspora (dispersion/scattering worldwide of the Jews from their homeland due to persecution) and rebuild the Land (Establish the State of Israel; This prophecy was fulfilled in 1948) that the War of Gog and Magog is expected to follow. The entire Nation of Israel will be plotted conspired against in regard to being ambushed from all sides. Many nations with anti-Semitic regimes have and will continue in scheming to destroy the State of Israel.

Israel is often referred to as a fig tree by the Hebrew Prophets and Jesus (Matthew 24:30-33). According to the Holy Bible, the budding of the fig tree (the birth of the State of Israel in 1948) is the single greatest clue that the last days are unfolding upon us. The Jews having regathered into their homeland of Israel, after such a lengthy exodus, was the total game changer for all biblical prophecy. In 1880, the Jewish population in Israel was zero. Then, then miracle occurred on May 14th, 1948, when the United Nations officially recognized the State of Israel.

The study of Biblical prophecies of the Book of Ezekiel in the Hebrew Bible (The Old Testament) indicates that Israel will survive a great invasion coming from the north (Ezekiel 38:6, 15; Ezekiel 39:1, 2; Invasion perpetrated by Rosh/Russia/Magog), at a time when Israel is being threatened by other hostile enemies (Ezekiel chapters 38 and 39). This intended invasion will be launched prior to the Seven Year Tribulation. The modern nations listed in Ezekiel 38:2-6 are threats to Israel and supportive of the Islamic-Arab agenda. Today, Magog, (the ancient land of the barbaric Scythians, who migrated to Russia), ruled by Gog, is comprised of Russia and the six former Soviet republics under Islamic influence. Also, Gog's allies include Meshech and Tubal (territories in Turkey), Gomer (Germany), Togarmah (Turkey), Persia (Iran), Cush/Euthiopia (Sudan), and Put (Libya). These nations will ultimately be part of the coalition that will march against Israel. The Battle or War of Gog and Magog is between the two Temple texts found in Ezekiel 37:26-28 and Ezekiel chapters 40-48, with both texts referring to the Millennial Temple. Ezekiel chapters 40-48 provides a graphic blueprint of the fourth earthly Israeli Temple, that is, the

Christ's Triumphant Appearance

Restoration Temple of the Millennial Age (The Millennial Temple). The account of Gog and Magog in Ezekiel chapters 38 and 39 will take place just prior to the rebuilding of Solomon's Temple.

In essence, the modern-day government of Russia will be doomed along with the Radical Muslims in its conspiracy against Israel. At least, that's what the Bible more than implies.

Gog is the leader of Magog and is identified as "the Prince of Rosh" (Ezekiel 38:2). Rosh is a common Hebrew word. Rosh is an identification with Russia. Rosh is a derivative, root word accepted by many expert scholars to be the correct translation, occurring about 750 times in the Bible. The grammar of the Hebrew Bible (the Old Testament) supports the translation of Rosh (Rus) as a proper noun denoting the geographical location of Russia. There are many who believe that Russia (Rosh) and Magog are one in the same. Gog's advancement to claim new territory and reclaim former Soviet satellite countries (as part of his agenda to, ultimately, invade Israel) will be totally based on propaganda and lies. And another major concern will be China joining forces with Magog (Russia).

"'Therefore, Son of man (Ezekiel, the Prophet), prophesy against Gog, and say, thus says the Lord God of Israel, Behold, I am against you, O, Gog, the Prince of Rosh. And I will turn you around and lead you on, bringing you up from the far north, and bring you against the mountains of Israel. You shall fall upon the mountains of Israel, you, and your troops, and the people who are with you. And I will send fire on Magog. So, I will make my holy name known in the midst of my people, Israel. Then, the nations shall know that I am the Lord, the Holy One in Israel. Behold, it is coming, and it shall be done,' says the God of Israel. 'This is the day of which I have spoken.'" (Ezekiel 39:1, 2, 4, 6-8)

Unlike the other names mentioned which indicate specific territories, "Gog" instead refers to an individual and identifies him as coming from "the land of Magog," and that he is "the Prince of Rosh" (the leader of Russia). "Gog" is mentioned a number of times in Ezekiel 38 and 39 and denotes the name or title of the leader of the forthcoming attempted invasion. He will become the most ruthless person in this deadly coalition of nations. "Gog" is not to be confused with the false messiah, who emerges at end of the War of Gog and Magog (toward the beginning of the Seven Year Tribulation), which is when "Gog" will meet with an unpleasant fate (Ezekiel 39:1-6).

Yet the horrible damage Gog (the Prince of Rosh) manages to inflict serves as a preview of the even worse catastrophe ahead at the hands of the false messiah. The Prince of Rosh will seem like a boy scout compared to the false messiah.

The overall tone of Ezekiel's prophecy also indicates that God will supernaturally place the desire for the invasion into Gog's mind, thereby influencing his will, just as the God of the Hebrew Bible shaped events by hardening Pharaoh's heart in the Book of Exodus. Yahweh demonstrated his sovereignty to the world when he delivered the children of Israel out of the bondage in Egypt. The same will hold true regarding the outcome of the Gog and Magog Invasion. The Lord fully intends to show an awesome display of his power.

But well before there is an Israeli victory in sight, a shared virulent anti-Semitic and anti-God obsession will be enough to override any historic differences between the Arabs and the Russians and motivate the formation of their union with each other.

Gog's intention is to take back the fourteen former Soviet satellite countries that they lost control of starting when the Berlin Wall was torn down in 1989. The complete list of the republics include: Kazakhstan, Kyrgyzstan, Uzbekistan, Turkmenistan, Tajikistan, Latvia, Lithuania, Azerbaijan, Armenia, Georgia, Estonia, Moldova, Belarus, and Ukraine.

All of the countries identified in Ezekiel chapter 38 are controlled by openly anti-Semitic Muslim governments who share the common goal of the extinction of Israel.

The Hebrew Bible states that this contemplated attack against the tiny country of Israel will be plotted from all sides, and this vast network of enemy nations extends all the way from Russia and its associated republics to the north, Iran to the east, Sudan in the south, and Libya to the west of Israel. To say that the Israeli army is greatly outnumbered would be the understatement of the twenty-first century.

However, this will only serve to highlight the supreme power of God's divine intervention when Israel's enemies are supernaturally defeated and destroyed.

There may have been peace treaties between the Israelis and the Arabs in the past, but there has been no enduring peace. Only the Israeli Messiah, Jesus Christ, can possibly bring stable, permanent resolve and remedy to this intense and complex situation. Everything else has miserably failed. The long and bloody history of conflict in the Middle East seems to indicate that more of the same can be expected in the future unless peace can somehow be established.

Current Islamic apocalyptic scenarios call for the establishment of a new caliphate whose capital is Jerusalem. The elimination of Israel is a prerequisite and mandate to Radical Muslims for the emergence of their global Islamic state.

The Gog and Magog War, which takes place prior to the Seven Year Tribulation, should not be confused with the Battle of Armageddon that takes place at the end of the Seven Year Tribulation. The Battle of Gog and Magog, predicted by Ezekiel, the Hebrew Prophet, accords well with our present world conditions, because the balance of power has shifted to Europe (EEC; The United States of Europe; The Common Market), a clear indication of prophecy coming to pass.

Russia (Rosh) has become economically dependent on the Arabs, and its current economic conditions and political instability have led Russia to forge military alliances with Islamic powers that continually call for Israel's destruction. Islam has become the fastest growing religion in the world, dominating the Middle East. Considering Russia's economic condition, there is a real threat that their government will be unable to control its arsenal of nuclear, chemical, and biological weapons. Many of these weapons are being sold as black-market items. Russia is a tragedy (waiting to happen) on its way to catastrophe, and the Arab countries and their allies are frantically arming themselves with the most dreadful weapons of mass destruction, with only one purpose, focus, and obsession in mind: The total annihilation of Israel.

Christ's Triumphant Appearance

NATO, the North Atlantic Treaty Organization (North Atlantic Alliance), an intergovernmental, military alliance between united member countries agreeing to mutual defense in response to an attack by any external party, will be limited in preventing Russia from advancing with schemes of hostile takeover.

Israel's overpowering military strategy combined with God's intervention in his own perfect timing in history will has been predicted to deprive those nations opposing Israel any chance of winning the Battle of Gog and Magog. The invading forces, confident of victory, will be no match for Israel. Surprisingly, the Bible claims that Israel will nip the situation in the bud. All the world, via satellite television, will vividly observe in awe as Yahweh, the Eternal One, makes it perfectly clear that he is the God who, ultimately, protects and defends Israel at all costs. This particular Islamic jihad (revolt) is foreseen not to succeed. At this point, more than any time in human history, people all over the globe, especially Radical Muslims, will be keenly aware that extremists just don't go taking the power of the God of Israel lightly. The attempted ambush (hostile takeover) of Israel proves to backfire. Israel remains the dominant military force in the Middle East.

The overwhelming display of power that Yahweh has shown to destroy Israel's enemies in the War of Gog and Magog has toned down the Islamic defiance enough to grant Israel her right to rebuild the Temple on the sacred Temple Mount. The only one rebellious enough to defy the God of Israel and the Israelis now will be the forthcoming false messiah.

Ezekiel chapters 38 and 39 uniquely details a future invasion attempt directed toward Israel by a huge alliance of foreign nations. This prediction, given to the prophet, Ezekiel, by God is one of the most dramatic prophecies found in all the Scriptures. The prophecy foretells of a planned attack on Israel by a multitude of nations and ends with the supernatural annihilation of these very enemies through God's direct intervention. Many of the nations, mentioned in these two chapters, that are sworn to oppose Israel, are the very countries that surround Israel. But the impending ambush is cleverly detected by Israel, allowing them to initiate the first move. Ezekiel chapters 38 and 39 depicts the most detailed prophecy found in the Hebrew Bible, in regard to outlining this future war. The fulfillment of the prophecy

Christ's Triumphant Appearance

(history written in advance) is clearly stated to take place in the "latter years" (Ezekiel 38:8) or "latter days" (Ezekiel 38:16). This forthcoming attempt to destroy Israel, meticulously detailed by Ezekiel over 2600 years ago, is bearing down upon us. This battle will take place just prior to the Seven Year Tribulation. Solomon's Temple (Israel's third earthly Temple) will be built just after the Battle of Gog and Magog and prior to the beginning of the Seven Year Tribulation. The restoration of Solomon's Temple will be made possible via a strong reaction to the incredible Israeli victory secured in the Battle of Gog and Magog. Israel's enemies temporarily back off in utter awe and shock, acknowledging that the God of the Jews must have, obviously, played a part in winning the war in the face of such overwhelming adversity. These Israeli foes will be so terrified that they will allow the Temple Mount to be sanctified to make way for Solomon's Temple to finally be rebuilt. The resulting joy of the Jewish people would, indeed, be abundant.

The Temple Mount is Ground Zero

It is universally conceded that there is no more volatile acreage on Earth than that of the Temple Mount. The Temple Mount has been the source of all the woes of mankind since the days depicted in the Bible. This struggle for control of the Temple Mount is the single most all-encompassing and embracing factor in determining the destiny of our planet, Earth.

When all aspects of the timing of the battle in Ezekiel chapters 38 and 39 are taken into consideration, it becomes clear that the event of the Battle of Gog and Magog will prepare the world to enter the final phase of Earth's history, which makes way for the Seven Year Tribulation followed by the Battle of Armageddon.

In Ezekiel chapter 38, names of a certain number of specific nations have been given that will be involved in the Battle of Gog and Magog. This battle will be nipped in the bud by the Israeli army (Ezekiel 37:10). The Battle of Armageddon, on the other hand, includes every single last one of the nations of the world, who will gather in the figurative Valley of Megiddo. Each and every strategy carried out in this war to end all wars will be a direct parallel reflection of all the forces of good and evil in the world converging and colliding with each other, and Jerusalem, Israel will be encompassed by her enemies (Zechariah 14:1-21; Psalm 122:6). Also, there is no mention in Ezekiel chapters 38 and 39 of the true Israeli Messiah or the false messiah concerning the Battle of Gog and Magog. Yet they both play major roles in the Battle of Armageddon all the way up to its dramatic conclusion. And Armageddon will offer no guarantee of success for either side. Its intensity will increase with each new confrontation. These are very important distinctions between the Battle of Gog and Magog and the Battle of Armageddon.

"And Satan shall go out to deceive the nations which are in the four quarters of the Earth, Gog and Magog, to gather them together to battle. The number of whom is the sand of the sea. And they went up on the breadth of the Earth, and compassed the camp of the saints about, and the beloved city (Jerusalem, Israel). And fire came down from God out of Heaven, and devoured them." (Revelation 20:8, 9; A passage regarding the Battle of Gog and Magog, mentioned in retrospect)

Once the dust settles from the Battle of Gog and Magog, Israel will become the major player on the political field in the Middle East. Just exactly how all of this plays out is anyone's guess.

CHAPTER FIVE

"I WOULD BE TRUE"
by Howard Arnold Walter
DAVIDSON HIGH SCHOOL
MOBILE, ALABAMA USA
SOMETIME IN THE 21st CENTURY

The Israeli Service And American Coalition, better known by its acronym, I.S.A.A.C., is a military exchange program agreed upon mutually by the United States and Israel in 2035. Israeli soldiers were transferred to bases all throughout the United States to be stationed and trained, while American troops, both officers and enlisted, were assigned to bases all throughout Israel. The success of this program, in terms of world security and protection, proved to be phenomenal, as the proximity of alliance between the two countries proved to be even more intimidating to those enemies who diametrically opposed the democratic comradery of the United States and Israel. The demographics of each country noticeably changed as well, as both nations got a good taste of each other's culture in the process.

Christ's Triumphant Appearance

BROOKLEY AIR FORCE BASE/BATES FIELD
THE MOBILE AEROPLEX AT BROOKLEY
MOBILE, ALABAMA USA

One way the United States expressed its eagerness for the I.S.S.A.C. military exchange program with Israel was to reopen, renovate, and expand the old Brookley Air Force Base in Mobile, Alabama {USA}. The base had been phased out in 1969 by the current Defense Secretary, Robert McNamara, and the biggest event to occur since its closing was the Airbus plan to assemble A319, A320 and A321 aircraft at the Mobile Aeroplex at Brookley. The landscape and dimensions of the base were greatly enlarged. The front gate of Brookley Air Force Base used to be close to the top of the ramp at Michigan Avenue, where drivers got off at Interstate 10. But now, the new front gate extended out miles further reaching all the way to Government Boulevard. In fact, expansions were made on all sides of the base, to make it one of the largest bases in America. The United States government bought acres and acres of houses along all the streets of Michigan Avenue, in between Interstate 10 and Government Boulevard. New acreage was procured all the way around the original base. And the brand-new improvements made, coupled with the latest and greatest fighter jets flying in and out, along with the top-notch personnel who transferred to become stationed at Brookley, all combined to make the upgraded base one of the greatest marvels in the United States. The additional square mileage acquired made Brookley Air Force Base, also referred to as the Mobile Aeroplex at Brookley, impressively massive. All the aerial activity caused Mobile to become a very noisy city but considering how much the economy had improved by leaps and bounds once the base was complete, no one complained very often. And the fine people of the Port City of Mobile, Alabama definitely felt more protected. They, certainly, weren't overly concerned about radical terrorists parachuting in.

Lieutenant Colonel Jesse Hartman, an Israeli Department Commander and Aerial Defense Combatant, was one of the first to enthusiastically endorse the I.S.A.A.C. Program and helped see it become a reality. He brought his son, David Hartman, to the base on the very first day he reported to Brookley. David was in his senior year of high school. The move from Israel to the United States inspired David to make Harvard University in Cambridge, Massachusetts USA the college he set as a goal to go to, rather

Christ's Triumphant Appearance

than the Hebrew University in Jerusalem, Israel. David planned on majoring in aeronautical engineering, to pursue a career as a fighter jet pilot, just like his father. All of David's ancestors were military men, and many of them were genuine Israeli heroes. They participated in the war that made it possible for Israel to become a State in 1948. They engaged in the Six-Day War of 1967 and the Yom Kippur War of 1973. David had relatives involved in wars prior to Israel becoming a State and others afterward. David's father was a decorated Israeli hero, and David had the very same ambitions. David's 6-foot, 2-inch tall, muscular build, with rugged features, handsome looks, jet black hair, deep brown eyes, and focused demeanor made him fit the part too. David had been going to Hartman High School in Jerusalem, an Orthodox Jewish school affiliated with the Shalom Hartman Institute. His developed ability at soccer, also referred to as football in Israel, had served to make him so athletic and agile that Coach Crenshaw at Davidson High School told David that he would give him a shot at trying out for the football team that is the home of the Davidson Warriors. David was looking forward to becoming Americanized. So, not going to the Hebrew University after high school would not be a big disappointment for him. Harvard University, along with MIT, would fit his plans perfectly. And, now, David was on a field trip with his father, inspecting the latest model fighter jets and their flight performance. For David, it was a glorious day being at the newly modernized, restructured, and expanded Air Force Base in Mobile, Alabama.

The climate can be quite humid in the Port City of Mobile and along the Gulf Coast, especially during the hurricane season. One of the major pastimes in Mobile, other than fishing, hunting and frolicking on the beach at Dauphin Island and Gulf Shores, Alabama under beautiful blue skies, is dodging category one to category five hurricanes. It's just like the old cliché that's said in Mobile: "If you don't like the weather in Mobile, stick around. It'll change."

The Israeli military and the American military had been working together on a top secret training program for fighter pilots, in conjunction with I.S.A.A.C. goals. And with every waking day, David aspired to follow in the footsteps of his father to one day become a fighter pilot himself. David wanted to excel at making his father and all of Israel proud of him.

Christ's Triumphant Appearance

DAVIDSON HIGH SCHOOL
MOBILE, ALABAMA USA

   The multi-colored leaves of orange, green, red, and brown were already being carried across the roads and yards by the fall wind as one clear indication that the classes at Davidson High School in Mobile were resuming. David is strolling down the hallway as a shuffle of students, from freshmen to seniors, race past him in between classes. David stops at the locker of an attractive senior, with an athletic build equal to his own in a feminine counterpart manner, and said, "Can I buy you lunch, Bathsheba?" Bathsheba Rosenberg, whose military parents had also been transferred from Israel, slowly closed her locker with books in her arms, and turned contemplatively to look up at David. She was wearing a pink angora sweater with a matching flannel skirt. Bathsheba had auburn hair, deep emerald-green eyes, and an athletic, olive tone color hardbody. Bathsheba is an Ann Margret look-a-like, as portrayed in the Elvis Presley movie, "Viva Las Vegas." And with a frisky look on her face, Bathsheba responded, "What's on the menu?" And, David said, "I'm not sure. I'm hoping it's a hamburger with some fries on the side. I'm getting a little fried on Kosher." Bathsheba laughed out loud, and said, "You are funny, David."

   David and Bathsheba got their trays of food in the Davidson High School Cafeteria and sat at the table against the wall where the windows provide a view of Pleasant Valley Road, the main street out in front of the school that

Christ's Triumphant Appearance

leads to both Azalea Road and Montlimar Drive. After they began eating, David says, "Bathsheba, I want to read something to you. It's a poem by Harold Walter Arnold:

"I would be true, for there are those who trust me.
I would be strong, for there is much to suffer.
I would be pure, for there are those who care.
I would be brave, for there is much to dare."

After David finished reading, Bathsheba looked back at him with an astonished look on her face, and said, "David, it is just unbelievable that a guy like you, who has the scientific aptitude you have, is such a major poet!"

"Well, I just love both literature and science, I suppose." David said.

"No, David. I mean it. You are a genuine poet. You've had a poet's heart ever since I've known you, when we were children. It's something that helps to give you reason in life." Bathsheba responded, with her eyes squinting and mouth half open. Bathsheba was dazzled by David, and the feeling was quite mutual of David's perspective of Bathsheba.

"Whoever loved that loved not at first sight? William Shakespeare. Romeo and Juliet." David quipped.

David was the one sitting at the table with the view of Pleasant Valley Road, and out of nowhere, Jonathan Diamond rushes closely to David's right side, sat down at the cafeteria table, and exclaimed, "David! You and I are on the roster to play football for the senior team! You're even being considered for quarterback, and the coaching staff is thinking about placing me in the position of tight end!"

David couldn't believe it.

"Have you been drinking some Mogen David Wine or something, Jonathan?" David retorted, half-way looking around like he was a little embarrassed.

Christ's Triumphant Appearance

"I'm not kidding, David," Jonathan confirmed. "Coach Crenshaw thinks we've both got what it takes, and he wants to win the championship really bad this year."

Jonathan was, hands down, David's best friend. Jonathan's parents also had transferred from Israel to participate in the I.S.A.A.C. Program. Jonathan, like David, was a handsome, athletic young man with dark features, and hazel eyes. David and Jonathan were destined to follow similar paths.

THE DAVIDSON HIGH SCHOOL WARRIORS
ON-CAMPUS STADIUM
MOBILE, ALABAMA USA
FRIDAY NIGHT

It was the big game to determine which high school team in the area would go to the State Championship. Coach Crenshaw, the Head Coach for Davidson High School and all of his staff were most proud of the Davidson High School Warrior Football Team uniformed in the school colors of gold and black, especially where David and Jonathan were concerned. Coach Crenshaw's hunches had paid off, and he felt that the blend of David Hartman and Jonathan Diamond was a winning combination for his team. Some of the American boys resented the Israeli guys moving in and "taking over," but Coach Crenshaw didn't care what anyone thought. They were playing the McGill-Toolen Catholic High School Yellow Jackets, whose colors are orange and black. The Yellow Jackets were a formidable team, a respected rival, and had knocked the Davidson Warriors out of the championship way too many times. This time, Coach Crenshaw was not taking any chances, and David and Jonathan were his ace in the hole.

THE DAVIDSON HIGH SCHOOL ON-CAMPUS STADIUM

It was a close football game all the way through. Now, it had gotten down to the wire of the game. The score was 14 to 17 in favor of the Yellow Jackets with 12 seconds on the clock in the fourth quarter. Davidson was on the 47 yard-line of McGill-Toolen. The Davidson Warrior Football Team was coming out of the huddle for what possibly could have been the final play of the game. David, the quarterback, just happened to look over to the

Christ's Triumphant Appearance

sideline, and noticed that Bathsheba, the head cheerleader, was giving David a timeout sign with her hands, as the other Davidson cheerleaders were yelling, "Go Warriors!" and making full use of their pom-poms. David relented, and made a timeout sign himself. The referee blew his whistle, as David ran in Bathsheba's direction, with coaches and football players grumbling on both sides of the field and spectators wondering what in the world was going on.

David made it to the sideline where Bathsheba was standing. She looked at David with tears in her focused eyes, and said, "You only make a play for me, right, David?"

David paused for just a second, as he tenderly looked at Bathsheba, and said, "That's right, Bathsheba, just for you." Tears began streaming down Bathsheba's face. "That we may choose something like a star to stay our minds on and be stayed, David," Bathsheba said.

David nodded his head in affirmation, "'Choose Something Like a Star,' that's my favorite poem by Robert Frost. My star would just so happen to be you, Bathsheba." David responded, feeling inspired, as he fought back showing his own emotions.

With that, David turned around and headed toward a newly formed huddle. Bathsheba immediately went back to twirling and throwing up her baton in an alluring and most impressive manner. Then, the ball was hiked, and David went back, as Jonathan ran in perfect form down the right sideline. David hurled the ball in Hail Mary fashion as Jonathan curved inward toward the middle of the field, out-dodging Yellow Jackets left and right. Jonathan leaped to catch the ball in mid-flight at the 31-yardline, only to, then, zigzag close to the left sideline of the field, out maneuvering two more tacklers before darting with great agility into the endzone, to secure the victory leading to the championship game. Davidson had just enough time left to kick the extra point, winning the game 21 to 17. So, the Davidson High School Warriors went to the State Championship that year. And they made Coach Crenshaw very proud, winning the championship with a score of 42 to 35. After the game, Coach Crenshaw made the remark to the entire football team: "You guys have sure made me look good today."

Yet they all were aware that they had won because David stayed his mind on Bathsheba, and Bathsheba stayed her mind on David.

THE DAVIDSON HIGH SCHOOL PROM AT THE LEWIS COPELAND AUDITORIUM LOCATED AT DAVIDSON HIGH SCHOOL

Bathsheba accepted David's invitation to go to the Davidson High School Prom with him, which was to take place at the Lewis Copeland Auditorium, located right on the Davidson High School campus. She wore a beautiful, blue dress, the same shade of sky-blue as the star and stripes on the Israeli flag. Bathsheba knew David would make a comment about the color. He loved America, and was proud to be a citizen, but he missed the country of Israel at times. The fact that Bathsheba was still with him in the United States practically signified that he was capable of taking the most important part of the country with him. And Bathsheba would continue to be with him, because they were both awarded academic scholarships to Harvard, with David also receiving a double scholarship to go to the Massachusetts Institute of Technology, better known as MIT. The opportunity to go to Harvard University and MIT gave David "a meant to be sensation," especially since Bathsheba and Jonathan would be there with him as well. Neither one of them regretted not attending the Hebrew University in Jerusalem.

David thought that Bathsheba looked absolutely stunning in her new prom dress when he picked her up in his red sports car. "My new dress was quite expensive, David. Do you think it was worth it?" Bathsheba asked, fishing for a compliment. "Worth dying for, seeing you wear it, Bathsheba!" David responded, as he opened the passenger side of his car to let her in. Bathsheba rendered a belly laugh and pushed David slightly on his chest out of jest, as David politely helped her into the car seat. "You look very handsome in that tuxedo, David." David closed Bathsheba's door, came around to the driver's side, got in, and asked, "You don't think I look too formal, do you?" Once again, David scored another sincere giggle from Bathsheba, as she looked up at him affectionately, and responded, "No." David leaned over, pinned a white rose corsage to the strap of Bathsheba's new blue dress, gave her a kiss, and said, "Now, with your new perfect-shade-of-blue dress and the white rose, you look just like the Israeli flag."

Christ's Triumphant Appearance

The Lewis Copeland Auditorium, named after a highly esteemed, distinguished, very prominent, former Davidson High School principal, had been greatly expanded since it was originally built. The building was extended all the way down to where the lap track used to be in the back of the building and enlarged all the way out to the fence adjacent to the student parking lot on the right side of the auditorium. There was a large open area created in the back of the newly built structure, which more than accommodated the entire senior student body for the Davidson High School Prom. And what was once the lap track is where the Davidson High School Warriors On-Campus Stadium now stood.

David and Bathsheba entered fashionably late to the Lewis Copeland Auditorium. They both had become such high school celebrities that their absence up to the time they arrived was noticed. And when the two suddenly appeared, you could almost hear a grasp, because the picture of the two of them coupled next to each other in their prom garb was most striking.

Christ's Triumphant Appearance

The large, designated room for the prom was moderately dark. There were strobe lights flashing different colored balls of light to create a soothing mood, as couples were slow dancing when David and Bathsheba entered in. The Disc Jockey in the back of the room was in his booth playing different requests of songs that were made of him, mostly by the ladies present. The DJ whole-heartedly congratulated the senior class for reaping the rewards of their hard-earned work, in between his musical renditions that entertained everyone.

All of a sudden, as David went to the punch table to get Bathsheba and himself some punch, the Disc Jockey decided to play the all-time favorite song of both David and Bathsheba, "Gypsy," sung by Stevie Nicks of Fleetwood Mac. It wasn't a coincidence. Bathsheba managed to make a request of the song while David was getting the punch and socializing with the principal of Davidson High School and his wife. Nevertheless, it caused chills to go up both David and Bathsheba's spines, considering the setting they were in, and that they were both prompted to seize the moment at hand.

"Oh, listen, Dear. It's our song!" David exclaimed. "May I have this dance?" He requested, as they set their punch glasses down on their table, and David led Bathsheba to the dance floor with a noticeable flair. The couple quickly became the center of attention. The song, "Gypsy," was not only David and Bathsheba's favorite song, but the video by the same name was their favorite musical video, highlighting Steve Nicks dancing in ballerina style and performing the Tango with Lindsey Buckingham. David and Bathsheba had every dance move of that video totally memorized, and they were mimicking each one of those moves in top form under the colored balls of the strobe lights, moving all around the prom night dance floor, and demonstrating that they had more than their fair share of practice doing the tango together. There were couples on the dance floor who stopped dancing, just so they could focus on watching David and Bathsheba. Many of the girls sitting down were swooning, some with goosebumps, because it looked so romantic. David and Bathsheba, ever since they arrived at Davidson High School, had exhibited that they were quite an item. But observing them now, dancing so much in sync with each other and so dressed up, was quite a phenomenon to behold. They looked like professional dancers, and the people observing could not take their eyes off of them. It was mesmerizing. David was twirling Bathsheba around, and

Christ's Triumphant Appearance

then, bringing her back close to him for an embrace. David was so dapper, debonair, and stylish in his bearing and composure. And, with every motion, Bathsheba met David with an intense, sultry gaze. They looked like a prince and a princess portrayed in a movie. It was a moment that the entire Davidson High School senior class on Prom Night got caught up in and would never forget.

And at one very special moment in the dance, when David could not be possibly dancing any closer to Bathsheba, he said, looking directly into her eyes, "I've never seen anything so beautiful in my life."

To which, Bathsheba responded, in an attractive manner, "You are all fair, my Love. Be careful what you ask for, David. You just might get it."

"Harvard, here we come, Bathsheba!" David replied.

"And who knows where after Harvard, David!" Bathsheba ventured to say.

HARVARD UNIVERSITY IN
CAMBRIDGE, MASSACHUSETTS USA

WHEN THE STUDENT IS READY, THE TEACHER WILL APPEAR

Harvard University in Cambridge, Massachusetts was founded on September 8th, 1636. The Ivy League College was named after its first benefactor, clergyman John Harvard, although the school has never been affiliated with any denomination. Harvard University is the oldest institution of learning in the United States, and the most prestigious college in the world. Harvard's library has the world's largest academic library system, and its muti-billion dollar endowment is the largest of any academic institution. Harvard has three campuses. The university's 209-acre main campus is centered on Harvard Yard in Cambridge, about three miles west-northwest of downtown Boston, and extends into the surrounding Harvard Square neighborhood. Including all three of Harvard's campuses, the university grounds have grown to 21 million square feet.

Established in 1879, Radcliffe College was a Women's Liberal Arts College that functioned as the female counterpart institution for the all-male Harvard College. In 1946, Harvard classes became co-ed. In 1977, there was a merger of Harvard and Radcliff's admissions. And then, in 1999, the female body of students merged completely into Harvard, and Radcliffe College became the Radcliffe Institute for Advanced Study. What used to be Radcliffe College is less than a one-minute drive away from Harvard University.

The Massachusetts Institute of Technology, better known as MIT, in Cambridge, Massachusetts, was founded on April, 10th, 1861 by its first president, William Barton Rogers, who had worked for years to organize an institution of higher learning devoted entirely to scientific and technical training. MIT was established in response to the increasing industrialization of the United States, and stressed laboratory instruction in applied science and engineering. MIT has been crowned the best university in the world for graduate employability. It has been named the number one university in the world. MIT is two miles away from Harvard University via Massachusetts Avenue. Many of those who going to MIT become trained aeronautical engineers in preparation of becoming experienced pilots.

Christ's Triumphant Appearance

Since 1945, Hanscom Air Force Base located in Bedford, Massachusetts, about a twenty-five mile drive from Harvard, emerged as the center for the development and acquisition of electronic systems, with key importance focused on radar. Yet in cooperation with the I.S.A.A.C. Program, the United States Air Force collaborated with Harvard and MIT in developing students to be fighter jet pilots. This program was a tremendous success, and the Aerial Combat Training at Hanscom Air Force Base had become so effective that it enhanced the careers of cadets desiring to be fighter jet pilots even more than the United States Air Force Training Academy. Hanscom Air Force Base, also, unbelievably, surpassed the excellence of Luke Air Force Base, the Air Education and Training Command Center (AETC), located fifteen miles west of Phoenix, Arizona.

Both David and Jonathan were given the opportunity to attend the United States Air Force Academy just North of Colorado Springs, Colorado. But they wanted to go to Harvard and MIT and participate in the I.S.A.A.C. Program at Hanscom Air Force Base, combining Officer Training School (OTS) and Fighter Jet Instruction. David and Jonathan were both awarded academic scholarships to Harvard and MIT, taking Aerospace Engineering courses at Harvard and working toward their Bachelor of Science Degrees in Aeronautical Engineering at MIT. Of course, David also was very enthusiastic about Harvard's enriching Liberal Arts curriculum, with a serious emphasis upon English and Literature. Bathsheba, along with many other Israeli students, was awarded an academic scholarship to Harvard too.

David's very first freshman class of the fall semester, in fact, was an English Literature Class at Harvard's Barker Center at eight o' clock on a Thursday morning. He would be coming to this particular class on every Tuesday and Thursday. David noticed on his schedule that the professor teaching the class was the well known Dr. Samuel Goldstein. David made his way to the classroom, managed to find a seat close to the front of the class, and waited along with the other students for the professor to arrive.

Eventually, an older gentleman, very distinguished looking, rather thin, of average height, with graying hair, and a mustache walked into the classroom wearing very impressive quality slacks and a vest. He had a book under his arm, took a seat at the front of the class, fully intending on making himself comfortable. He spoke in a firm, yet joyful manner: "Good morning

Christ's Triumphant Appearance

to you, one and all, and welcome to Harvard. I know this must be your initial class at the university, considering this is a freshman course, this is our first day of attendance, and it's eight o'clock in the morning. I'm Dr. Samuel Goldstein, and I'll be your host over the next few months, exploring with you the wonderous world of English Literature. We'll save the amenities for another time, as I am quite certain we will, in the course of this adventure, become acquainted with each other very well. So, for right now, please turn with me in your English Literature book to page 187."

As Dr. Goldstein made the page request, he stood up from his desk, and began walking around the room, with a stack of papers ready to be distributed, as he spoke: "This syllabus that I am providing each of you clearly outlines what will be expected of you each and every time you come to class in the course of this semester. It may seem in your view somewhat random of me to begin our curriculum today on page 187, rather than page 1, but I find immense satisfaction in introducing my students to this course of English Literature with a poem from Rudyard Kipling. He was awarded the Nobel Prize in Literature in 1907. Dr. Goldstein proceeded to discuss the life of Rudyard Kipling in an intriguing fashion, and as David was observing Dr. Goldstein, his mind began to unexplainably flashback to a time that gave him very powerful impressions of déjà vu. David's mind uncontrollably altered back and forth between the classroom where Dr. Goldstein was teaching that morning and a period of time that could easily be described as Before Christ (B.C.). And, David, who knew his Hebrew Bible, had a particular verse that kept coming to mind from the First Book of Samuel: "Then, Samuel took the horn of oil, and anointed him in the midst of his brethren. And the Spirit of the Lord came upon David from that day forward." I Samuel 16:13

Then, the alternating finally stopped, but David was no longer in Dr. Goldstein's English class, but, obviously, over two millenniums back in time. David was a young shepherd boy in this vision (Joel 2:28, 29; Acts 2:17, 18), and Samuel, the Israeli Prophet, who looked exactly like Dr. Goldstein, was anointing David to be king over all of Israel. And, for that moment, David's mind was not even close to being in an English class at Harvard. For that intense, real instant, David perceived that the God of Israel had just anointed him to be king in another era. Then, Samuel said to David: "The Lord God of Israel has sought him a man after his own heart, David,

Christ's Triumphant Appearance

and you are that man, and he has commanded you to be captain over his people, Israel." David was living in that moment, as he had once before. He was there again, without question. He was in a place that was fully recognizable. And the realization of reliving that life more than implied that a new cause, a new purpose would be just ahead. And as much as David, back in another time, immediately, went on to defeat Goliath after his first anointing, so would it be that David would straightaway find his imminent destiny after this renewed anointing in a modern day world. And the Spirit of the God of Israel came upon David from that day forward. It was God's intention to use David to beat down the foes of Israel, and to establish the Throne of David forever, as the God of Israel had always promised. Just as much as David and Jonathan swore an oath to each other, God had sworn an oath to preserve David and Jonathan, and to maintain a man on the Throne of David from one generation to the next. Just as much as David of the Hebrew Bible was used in the preparation of building the first Temple, it was God's desire to use David of a more contemporary time to restore the Temple on an appointed day in the near future, an event that would come to pass in the God of Israel's perfect timing. It was an expectation whose time had come.

I HAVE FOUND DAVID, MY SERVANT.
WITH MY HOLY OIL, I, THE GOD OF ISRAEL,
HAVE ANOINTED HIM. PSALM 89:20

Christ's Triumphant Appearance

Then, once David had completely absorbed what had occurred, he began fading back to the classroom, with Dr. Goldstein's voice practically serving as a beacon: "And, so, in conclusion of today's meeting, as promised," Dr. Goldstein said, "I would like to share with you a special poem by Rudyard Kipling, that I intentionally wanted you to remember on your first day of class at Harvard University, a poem that you may very well carry with you as a keepsake in life. The poem is entitled, "IF ---." And it goes something like this, as I will be paraphrasing here and there:

'If you can keep your head, when all about you are losing theirs and blaming the situation on you. If you can trust yourself, when all men doubt you ... If you can wait and not be tired by waiting. Or be lied about, and not deal in lies. If you can be hated, and not give way to hating. And yet, not intend to look too good in the eyes of others, nor talk too wise. If you can dream --- and not make dreams your master. If you can meet with triumph and disaster and treat those two impostors just the same. Or watch the things you gave your life to become broken, and stoop and build them back up with worn out tools. If you can make one heap of all your winnings, and risk it on one turn of pitch-and-toss, and lose, and start from the beginning, and never breathe a word about your loss. If you can talk with crowds and keep your virtue. Or walk with kings, and not lose the common touch. If neither foes nor loving friends can hurt you. If all men count with you, but none too much. If you can fill the unforgiving minute with sixty seconds worth of distant run. Yours is the Earth and everything that's in it.'"

Dr. Goldstein concluded the poem with just one final comment: "With that, ladies and gentlemen, you are dismissed. Welcome to Harvard!"

David remained seated for a moment as the other students made their way out of the classroom. He had a laser beam focus on Dr. Goldstein. Eventually, David got up, and walked over to Dr. Goldstein, who was organizing his desk. David looked at him in amazement, and said, "I know you!"

Dr. Goldstein looked up at David, with a wise, joyful, grandfatherly expression on his face, "I'm fully aware of that, David."

Christ's Triumphant Appearance

David responded, "But, how can this be? I've never met you before today. But something --- something really is happening!"

Dr. Goldstein concurred, "Yes. Something is happening, indeed, and we need to talk about it, that is, you, myself, and, of course, Jonathan Diamond and Bathsheba Rosenberg."

"You're familiar with Bathsheba and Jonathan?" David asked, exclaiming. "Wait a minute! You're Israeli, aren't you?"

"Born and raised in Israel, my boy," Dr. Goldstein confirmed. "Let's just say that this is perfect timing for us to cross paths, you and I."

"Perfect timing," David mumbled to himself, "I can sense that it's important for us to talk, all four of us."

"Not to sound too urgent, David, but it's critical that we all discuss some matters. Are you familiar with Harvest Restaurant?" Dr. Goldstein asked.

"Yes. I recently heard about it," David said. "It's just off campus. I understand it's quite a nice place."

"It's a superb restaurant for you to take Bathsheba on a regular basis. There's a very romantic quality about Harvest Restaurant." Dr. Goldstein relayed, with David appreciating the tip. "Shall we say this Saturday evening at seven-ish? I'll make the reservations. They know me all too well at Harvest. I have a special table there that I frequent. The restaurant has a very relaxing atmosphere. Let Bathsheba and Jonathan know that it'll be my treat."

"Sounds great!" David said. "I know this is right on target."

"And, David," Dr. Goldstein said in a serious tone, "I want you to keep something in mind until we all meet Saturday night. It can be summed up in five very powerful words."

David stood there before Dr. Goldstein in total suspense.

"Everything has come full circle," Dr. Goldstein emphasized, as he took David's hand to shake it. "Everything has come full circle, young man. I look forward to seeing you all Saturday night. Here's my telephone number just in case you need to call me." Dr. Goldstein handed David a card with his other hand. "Dress business casual. It's going to be intriguing!"

As David turned to walk out the door, he took a glance at the card:

Dr. Samuel Goldstein
Harvard University English Department
Barker Center, 12 Quincy Street, Cambridge, MA 02138
617-495-6070, Ext. 777
"Be ashamed to die until you have won
some victory for humanity."

THE HARRY ELKINS WIDENER MEMORIAL LIBRARY HARVARD UNIVERSITY
Camelot Lost. Camelot Restored. (King Arthur and his Court)

It would be a couple of days before David would be seeing Dr. Goldstein again. And before the semester got fully cranked up, he wanted to pay a visit to Harvard's main library, the Harry Elkins Widener Memorial Library, part of the Harvard Library System. There are over seventy different libraries on Harvard's campus, but David wanted to check out the main library first. The total number of libraries collectively comprise the Harvard Library, a most impressive system that carries the largest research collection anywhere around the world in print and digital formats, incapable of being matched by any other library.

David's main topic of interest was United States President John F. Kennedy. And what better place could there be for David to learn more of this great man that he admired so much other than Harvard University? After all, this was the very college where the Thirty-Fifth President of the United States had graduated.

Christ's Triumphant Appearance

After reading a choice selection of books regarding the 35th President's upbringing, his stay in England when his father, Joseph P. Kennedy Sr., was appointed by Franklin Delano Roosevelt as Ambassador to England, JFK's education, his military service during World War II as Commander of PT-109 in the United States Navy, the tragedies involving his brothers, Joseph P. Kennedy Jr. and Robert Francis Kennedy, his sister Kathleen, better known as "Kick," who died in an airplane crash, his rise to the Congress and Senate, and taking Jacqueline Lee Bouvier as his wife. David watched many of the documentaries of the president on a monitor and absorbed the words of JFK into his very soul, serving to greatly inspire him.

The humor of John F. Kennedy dazzled David, including a quote made by JFK in his youth: "A life of complete leisure is the hardest work of all."

David, also, watched portions of all four presidential debates between JFK and Vice President Richard M. Nixon, who had served under President Dwight D. Eisenhower for the past eight years. They were the very first televised presidential debates in United States history. The one single moment that caught David's attention the most in the first debate was Kennedy's response to Nixon, when the Vice President remarked that JFK had a responsibility to be right in his criticism of the country, and that he was downgrading America by "running her down." The next future president slightly turned toward Nixon and said: "I really don't need Mr. Nixon to tell me about what my responsibilities are as a citizen. I've served this country for fourteen years in Congress and before that in the service. I have just as high a devotion, and just as high an opinion. What I downgrade, Mr. Nixon, is the leadership the country is getting, not the country."

David concurred with JFK's attitude about some of the dreams he wanted to inspire and accomplish during his presidency, like seeing peace in the world, by stating: "I'm an idealist without illusions."

David admired the social skills Kennedy possessed and the connections he had with so many Hollywood celebrities, like when, on May 24th, 1961, he and the First Lady, Jacqueline Bouvier Kennedy, entertained Princess Grace Kelly, the former Hollywood movie star, and her husband, Prince Rainer II de Grimaldi of Monaco, at the White House.

Christ's Triumphant Appearance

David viewed another video, where on May 25th, 1961, before a joint session of Congress, John F. Kennedy boldly shared a vision destined to come to pass in July of 1969, stating: "I believe that this nation should commit itself to achieving the goal, before this decade is out, of landing a man on the moon and returning him safely to the Earth.

JOHN F. KENNEDY

And there was, of course, the Cuban Missile Crisis that shocked the United States and the world, when Russia transported missiles to Cuba, just off the coast of Florida. David was dazzled by JFK's handling of this dangerous situation and hung on to every word he said in his televised speech of October 22nd, 1962, especially when he challenged the Russian dictator: "I call upon Chairman Khrushchev to halt this clandestine, reckless, and provocative threat to world peace and to stabilize relations between our two nations." Rather than initiate a full-scale retaliatory nuclear war against Russia as his military advisors insisted, President Kennedy, with his brother, Attorney General Robert Francis Kennedy, by his side, chose to verbally confront the Russian Chairman in an incredibly dangerous poker game with the entire world at stake. And in the end, Khrushchev folded, detouring all the nuclear warheads away from Cuba that he had sent.

David became very enamored and awestruck with President Kennedy when he met with the current Israeli Labor and Foreign Minister, Golda Meir, in Palm Beach, Florida on December 27th, 1962. It was on this occasion that JFK expressed his devotion to Israel, when he said: "Israel was not created in order to disappear. Israel will endure and flourish. Israel is the child of hope and the home of the brave. Israel can neither be broken by adversity nor demoralized by success. Israel carries the shield of democracy, and Israel honors the sword of freedom." Golda Meir went on to become David's favorite Prime Minister of Israel. Her first term began on March 17th, 1969.

Although David was training to become the best fighter jet pilot he could possibly be, he shared President Kennedy's views concerning the weapons of war:

"Mankind must put an end to war, or war will put an end to mankind."

"The weapons of war must be abolished before they abolish us."

This included the day when JFK addressed the General Assembly of the United Nations on September 25th, 1961, and stated: "Every man, woman, and child lives under a nuclear sword of Damocles, hanging by the slenderest of threads, capable of being cut at any time by accident, or miscalculation, or madness."

And with all the worldwide civil unrest that was taking place in David's day, he felt that the diplomatic words in JFK's televised speech on June 11th, 1963 were most applicable to his own time. Even in the modern, super technological period that David lived, there were horrible upheavals in society that existed, created by civil chaos and racial tension. Pandemonium was created by the riots that were breaking out, and civil rights protesters were filling the streets worldwide on a regular basis. The entire planet was on edge. And it didn't appear that any progress had been made in regard to achieving social justice since the time of President Abraham Lincoln or the calamity of President John F. Kennedy's Administration. Mankind had not grown to learn a single thing concerning equal rights for all, not only in the United States but around the world as well.

Yet unlike the world leaders of David's day, who lacked the ability to offer sympathetic comfort in the midst of this ongoing crisis, the words that President John F. Kennedy incorporated in a televised speech served to appease the nation, even in the midst of a pandemic. The plague of inequality was even exceeding the turmoil of the pandemic at hand. The words JFK rendered came from his heart and soul, and still prevail:

"Good evening, my fellow citizens. I hope that every American, regardless of where he lives, will stop and examine his conscience. This nation was founded on the principle that all men are created equal, and that the rights of every man are diminished when the rights of one man are threatened.

Today, we are committed to a worldwide struggle to promote and protect the rights of all who wish to be free. It ought to be possible, in short, for every American to enjoy the privileges of being American without regard to his race or his color. In short, every American ought to have the right to be treated as he would wish to be treated. This is not a sectional issue. Nor is this a partisan issue. This is not even a legal or legislative issue alone. It is better to settle these matters in the courts than on the streets, and new laws are needed at every level, but laws alone cannot make men see right.

We are confronted primarily with a moral issue. It is as old as the Scriptures and as clear as the Constitution. The heart of the question is whether we are going to treat our fellow Americans as we want to be treated. And this nation, for all its hopes and all its boasts, will not be fully free until all its citizens are free. Now, the time has come for this nation to fulfill its promise. The fires of frustration and discord are burning in every city. We face, therefore, a moral crisis as a country and a people. A great change is at hand, and our task, our obligation, is to make that revolution, that change, peaceful and constructive for all.

My fellow Americans, this is a problem which faces us all. It seems to me that these are matters which concern us all, not merely Presidents or Congressmen or Governors, but every citizen of the United States. This is one country. It has become one country because all the people born here and all the people who came here had an equal chance to develop their talents. Therefore, I am asking for your help in making it easier for us to move ahead and to provide the kind of equality of treatment which we would want ourselves. This is what we are talking about, and this is the matter which concerns this country and what it stands for. And in meeting it, I ask the support of all our citizens. Thank you very much."

After hearing this speech, David considered that mankind's general response to remedy civil unrest (in the last days), even in the midst of a pandemic, appeared to be worldwide violence in the streets.

David was amazed that the civil unrest occurring during Kennedy's presidency was not so much different than the days in which he lived, and that no progress seemed to have taken place on this vital issue. So, civil unrest persists to this very day. Because social justice will not come until there is a strong component of trust for our respective world leaders. And those leaders must be trustworthy enough for the people to honestly believe that these elected officials have the best interests for the people at heart, leading their constituents with at least some degree of understanding. And also that, somehow, all people would be willing to make it their number one priority to be in harmony with each other.

And then, just a little more than two weeks after President Kennedy's speech on civil rights, he delivered David's favorite speech of all time to the people of West Berlin, Germany on June 26th, 1963:

"You live in a defended island of freedom, but your life is part of the main. So, let me ask you as I close to lift your eyes beyond the dangers of today to the hopes of tomorrow. Beyond the freedom merely of this city of Berlin or your country of Germany to the advance of freedom everywhere. Beyond this wall to the day of peace and justice. Beyond yourselves and

Christ's Triumphant Appearance

ourselves to all mankind. Freedom is indivisible, and when one man is enslaved, all are not free. When all are free, then, we can look forward to that day when this city will be joined as one and this country and this great Continent of Europe in a peaceful and hopeful globe. When that day finally comes, AS IT WILL (Matthew 24:27, 30, 31), the people of West Berlin can take sober satisfaction in the fact that they were in the front lines for almost two decades."

And it was on June 10, 1963, at a Commencement Address at American University in Washington D.C., President John Fitzgerald Kennedy spoke no truer words concerning international affairs:

"No government or social system is so evil that its people must be considered as lacking in virtue. For in the final analysis, our most basic common link is that we all inhabit this small planet. We all cherish our children's future. And we are all mortal. Confident and unafraid, we labor on --- not toward a strategy of annihilation, but toward a strategy of peace."

The assassinations of John F. Kennedy, Robert F. Kennedy and Martin Luther King Jr. in the 1960's were also pivotal in bringing the world to such an ominous place of difficult times. These assassinations carried a ripple effect that were even affecting so many people in David's modern era.

No one summed up the situation more appropriately than JFK's wife, Jacqueline Kennedy, concerning the loss of one of America's greatest presidents, when she said:

"Now, I think I should have known that he was magic all along. I did know it, but I should have guessed that it would be too much to ask to grow old with him and see our children grow up together. So, now, he is a legend when he would have preferred to be a man."

HARVEST RESTAURANT
CAMBRIDGE, MASSACHUSETTS

David, Bathsheba, and Jonathan arrived at Harvest Restaurant promptly at 7:00 P.M. David and Jonathan both looked dapper wearing dress slacks, sports coats, and shirts with an open collar. Bathsheba was looking

Christ's Triumphant Appearance

especially sensational in an exquisite, classic style evening dress. The maître d' was expecting them and knew exactly which table to escort them to, as he had known Dr. Goldstein for many years, and had frequented him to the same cozy corner of the restaurant on a number of occasions. As David walked to the table, he couldn't help but be reminded of the five immortal words that Dr. Goldstein had stressed to him: "Everything has come full circle."

DR. SAMUEL GOLDSTEIN'S COZY LITTLE CORNER AT HARVEST RESTAURANT

"Thank you for coming. Your presence here tonight is a statement that we are all on the same page or, shall we say, wavelength." Dr. Goldstein said. "Using the word, 'page,' is far too much of a pun coming from an old English professor such as myself. Please make yourselves comfortable."

"Well, this restaurant, certainly, is everything you said it would be," remarked David. "What a great atmosphere!"

"Yes. I like it. It's the atmosphere of Harvest Restaurant that has prevented me from going anywhere else for quite some time now," Dr. Goldstein responded. "And, of course, you are Bathsheba and Jonathan. What a joy it is to meet you and have all three of you dine with me on this divine appointment. And Bathsheba, you are just as beautiful in person as I thought you would be. You and David make such a handsome couple together."

"Thank you, Dr. Goldstein," Bathsheba replied, most impressed with his charming, courteous demeanor.

Jonathan acknowledged what a pleasure it was to meet Dr. Goldstein, having heard so much about him from David. He, as well, was very impressed with how much of a refined, distinguished gentleman Dr. Goldstein appeared to be.

"All three of you are getting settled here at Harvard I trust. That is, has it been a smooth transition for you?" Dr. Goldstein inquired.

"Oh, yes!" Bathsheba said, beating David and Jonathan to the response, thinking how nice it was of Dr. Goldstein to ask such a considerate question. "I know this is going to be a wonderful experience."

All four of them chatted casually for a while, and then, decided to order their meals.

Dr. Goldstein summoned Abagail, his favorite waitress, over to the table, and introduced her to David, Bathsheba, and Jonathan. After the amenities with Abigail, leaving no room for doubt of her affability, they were all ready to order.

"I'll have New England Seafood Boil," Bathsheba requested, with David ordering the same.

Christ's Triumphant Appearance

"And the Roasted Beets and Apples as an appetizer," Bathsheba added.

"Excellent choices," Abigail said.

"I'll go with the 14-ounce Brandt Prime Beef Sirloin." Jonathan said.

"And I'll have my usual, Abigail," Dr. Goldstein stated, which meant that he also wanted the 14-ounce Brandt Prime Beef Sirloin, like Jonathan.

"Very good," Abigail responded, and then, focused on Dr. Goldstein's guests. "I hope you three realize that you're in the hands of an exceptionally fine host. He is good company. Trust me, especially when he's in the relaxing domain of Harvest Restaurant. I'd like to officially welcome all three of you as our special guests."

David, Bathsheba, and Jonathan all nodded in appreciation.

Dr. Goldstein, then, paused for a few seconds after Abigail had left, as if to gather his thoughts, "Well, David has probably mentioned to you that, just like yourselves, I was born and raised in Israel. While I do have a great inclination and imagination for written works, as you know, being David's English Literature professor, I also have an aptitude for music, and have served as a cantor in the synagogue for many years. I've even married a number of couples, having the authority to do so. I consider myself to be an Orthodox Jew, but, of course, I'm very well read, and I have an open mind. I happened to get wind of David and Jonathan's victory for the State Football Championship when you were students at Davidson High School, not terribly long ago. It's quite an extraordinary story how I came across the article, as I was doing some research on an unrelated topic. And go Davidson Warriors, by the way! But, when I say that I have an open mind, I am mostly referring to very deep topics.'"

"Yes!" Bathsheba exclaimed, in support of David and Jonathan, most impressed with Dr. Goldstein's knowledge of them. "I suppose you can safely say that they are not only all-Israeli boys, but also all-American boys as well."

Christ's Triumphant Appearance

"Yes, the very best of both worlds, Bathsheba. Dr. Goldstein concurred. Of course, all four of us, having been born in Israel, are of a unique and special kindred spirit. But let me ask all three of you, at the risk of opening a serious discussion: "Have either one of you ever heard of the Restoration of the Throne of David?"

"I think I can speak for all three of us, Dr. Goldstein." David replied. "We all know what you mean. It concerns Israel with the Coming of the Israeli Messiah, Mashiach ben David, to build his Temple and establish his kingdom once and for all. Ever since the second Temple was destroyed in 70 A.D., the Israelis have desired to see the Temple built again."

"Very good, my boy!" Dr. Goldstein exclaimed, as his face lit up. "And, of course, I'm sure you're fully aware where the Temple must be built, and the hindrances that are keeping it from being built."

"Yes," Jonathan quickly spoke up. "It is absolutely imperative that the Temple be built on the Temple Mount. The Temple Mount would need to be ritually sanctified before the Temple would be allowed to be built."

"My goodness! It's quite apparent that I'm in good company tonight. There's no doubt that control over the Temple Mount is the single most volatile factor in determining the destiny of our planet." Dr. Goldstein interjected. "That fact is universally conceded. There have been peace proposals, plans, agreements, and accords considered and attempted, but alas, a formal, lasting peace between all parties involved in the Middle East has apparently been an impossibility. Perhaps, it should be submitted that only the Israeli Messiah will be successful in bringing about everlasting, never-ending peace to the Middle East and the world. Any and all efforts of men will fall through. And everlasting peace will not be witnessed when Solomon's Temple is rebuilt. It will be documented seven years later, after the Tribulation, when the Millennial Temple is built by the Israeli Messiah, and the Messiah alone. Both the major and the minor prophets in the Hebrew Bible," Dr. Goldstein elaborated, "have prophesied that the Millennial Temple will be built. And it's abundantly clear that there will be two Temples built after Israel becomes a State, which, of course, gloriously occurred in 1948. The fulfillment of the prophecy of Israel regaining control of her country again gave us good cause to celebrate the confirmation that

Christ's Triumphant Appearance

the rebuilding of the Temple is within reach. This will be Israel's third Temple, otherwise referred to as Solomon's Temple Rebuilt, that, in turn, becomes the Tribulation Temple, and is destroyed at the end of the Seven Year Tribulation. Then, at that point, the Millennial Temple will be created by the Israeli Messiah, without any need of assistance from human hands. In fact, there are a number of prophecies that have come to pass after Israel was formed as a nation in 1948. And there are not many prophecies remaining to be fulfilled before Solomon's Temple is rebuilt. The destructive psyche of human depravity is a component of mankind that makes war an inevitable reality. The Israeli Messiah will make it possible for the Jews and their allies to rise above that depravity and reach out for peace. That may be the very reason why the Messiah is referred to as the Pearl of Great Price. God's plan for the Temple was first revealed to Moses at the foot of Mount Sinai. Out of the thunders of Mount Sinai, the God of Israel revealed his plan by which the Tabernacle of God would be constructed. The connection between the Tabernacle, the first and second Temples, and the two latter day Temples is unmistakable. The God of Israel said to Moses: "Let them construct a Sanctuary for me that I may dwell among them." And the Israelis today are more than ready to rebuild Solomon's Temple, despite the fact that the third Temple is marked in the Hebrew Bible as doomed, according to Daniel, the Prophet. The Israeli people believe that the two Israeli Temples of the future, Solomon's Temple Rebuilt and the Millennial Temple, must be built on Mount Moriah in Jerusalem, which, of course, is equivalent to the exact location of the Temple Mount. It is also the same place where Abraham, the father of the Jews, built an altar, and where King David bought a parcel of land in high hopes of the Temple being built on that very spot. Mount Moriah is interpreted as the mountain of God's inheritance. Even Moses predicted the Messiah alone would build the Millennial Temple to secure the Israelis, when he said: "You shall bring your people in, and plant them in the mountain of your inheritance, in this place, O, Lord, which you have made for yourself to dwell in the Sanctuary, which your hands have established." The Temple, as you know, David, Bathsheba, and Jonathan, is extremely important to Israeli nationality. The Temple is essential to establishing and preserving the national and international unity and integrity of Israel. The Temple is a representation of Israel's national sovereignty. And the Temple brings about a unique measure of stability for the Israeli people. Yet while there are, certainly, many peace-loving Muslims in the world, the Radical

Christ's Triumphant Appearance

Muslims advocate a very dangerous brand of Islam. As you said Jonathan, the elimination of Israel is a prerequisite for the emergence of the global Islamic state, from the viewpoint of all Radical Muslims and those supporting their cause. Therefore, there is a realistic question as to whether or not the Jewish Temple can be built on the Temple Mount, that is, without the possibility of annihilating the entire world."

"Excuse me, Dr. Goldstein," Abigail said, "I hate to interrupt you, but I have your entrees." Abigail had already slipped the appetizers in, during their conversation. She had expedited the meals for Dr. Goldstein's table.

"All right, the New England Seafood Broil for David and Bathsheba, and the 14-ounce Prime Beef Sirloin for Jonathan and Dr. Goldstein," Abigail politely said, being a superb, first-class waitress. "I trust that Dr. Goldstein is keeping his guests well entertained."

"Oh, yes. He's fascinating." Bathsheba confirmed eagerly.

"I'm not surprised one bit," Abigail said. "He and I have engaged in some very enlightening discussions through the years. He's been a good friend to me. Okay, you continue to mingle, mingle. Enjoy your meals and let me know if I may assist you in any way."

"She is quite academic herself," Dr Goldstein said after Abigail had left. "Now, let's shift gears somewhat, and focus on Israel's solution to this matter. We have made reference to the Restoration of the Throne of David. As you had mentioned, David, the Jewish Messiah is Mashiach ben David. The existence of the modern-day State of Israel today, formed against all odds, is the number one exhibit of evidence that all the other prophecies of the prophets, great and small, of the Hebrew Bible, concerning every single issue of the end time, are expected to, literally, be fulfilled. As mentioned, the Jewish people's return to the Promised Land of Israel is one of the single most significant fulfilled Biblical prophecies of all time. It, certainly, serves to signify the greatest sign that the latter days are upon us. The entire world observed the Jew's return to Israel in awe as the prophecies of the Hebrew prophets unfolded in high drama. Many Israelis felt that this occurrence would, in and of itself, usher in the appearance of the Israeli Messiah, but other prophecies needed to be fulfilled first. The first great miracle of

Christ's Triumphant Appearance

fulfillment occurred on May 14th, 1948, when the United Nations officially recognized Israel as a State. The loss of the second Israeli Temple in 70 A.D. brought about an ongoing threat concerning Israel's continued national existence. Yet now, hope has been renewed that all the other prophecies, especially concerning the Temple, will follow suit. The Millennial Temple becoming a reality in the future at the hand of the Messiah will be the ultimate proof that the prophets knew what they were talking about, and that they were inspired. The Israelis and all our ancestors cannot, by any means, reach their proper spiritual status without the Temple being rebuilt on the Temple Mount in Jerusalem. The Temple, of the last days, will be the supreme statement of Israeli sovereignty. There will be a new level of spiritual attainment achieved through the building of the Millennial Temple. And the Millennial Temple will shine as a beacon to the entire world. The Restoration of the Throne of David is dependent upon the building of the Millennial Temple by the Israeli Messiah alone. As it is written by Zechariah, among others: "The Jewish Messiah shall build the Temple, and he shall sit and rule upon his Throne." And Zechariah, also, made it clear that the trademark of the Messiah's reign will be peace, everlasting peace. Isaiah, the Prophet, pointed out that the Messiah is the Prince of Peace, and that the increase of the Messiah's government and peace will have no end upon the Throne of David and his kingdom. And that he will establish his kingdom forever."

"The Israelis have returned and resettled in their own land. They will never be removed again." David firmly said with confidence.

"It's interesting that you would be the very one to point that out. I'm very proud of you, David. I can see that my English Literature class this semester is going to be a wonderful growth experience for both of us," Dr. Goldstein said, once again in a protectively grandfather fashion. "With a population approaching a considerable number of Israelis around the world, modern-day Israel has harnessed political, military and economic ties with the world's democratic superpowers, and has an arsenal that includes an incredible number of nuclear weapons considering the size of our country. It appears, on the surface, that the State of Israel will continue to exist. Despite the fact that Israel's enemies have acquired nuclear and chemical weapons, that they either produced themselves or smuggled in through the black-market, Israel remains one of the world's strongest military powers.

Christ's Triumphant Appearance

And, more often than not, we've been victorious in battles facing insurmountable odds, such as the classic Six Day War and the Yom Kippur War, that allowed us to gain back a lot of our land and then some, to extend our borders. And God has just begun the process of expanding the borders of Israel. The Israeli victories thus procured is a show of strength that has been nothing short of miraculous. The fact that the God of Israel has intervened to secure these victories is what gives Israel the edge on being unmatched militarily. The Book of Ezekiel makes it quite clear that the Israelis will dwell in their own land, the Eternal Promised Land. This is referring to the land that our ancestors, and their children, and their children's children were intended to abide in forever. And that the God of Israel's servant, David, will be their prince forever. The prophet goes on to say that God has devised a Covenant of peace. And that it will be that very everlasting Covenant that he wants to put in place. We are destined to enter into the Eternal Land of Promise. The God of Israel desires to set up his Sanctuary, the Millennial Temple, in the midst of us forever. You see, the Israeli Messiah is of the lineage of David. He is a descendant of David. And yet, paradoxically, he has been around since prior to the very foundation of the world as well."

"Is everything okay?" Abigail broke in and asked.

"Everything is just fine," Jonathan quickly responded. "It couldn't be better."

Everyone was nodding in accord.

"The food is absolute cuisine," Bathsheba added.

"And I couldn't help but notice that Dr. Goldstein has your undivided attention," Abigail said cheerfully. "He's had me spellbound a number of times. He can be quite dazzling."

"You're too kind, Abigail." Dr. Goldstein said, seeming a little embarrassed with a red face. "You folks would think that Abigail is one of my nearest kin, rendering compliments like that. But she, literally, is like family to me. You are very special to many people who are patrons of Harvest Restaurant, Abigail."

Christ's Triumphant Appearance

"I feel that same way about you," Dr. Goldstein. "You are special to all of us here at Harvest Restaurant. Is there anything else that I can get for any of you? May I entice you with some dessert? The coconut chocolate mousse cake is incredible."

"No, thank you," Bathsheba responded. "That sounds a little too divine for me, calorie-wise. Everything is just fine."

"She's trying to maintain that girlish figure of hers." David said, with Bathsheba giving him a glare."

"Well, she's certainly managing to do that," Abigail responded. "How about the rest of you?"

"I'm good," Jonathan said.

"The same here. Thank you for everything." David concurred.

"We're all fine, Abigail," Dr. Goldstein added. "As usual, you've been superb and a joy to see."

"Thank you," Abigail said. "Be sure to come again. It's been a wonderful pleasure meeting all of you."

"What I'm leading up to concerning the Restoration of the Throne of David is that since the throne is going to be restored, then, people are being restored as well," Dr. Goldstein emphasized. "The prophet, Joel, said that the Israeli Messiah would restore his people and raise up his great army, of which he would designate David to lead the way as his commander. David, of the end time, will be just as much a man after God's own heart as David was in the Hebrew Bible. We shall know that the Messiah is in our midst, and he will put his Spirit upon us, that we may be empowered. And you must know that I can say with total assurance that you are the Restored David, Bathsheba, and Jonathan. I am not referring to reincarnation or anything mystical of that nature. It's just like I mentioned to you when we first met in my class, David. Five words that sum it all up: 'Everything has come full circle.' And you three, among many, many others as well, of

Christ's Triumphant Appearance

course, are obviously most special in the eyes of our God. That is, certainly, no exaggeration in your case."

"I've had flashbacks about this --- recollections --- glimpses. Just like in your class, when I pictured you anointing me many years ago," David said, without doubting one bit that Dr. Goldstein was absolutely correct. It made perfect sense to David.

"There is much more to say along these lines to verify what I'm saying," Dr. Goldstein added. "David, you and Jonathan are, indeed, the Two Anointed Ones mentioned in the Hebrew Bible, who will be empowered by Moses, Elijah, and the Israeli Messiah. You are also referred to as the Two Olive Trees. Some will try to say that the Two Anointed Ones are Zerubbabel, who built the second Temple after the Jews were released from Babylonian captivity, and the High Priest, Joshua, but that belief is in error. Zechariah, the Prophet, states that these two will not be operating in their own strength or power, but strictly by their God's power. Also, according to the eleventh chapter of the Book of Revelation in the New Testament, the Two Anointed Ones of the Book of Zechariah in the Hebrew Bible are referred to as the Two Witnesses, the Two Olive Trees and the Two Candlesticks. In all reality, these two are, indeed, the restored David and Jonathan of the last days, who are expected to be great heroes for Israel, especially in the final week of the Seventy Weeks of Years, commonly referred to as the Seven Year Tribulation mentioned in the Book of Daniel. Moses and Elijah will, at a critical point, converge upon the Restored David and the Restored Jonathan of the latter days. These two men will have the power, as Elijah did in the Hebrew Bible, to shut the skies so that no rain will fall, and, also, like Moses, having the power to turn rivers and oceans into blood, and to send every kind of plague upon the Earth. These Two Anointed Ones will have the power to perform the same miracles of Elijah and Moses, plus much more, considering the task ahead of them. David and Jonathan, who have a sacred, eternal oath with each other, reinforced by God, are, indisputably, the Two Anointed Ones in our modern time. The Ark of the Covenant is also mentioned in the eleventh chapter of Revelation, the exact same chapter where the Restored David and Jonathan are referred to in the New Testament of the Bible. This fact is highly significant, especially for David. The prophets of the Hebrew Bible foresaw many, many years ago that the latter day David and Jonathan would blaze the way

Christ's Triumphant Appearance

for Israel's restoration. And David and Jonathan themselves solidified the prophecies of the prophets by making an oath with each other, in the Book First Samuel, that God, in His name, would abide between David's descendants and Jonathan's descendants for all time, until everything comes full circle, and they unite again in person. And I know it's safe to say that the God of Israel is honoring that oath between David and Jonathan this very evening. And, by the way, since I've been making reference to the Book of Revelation, no one needs to remind me that any Jew who advocates the New Testament is regarded by many other Jews as not being a legitimate Jew. But, as I said, to make a very long story short, I've been around the block with all this, and it's forced me to have an objective, open mind."

"Wow!" Bathsheba reacted.

"There's more," Dr. Goldstein continued. "In the Book of the Song of Solomon, that is, Song of Solomon 6:10, there is a reference to Bathsheba, 'who looks forth as the morning, fair as the moon, clear as the sun, and terrible as an army of banners.' This is a highly significant verse referring to you, Bathsheba. David is a military man, as predicted in Ezekiel 37:10 to lead Israel's army in the end time. Bathsheba is the wife of an Israeli military man, and she is a woman of war. Also, in the twelfth chapter of the Book of Revelation, Bathsheba is spoken of as a woman appearing as a great wonder in Heaven. She is clothed with the sun, which is a metaphor referring to you, David, and the moon is under her feet, which is a metaphor referring to you, Bathsheba. And a crown of twelve stars, symbolic of the Twelve Tribes of Israel, is on her head. She is pregnant with a male child. This child will be you and David's future son, Bathsheba, the Restored Solomon, whose presence in the world will be instrumental in the rebuilding of Solomon's Temple. It goes on to say that the devil, described to be a Red Dragon, is ready to pounce upon this boy as soon as he is born. The devil also spews out a flood of destruction toward the woman, but the Earth is opened up to swallow the flood. And she is also given two wings of a great eagle by the God of Israel, who equips her with his Spirit and power like the eagles mentioned in Isaiah 40:31, to escape the devil's relentless pursuit."

"I'll say it backwards. Wow!" Jonathan exclaimed.

Christ's Triumphant Appearance

"I believe I've said enough for now," Dr. Goldstein said, "but I should emphasize, without just blurting it out in an insensitive manner, that the three of you are in grave danger. And the main reason for all the imminent peril will be the rise of a madman, who will come to be known as the false messiah. As civilization speeds toward its final destiny, a powerful world leader will emerge to center stage and assume his much-desired place."

Dr. Goldstein went on to conclude, without skipping a beat, "With this soon to come maniac, the false messiah, emerging into the world picture, only to bring so much war, destruction, and bloodshed on Earth, all optimistic hopes and dreams of the future will one day smolder in the ashes of a world gone crazy. He will appear in between the period after the Battle of Gog and Magog and the rebuilding of Solomon's Temple and make his move. He will operate in what he considers to be his own perfect timing, mocking God's perfect timing. He will arise promising lasting peace in the Middle East. He will be one of the people signing a seven-year treaty with Israel, involving negotiations with Israel's harshest enemies. The Bible predicts this treaty between Israel and this powerful world leader will bring about a bogus, fraudulent peace and prosperity between the country of Israel and her surrounding enemy nations. This peace will be short-lived, and only last for three-and-a-half years, that is, the first half of the Seven Year Tribulation. At that point, this world leader will break his covenant with Israel. He will, then, go on to violently persecute the people of Israel for the next three and a half years. The last three and a half years of the Seven Year Tribulation will be the Great Tribulation or "Jacob's Trouble" as prophesied in the Book of Jeremiah, the Book of Daniel, the Book of Revelation and the Book of Matthew, by the Israeli Messiah himself. And, in the midst of the Seven Year Tribulation, the false messiah will cause the sacrifices and offerings at the altar of the Temple to cease, and he will blaspheme the God of Israel in the Holy of Holies, proclaiming that he is the Most High God, as prophesied by Isaiah, Daniel, and Paul, the Apostle, in II Thessalonians 2:3-9. The chaos created will pave the way for him to rise as a new world leader, as he pleases. Satan has battled Israel at every turn throughout history, waiting for the right moment to indwell the right person as his final masterpiece. the false messiah will be the absolute embodiment of evil, and carry out his dirty work throughout the entire world. He will establish the new Roman Empire, equivalent to a modern-day Babylon. And he will do whatever it takes to destroy God's people and prevent the Millennial Temple from being built by Mashiach ben David."

Christ's Triumphant Appearance

Dr. Goldstein hesitated for a moment, as if to gather his thoughts just one more time for the evening, and then, proceeded.

"And, as a priority, keep this in mind: Don't be misled by modern-day false prophets making bogus claims as to when the Messiah is coming. The Messiah has already stated that he will come quickly enough. And the countless number of souls who died waiting for the Great and Terrible Day of the Lord, that is, the brightness of the Coming of the Lord Jesus Christ to take place will suddenly find themselves in the Eternal Promised Land of Israel at last!" Dr. Goldstein said emphatically.

"The only way I'm going to be flying off is in a fighter jet," David quipped.

"There goes that disarming charm of yours again," Bathsheba retorted, with a big smile.

"She's the only one who laughs at my jokes," David said sincerely, although others did appreciate his sense of humor and levity.

"Yes. You two have a fascinating rapport with each other." Dr. Goldstein said, seeming just as amused with David's remark.

"Now, also of great importance is that you be aware that the false messiah will be more than merely a comrade of the devil," Dr. Goldstein elaborated. "The false messiah will be the devil incarnate. Successfully destroying the false messiah would be the direct equivalent of annihilating Satan. And of course, this is an extremely precarious situation which entails many risks, because we don't know the intricate details. Only Almighty God knows. But one thing I do know: Defeating Satan cannot be done without the assistance of the Israeli Messiah. And I also know that our world will not have a chance of procuring peace as long as the false messiah has his way. So, take this as a nugget of wisdom and perspective: Satan may be able to discern when the Seven Year Tribulation is forthcoming, and act accordingly with his plans, but the devil does not possess all the complex information as to how matters will come to pass. Satan is left to speculate on many issues that the God of Israel already had figured out before anyone else came along. A good example of us knowing the broad details is the fact that all four of us are aware that the Ark of the Covenant will somehow be restored to the Millennial Temple after the Messiah builds it. I would venture to say that the responsibility of getting the Ark back to its rightful place has been laid on your shoulders in a large respect, David," Dr. Goldstein stressed.

"Well, despite all the myths and theories, such as the Knights Templar, the Qumran caves in Israel where the Dead Sea Scrolls were found, the Church of Our Lady Mary in Aksum, Ethiopia, and so forth, Dr. Goldstein," David replied, "I, honestly, know where the Ark of the Covenant may be found."

"I don't doubt that one bit, my boy," Dr. Goldstein said. "Of all the people who are living today, I am not at all surprised that you are privy to having information concerning the Ark. You, certainly, qualify in the God of Israel's eyes. The Ark of the Covenant disappeared after the first Temple and Jerusalem were destroyed by the Babylonians. It is absolutely imperative that the Ark of the Covenant be restored to the Millennial Temple. But we do not want to allow the Ark to enter the Tribulation Temple, that is, Solomon's Temple Rebuilt, because it's been prophesied by Daniel, the Prophet, in the Book of Daniel, that it will be unavoidable to keep the false messiah from blaspheming our God from the location of the Holy of Holies, where the Ark is usually in place. This event will be referred to as the Abomination of Desolation, as predicted by Daniel, the Prophet, in the Book of Daniel and by Jesus Christ in the twenty-fourth chapter of the Book of Matthew. We don't want the Ark to be in place when this horrible event of the Abomination of Desolation occurs. And, considering that the Abomination of Desolation is a legitimate Hebrew prophecy, then, we can more than assume that it, very unfortunately, is something that will actually occur. But there is sound assurance, according to the prediction of Daniel, that a time will come when the God of Israel's kingdom will destroy all the other kingdoms of the world. Daniel, also, prophesied that the God of Heaven will set up a kingdom that will never be destroyed. No one is going to ever conquer it. God's kingdom is fully expected to shatter these evil kingdoms into nothingness, and his kingdom will stand forever. We know the overall blueprint, but we do not know the complicated fine points."

Christ's Triumphant Appearance

"Wouldn't you say that would open things up for us to play with destiny?" David said. "Do we have the right to outguess God, who is omniscient?"

"That's the million-dollar question, David. Is God even in control of all the smaller details, or are we making decisions on our own, subject to error, to the extent that our mistakes are fatal enough to cause us to lose the victory and plummet the world into eternal darkness." Dr. Goldstein responded.

"That's deep! Considering that so many lives are at stake." Jonathan noted.

"There are so many people involved in this big picture who have passed away, such as, our forefathers who looked forward to the day when all of the prophecies of the Bible would come to fulfillment. Moses, who was chose by Yahweh, the father of spirits (Hebrews 12:9), to lead the Israelites out of Egypt by way of the Red Sea and through the wilderness, with God going before them by day in a pillar of cloud showing the way, and by night in a pillar of fire to give the light (Exodus 13:21). There are people from all different backgrounds counting on the Eternal Promised Land to be within their grasp," Dr. Goldstein said in closing. "I must, indeed, admit that the entire scenario is a very terrifying prospect. And David, Bathsheba, and Jonathan, while all four of us may have an idea of the overall picture and scheme of things, we are still at a loss to know everything that's going to be necessary to fill in the gaps. Therefore, how do we know that we have any guarantee of success, other than including faith into the equation?"

"And with all that said, Dr. Goldstein," David responded, "considering that your three guests this evening here at Harvest Restaurant represent the Restored David, Bathsheba, and Jonathan of the last days, then, it would, apparently, follow suit that you are the Restored ..."

David was interrupted. Dr. Goldstein quickly addressed David's astute, logical deduction.

"That's exactly right, David. The Restored Samuel, the Prophet," Dr. Goldstein interjected, confirming what David, Bathsheba, and Jonathan knew all along.

CHAPTER SIX
THE PROPHETIC PATH OF NO RETURN

HATZERIM AIRBASE
THE ISRAELI AIR FORCE FLIGHT ACADEMY
TOP GUN TRAINING
BEER SHEVA, ISRAEL
44 MILES SOUTHWEST OF JERUSALEM

Before leaving Hanscom Air Force Base in the United States, David Hartman and Jonathan Diamond participated in a special ceremony there to receive their fighter pilot call signs. David was designated the call sign, Soaring Eagle, because he always flew a fighter jet as gracefully as an eagle soars across the sky. Observing David rising so effortlessly in his F-22 Raptor Stealth Fighter Jet was just like watching someone breaking free of every troubling care in life. And Jonathan was given the call sign, Greased Lightning, because he loved to fly so fast in his F-35 Lightning IV Stealth Fighter Jet, propelled by the Spirit of God, gliding him upon the wind, causing onlookers to somehow recapture the simplicity of God that escapes man. It was as if David and Jonathan were both reaching for the Eternal One, Yahweh, in flight. The interaction of this charismatic duo, soaring together in such a synchronized fashion as Fighter Wing Leader and Wingman, was an infinite mystery that couldn't be explained away. It was the vivid phenomenon of two men revealing God's own unique purpose in

Christ's Triumphant Appearance

their lives, that is, the kind of meaning that most people search for without end. As people in Israel stood and stared upwards at the sky day by day, they were inspired with the sensation that David and Jonathan had somehow miraculously discovered the secret of where all new-born life originates, beyond what human intellect was capable to reason. There was no more of a glorious sight on Earth. And these two respective call signs would follow them for the duration of their flying careers, and that, of course, was no less true when they transferred to Hatzerim Airbase in Beer Sheva, Israel, after being accepted to the Israeli Air Force Flight Academy for Israeli TOP GUN Fighter Jet training.

Both David and Jonathan had graduated with honors from Harvard and MIT and excelled in their education to become fighter jet pilots at Hanscom Air Force Base in the United States. They acquired distinguished recognition in Officer Training School (OTS). And their dream came true to be accepted to the top secret Israeli Air Force TOP GUN Flight Academy in Israel to receive training to compete to become the best of the best as Israeli TOP GUN Fighter Pilots.

The hard-fast-and-continuous TOP GUN Fighter Jet training for David and Jonathan's class had been intense. There was a review of the basic instruction of aerodynamics, tactics, and maneuvers, and, of course, there was a great deal of advanced learning.

Of all the instructors and mentors who David and Jonathan would draw from, Commander Ariel Rosenberg, Bathsheba's father, stood out as an outstanding model for all of the young TOP GUN Fighter Pilots to emulate. He was a genuine Israeli hero, and his style of teaching stood out from all the rest. Physically, he towered over most men being six foot, four inches tall, with a muscular build and rugged features. Of course, another big factor that specifically stood out to David was that Commander Rosenberg was Bathsheba's father. He was also a very good friend of David's father. One statement made by Commander Rosenberg at the very beginning of TOP GUN training that really stood out to both David and Jonathan was: "Aggressiveness, determination, patience, and a cool head have distinguished the successful pilot from all others throughout the history of aerial combat. The pilot who makes the fewer gross mistakes is the pilot who wins."

Christ's Triumphant Appearance

It was pointed out that there are major rules of engagement in Israeli military science. There is an official approach and diplomatic protocol that must be abided by. Just as there had been a need for the Haganah, Hebrew for "the defense" of Israel (from 1920-1928), the establishment of Israeli TOP GUN had proven to be a vital component in the Israeli Defense Forces (IDF). Israeli TOP GUN had become perfectly designed and tweaked to protect the citizens of Israel. And these newly commissioned officers had been in Israeli TOP GUN Flight School to learn how to become strategists.

Israel has the most technologically advanced military on Earth. And more than any other country that gathered information from all around the world, Israel had to rely on the Mossad, Israeli Intelligence, to provide regular, ongoing, never-ending collection of international confidential knowledge for its very survival, most of it being top secret.

It would be emphasized by the more experienced pilots that aerial combat at such a high level, with all of its risks, is the most dangerous game in the world. It was here the students would learn resilience, versatility, agility, the ability to maneuver according to circumstance, and how to make split second decisions instinctively. It would be here they learned to master detail without wallowing it or being overwhelmed by it. It would be here they would learn how to encounter and survive every kind of hazard and opposition known to mankind. Some of the Israeli TOP GUN Fighter Jet training included: Israeli TOP GUN Aerial Combat Tactics and Maneuvers, mathematical solutions for even the messiest of fighter jet battle engagement problems, Fighter Jet Physics, modern-day dog fights, when to use guns and when to use missiles, Guided Rockets and Unguided Rockets, Aircraft Center of Gravity, the various fighter jets flown by TOP GUN Pilots, Lead Angle, Time-of-Flight, Velocity Vector, Line-of-Sight, cockpit devices such as the display unit, a gyroscope and the computer, tracking targets by holding the pipper steady in relation to the saddle, Air-to-Air Missiles, Surface-to-Air Missiles, Heat Seeking Missiles, Radar Guided Missiles, Cruise Missiles, gun firing situations that include Tracking Shots and Snapshots, the dangers of overshooting your jet in relation to the target, the rate of G increase, avoiding games of chicken, not allowing an enemy aircraft to get in firing range from behind, judging the changing flight path of a Guided Missile, Thrust-to-Weight Ratio, Guard Frequency, Nuclear Warheads, Atomic and Hydrogen Bombs, Tracking Radar Systems, Fire-

Christ's Triumphant Appearance

Control Computers, Hologram Computers, Quantum Computers, Angle-of-Attack, Jet Thrust Drag, Break Turns, Rolling Turns, Missile Guidance Trajectory, the physics and techniques of primary maneuvers, Pursuit Curves, Lag Pursuit, Lag Rolls, the High Yo-Yo and Low Yo-Yo Maneuvers, Turn Radius, Evasive Maneuvers, the Flat Scissors Maneuver, Vertical and Oblique Turns, Radical Acceleration being the Vector Sum of Load Factor and Gravity, Angle-of-Attack Fight Tactics, Energy Fight Tactics, the Zoom Climb Tactic, Basic Fighter Maneuvering (BFM), Section Engaged Maneuvering (SEM), Reengaging, Lead Turns, Vertical Maneuvering Speed, the Diving Spiral, 180 Degree Rolls, 360 Degree Rolls, Horizontal and Vertical Maneuvering, Rear-Quarter Shots, Beautiful Look-up Shots, Lift Vector, Turn Performance, Instantaneous Turn Performance, Sustained Turns, Maximum Turn Performance, G-Capability, Turbocharged Fighter Jets, Pure Pursuit, Supersonic Fighter Aircrafts, Hit-and-Run Tactics, Ballistic Flight Paths, Quantum Mechanics, the Theory of Relativity, the Electrodynamics of Moving Bodies, Brownian Motion, Hovering V/STOL Fighter Aircrafts such as the British Harrier and Boeing AH-64 Apache Attack Helicopter, Thrust Vector in Forward Flight, Fighter Wing Leaders, Wingmen, the Double Attack, Maneuvering Flexibility, the Offensive Spilt, the Defensive Split, the High/Low Split, Vertical and Horizontal Splits, not to engage unless you have the advantage, Cross Turns, Split Plane Maneuvering, Calculated Risks, Padlocking, the various aircraft formations, fighter jets escorting bombers, handling sensory overload, communications with Air Traffic Control, Ground Control, Israeli Command (Joshua) and other fighter pilots, Maximum Altitude Advantage, utilizing radar to detect targets in heavy clutter, Spins, Electronic Surveillance, Afterburners, Radar Jamming, the Bracket Attack, the Hook, the Sweep Tactic, Lift Limit, True Airspeed, Kinetic Energy, Potential Energy, Nuclear Physics, Mach Drag, Sustained G-Capability, Acceleration Performance, Lift-to-Drag Ratio, Lift-to-Weight Ratio, the effect of gravity on Turn Performance, Roll Performance and Aerodynamic Roll Controls. The Israeli TOP GUN Pilots were entrusted with many top secret details. Some of the Israeli TOP GUN Fighter Jet training was a review of what David and Jonathan picked up at Harvard, MIT, and Hanscom Air Force Base, but most of it was brand new. The bottom line to everything was to instill a second nature making accurate, split-second decisions.

Christ's Triumphant Appearance

**DAVID'S CALL SIGN: SOARING EAGLE – ISAIAH 40:31
THE GREAT EAGLE REVELATION 12:14**

David's call sign is Soaring Eagle as an Israeli TOP GUN Fighter Pilot. David flies a Lockheed Martin F-22 Raptor Stealth Fighter Jet. The definition of the word raptor is "a large, strong bird of prey, such as an eagle." Hence, the call sign, Soaring Eagle. Another very strong reinforcement to David having this particular call sign is that his favorite verse in the Hebrew Bible is Isaiah 40:31.

"They that wait upon the Lord shall renew their strength. They shall mount up with wings as eagles. They shall run, and not be weary. And they shall walk, and not faint." (Isaiah 40:31)

Christ's Triumphant Appearance

F-22 RAPTOR --- COMMANDER DAVID HARTMAN

Jonathan flies a Lockheed Martin F-35 Lighting IV Stealth Fighter Jet, hence, the call sign, Greased Lightning.

"And the fire was bright. And out of the fire came forth lightning." (Ezekiel 1:13; Matthew 24:27)

JONATHAN'S CALL SIGN: GREASED LIGHTNING

Christ's Triumphant Appearance
EZEKIEL 1:13 --- MATTHEW 24:27

F-35 LIGHTNING IV
COMMANDER JONATHAN DIAMOND

"I have found David, my servant. With my holy oil have I anointed him. With whom my hand shall be established. My arm also shall strengthen him. My mercy will preserve him forevermore, and my Covenant shall stand fast with him. His seed also will I make to endure forever, and his Throne as the days of Heaven." (The Lord God of Israel; Psalm 89:20, 21, 28, 29)

"Lord, remember David, and all his afflictions. How David swore unto the Lord God of Israel and vowed unto the mighty God of Jacob. Surely, I will not come into the comfort of my house, nor lay in my bed, or give to sleep to my eyes, or slumber to my eyelids, until I have found a place of rest for the Lord, a Habitation (The Millennial Temple; a permanent dwelling place) for the mighty God of Jacob." (David; Psalm 132:1-5)

"For I will defend this city (Jerusalem, Israel), to save it for my own sake, and for the sake of David, my servant." (The Lord God of Israel; Isaiah 37:35)

Christ's Triumphant Appearance

"The task of a leader is to get his people from where they are to where they have not been." (Former United States Secretary of State, Henry Kissinger)

"Nevertheless, for David's sake did the Lord his God give him a lamp in Jerusalem to set up his son (Solomon) after him, and to establish Jerusalem. Because David did that which was right in the eyes of the Lord."
(I Kings 15:4, 5)

"And God (Yahweh, the Eternal One) said unto him, 'Your name has been Jacob. But your name shall not be Jacob any longer, but Israel shall be your name.' And God called his name, Israel. And God said unto him, 'I am God Almighty. Be fruitful and multiply. A nation and a company of nations shall come from you, and kings shall be born unto you. And the land which I gave unto Abraham and Isaac, I give to you as well, and to your seed after you, I will give the land (The Eternal Promised Land of Israel).'"
(Genesis 35:10-12; Genesis 32:24-30)

Christ's Triumphant Appearance

Moses, the receiver of the Ten Commandments (Exodus 20:1-24; Exodus 31:16-18; Exodus 32:15, 16) at Mount Sinai (Mount Horeb), and Elijah, the Hebrew Prophet, will both appear "before the coming of the Great and Dreadful Day of the Lord (Jesus Christ, the Israeli Messiah)." Moses and Elijah will assist the Restored David and Jonathan (The Two Anointed Ones; The Two Olive Trees; The Two Witnesses; The Two Prophets). (I Samuel 20:42; Zechariah 4:9-14; Malachi 4:4-6; Revelation 11:1-19)

"Then, the God of Israel said unto me (Ezekiel, the Prophet), 'Prophesy unto to the wind, prophesy, Son of man, and say to the wind, Thus says the Lord God. Come from the four winds, O breath, and breathe upon these slain, that they may live.' So, I prophesied as he commanded me, and breath came into them, and they lived, and stood up upon their feet, an exceeding great army." (Ezekiel 37:9, 10)

"These are the Two Anointed Ones, that stand by the Lord of the whole Earth." (Zechariah 4:14; The Restored David and Jonathan)

"Remember the Law of Moses, my servant, which I commanded unto him in Horeb (Mount Sinai) for all Israel, with the statutes and judgments (The Ten Commandments; The 613 mitzvot found in the Torah; Mitzvot means commandments or good deeds). And behold, I send you Elijah, the Prophet, before the coming of the Great and Dreadful Day of the Lord (Jesus Christ; King of kings and Lord of lords)." (Malachi 4:4, 5)

"And I will give power unto my Two Witnesses, and they shall prophesy a thousand two hundred and threescore days (1,260 days; 3 ½ years; the Great Tribulation), clothed in sackcloth. These are the Two Olive Trees and the Two Candlesticks standing before the God of the Earth. And if any man attempts to hurt them, fire will proceed out of their mouths, and devour their enemies. These have the power to shut Heaven, so that it doesn't rain in the days of their prophesy (just like Elijah; I Kings 17:1). And they will have power over the waters, that is, to turn them into blood (just like Moses; Exodus 7:14-17, 20), and to smite the Earth with all plagues (just like Moses; the eighth chapter through the twelfth chapter of the Book of Exodus), as often as they will." (Revelation 11:3-6)

Christ's Triumphant Appearance

David is depicted in Bible passages as thoroughly mortal, which is to say that he is susceptible to all of the failings, all the sins, and all the shortcomings that afflict every human being anywhere. This causes some to wonder how David could be considered by the Lord to be "a man after God's own heart." (I Samuel 13:14; Acts 13:22, 23) This seems to be an unsettling contradiction. Yet these very same people who question David are always ready to forgive David. And Yahweh is the God who consistently loves and pardons David. David's life offers an enduring definition of what it means to be human. David always manages to live and survive. That's because David possesses an indomitable will to live and survive, and his motivation is for Bathsheba and all of God's people.

God's eternal Covenant with Israel is not a code of law. It is based on the sure mercies of David. (Isaiah 55:3, 4; Acts 13:33, 34)

"But now, the Lord has sought him a man after his own heart, and the Lord has commanded him to be Captain over his people." (Samuel, the Prophet, referring to David; I Samuel 13:14; Acts 13:22, 23)

"And the God of Israel raised David up unto the people of Israel to be their king, to whom the Lord also gave testimony, and said, 'I have found David, the son of Jesse, a man after my own heart, who shall fulfill all my will.' Of this man's seed has God, according to his promise, raised unto Israel a Savior, Jesus." (Acts 13:22, 23)

"I will make an everlasting Covenant with you, even the sure mercies of David. Behold, I have given him for a witness to the people, a leader and commander to the people." (Isaiah 55:3, 4; Acts 13:33, 34)

One moment David is watching over a flock of sheep grazing in the meadow. The next moment he is being anointed to become the future king of Israel.

David officially goes from being a shepherd to becoming a man of war in Yahweh's army, still a man after God's own heart. David's path would take him, by the grace of God, from pasturing sheep to ruling over Israel.

Christ's Triumphant Appearance

"Now, therefore, so shall you say unto my servant, David, 'Thus says the Lord of hosts, I took you from the sheepcote, from following the sheep, to be ruler over my people, over Israel.'" (II Samuel 7:8)

"And the God of Israel built his Sanctuary like the high places, like the Earth which he has established forever. He chose David also to be his servant and took him from the sheepfolds. From following the ewes great with young, he brought David to feed Jacob, his people, and Israel, his inheritance. So, he fed them according to the integrity of his heart. And he guided them by the skillfulness of his hands." (Psalm 78:69-72)

"'As for you, O my flock,' Thus says the Lord God of Israel, 'I will set up one shepherd over them, and he shall feed them, even, my servant, David. He shall feed them, and he shall be their shepherd.'" (Ezekiel 34:17, 23)

"Afterward, the children of Israel shall return, and seek the Lord their God, and David, their king. And they shall fear the Lord and his goodness in the latter days." (Hosea 3:5)

"Now, it was in the heart of David, my father, to build a House for the name of the Lord God of Israel." (King Solomon; I Kings 8:17; II Chronicles 6:7)

"And when the Philistines heard that David was anointed king over all Israel, all the Philistines went up to seek David. And David heard of it and went out against them." (I Chronicles 14:8)

"For the Lord has spoken of David, saying, 'By the hand of my servant, David, I will save my people, Israel, out of the hand of the Philistines, and out of the hand of all their enemies.'" (II Samuel 3:18)

To be an Israeli is to be a warrior in spiritual battle (Ephesians 6:10-19).

"War is the trade of all kings." (John Dryden, "King Arthur")

"I am and will always continue to be a man of war." (David; I Chronicles 28:1-3)

Christ's Triumphant Appearance

"The Lord is a man of war." (Exodus 15:3)

"The Lord will have war." (Exodus 17:15, 16 "Jehovah-nissi")

"If ye will go armed before the Lord to war, you all will go armed over Jordan before the Lord, until he has driven out his enemies from before him. And the land will be subdued before the Lord, and before Israel. And this land shall be your possession before the Lord." (Numbers 32:20-22)

"For the battle is the Lord's." (David; I Samuel 17:45-47)

"The war was of God." (I Chronicles 5:22)

"And the men of Judah came, and there they anointed David king over the House of Judah." (II Samuel 2:4)

"Then, came all the Tribes of Israel to David unto Hebron, and spoke, saying, 'The Lord said unto you, You shall feed my people, Israel, and you shall be a captain over Israel.' So, all the Elders of Israel made a league with King David in Hebron before the Lord. And they anointed David king over all Israel." (II Samuel 5:1-3)

"All these men of war came with a perfect heart to Hebron, to make David king over all Israel. And all the rest also of Israel were of one heart to make David king." (I Chronicles 12:38)

"And David perceived the Lord had established him king over Israel, and that the God of Israel had exalted his kingdom for his people Israel's sake." (II Samuel 5:12; I Chronicles 14:2)

"And all Israel and Judah loved David, because he went out and came in before them." (I Samuel 18:16)

David's very name means, "Beloved."

"And David behaved himself wisely in all his ways, and the Lord was with him." (I Samuel 18:14)

Christ's Triumphant Appearance

"Prepare for war and wake up the mighty men. Let all the men of war draw near. Let them come up." (Joel 3:9)

Throughout history, the technology of war has continually changed. But the art of war, how a commander commands, has remained more or less the same. Nations have gone out of existence because of their failure to understand what war is all about, including its diplomatic, economic, and social elements. A great commander, one way or another, always seems to understand how all of these forces are interrelated.

"According to the commandment of David, and of Solomon, his son." (Nehemiah 12:45)

"In that day shall the Lord defend the inhabitants of Jerusalem. And he that is feeble among them at that day shall be as David. And the House of David shall be as God, as the angel of the Lord before them. And it shall come to pass, in that day, that I will seek to destroy all the nations that come against Jerusalem." (The God of Israel; Zechariah 12:8, 9)

David becomes a warrior-king.

Israel and her allies make up of a handful of brave men, women, and children (Israeli warriors) who are willing to give their lives for what seems to be a forgotten word: Honor.

The war we are engaged in these days is strictly spiritual in nature. It really is a new kind of war.

"'Behold, I will send my messenger, and he shall prepare the way before me. And the Lord (Jesus Christ), whom you seek, shall suddenly come to his Temple (The Millennial Temple; The fourth Israeli Temple on Earth), even the Messenger of the Covenant, whom you delight in. Behold, he shall come,' says the Lord of hosts. 'But who may abide the day of his coming? And who shall stand when he appears?'" (Malachi 3:1, 2)

"And the Lord God of Israel shall utter his voice before his army. For his camp is very great. For he is strong that executes his Word. For the day of the Lord is great and very terrible. And who can abide it?" (Joel 2:11)

Christ's Triumphant Appearance

"For the great day of the Lord's wrath has come. And who shall be able to stand?" (Revelation 6:17)

"Where there is no vision, God's people will perish."
(Israeli TOP GUN; Proverbs 29:18)

The word "Israel" means, "Ruling with God."

Judaism has a claim to Jerusalem and the Temple Mount.

The Israelis are waiting on Elijah, Moses, and the Jewish Messiah (Jesus Christ; "Mashiach ben David" in Hebrew; Daniel 9:24, 25) to resolve all of the complex issues of bringing about the Restoration of the Throne of David.

The Jewish Messiah is an Israeli warrior.

"That David, my servant, may have light always before me in Jerusalem. The city where I have chosen to put my name is Jerusalem." (I Kings 11:36; Jerusalem is the City of David)

"And the Lord said to David and to Solomon, his son, 'In this House, and in Jerusalem, which I have chosen, will I put my name forever.'"
(II Kings 21:7)

"But I have chosen Jerusalem (The City of David), that my name might be there. And I have chosen David to be over my people, Israel."
(II Chronicles 6:6)

"Blessed is the nation whose God is the Lord. And the people whom he has chosen." (Psalm 33:12)

David and Jonathan fly their jet fighters in parallel a lot as the Fighting Wing Leader and the Wingman, respectively. (Israeli TOP GUN)
At the helms of their fighter jets, both David and Jonathan can leave any other fighter pilot in their dust, at any given second. When it comes to flying fighter jets, David and Jonathan are both into speed. Neither one of them can go fast enough.

Christ's Triumphant Appearance

The Israeli TOP GUN Elders are always keeping track of David and Jonathan out of the corner of their eyes, ready to make their move should David and Jonathan become overwhelmed with crossfire in battle. The Elders have done it many, many times (practically in their sleep) while they are casually playing cards, that is, always monitoring David and Jonathan via a scope. The Israeli TOP GUN Elders can spring into action in a split second to cover David and Jonathan's backs, if need be. They have been doing it ever since David and Jonathan were born, always protective of their young, outstanding prodigies. The TOP GUN Elders of Israel taught David and Jonathan everything they know. The Israeli TOP GUN Elders have nerves of steel.

Both David and Jonathan could be easily accused of flying by the seat of their pants. But it has been proven time and time again that their aerial acrobatics are effective for all of Israel.

"It's a good thing that you and I are of a kindred spirit, Jonathan." (David)

Should a squadron of Israeli TOP GUN Fighter Jets piloted by the Elders ever move in on you, you're definitely going to realize it. These guys do not play when they are in a serious mode.

It's not a good idea to cross the path of an oncoming Israeli TOP GUN Fighter Jet.

When Soaring Eagle and Greased Lighting are doing a fly-by, in parallel with each other, past an Israeli aircraft carrier, David tends to tilt his fighter jet during the process.

Judah is the Israeli Tribe of Royalty. With a few exceptions, most Israeli TOP GUN Fighter Jet Pilots come from the Tribe of Judah, Israel's Tribe of war. A classic example of an exception to that rule would be Jonathan, David's best friend, who is from the Israeli Tribe of Benjamin. Jonathan is an honorary member of the Tribe of Judah. (I Samuel 13:2, 3)

Judah is the Israeli Tribe of war (appointed by Yahweh for the divine protection of Israel and her allies). Jesus Christ is of the Tribe of Judah.

Christ's Triumphant Appearance

"The Lord has sought him a man after his own heart. And the Lord has commanded David to be a Captain over his people, Israel." (I Samuel 13;14; Acts 13:22, 23)

"The Lord raised up unto them David to be their king. To whom he also gave testimony, and said, 'I have found David, a man after my own heart, who shall fulfill my will. Of this man's seed has God, according to his promise, raised unto Israel a Savior, Jesus." (Acts 13:22, 23)

"I will give you the sure mercies of David." (Acts 13:34)

"So, Ezekiel prophesied as the God of Israel commanded him, and breath came into them, and they lived, and stood up upon their feet, an exceeding great army." (Ezekiel 37:10)

Jonathan and David are connected in a metaphysical sense, and they are best friends. They were best friends in the Hebrew Bible, and they are best friends in the eschatological end time as well, when they are miraculously rejoined in true form. They are both exceptional, expert ("the best of the best") Israeli TOP GUN Fighter Pilots in modern days, and they maneuver together quite effectively in combative situations. The Restored David and the Restored Jonathan of the last days were prophesied many Israeli moons ago. (I Samuel 20:42)

"And Jonathan said to David, 'Go in peace, forasmuch as we have sworn in the name of the Lord, saying, the Lord be between us, and between my seed and your seed forever.'" (I Samuel 20:42)

David and Jonathan gained ample training under their belts between Harvard, MIT, and Hanscom Air Force Base, and all of that combined academia was enough to qualify them when they were put to the test, enduring the rigors and challenge of the Battle of Gog and Magog. The victories procured by the Jews in the war securing Israel as a State in 1948, the Six-Day War (1967), the Yom Kipper War (1973), and all subsequent Israeli wars had ended quite miraculously indeed. The Battle of Gog and Magog going in Israel's favor, with David and Jonathan forging away showing impassioned determination, was enough to turn a shaky situation into a triumphant celebration, proving to be no less miraculous of a victory.

Christ's Triumphant Appearance

Now, preparation was being made, in a monumental fashion, as the world braced itself for the much-prophesied war to win all wars, the Battle of Armageddon.

GOG AND MAGOG
Ezekiel 38-39

"Therefore, thou Son of man (Ezekiel, the Prophet), prophesy against Gog, and say, 'Thus says the Lord God of Israel, Behold, I am against you, O, Gog. And I will send fire upon Magog. And you shall know that I am the Lord." (Ezekiel 39:1, 6)

And, so, it would be. The enemies of Israel were so taken back and in fear of the superior performance of the Israeli army during the Battle of Gog and Magog that no one could deny that the God of Israel had intervened on behalf of the Jews. The apprehension and hesitation of Israel's foes to not risk another encounter of that magnitude was visibly noticeable to the entire world. And it opened the door to make way for Solomon's Temple to be rebuilt. Therefore, the third Israeli Temple on Earth, Solomon's Temple Rebuilt, became a reality, and, hence, the Tribulation Temple as well, that is, at the outset of the Great Tribulation.

And with the victory of the Battle of Gog and Magog, David mustered up the courage to finally ask for Bathsheba's hand in marriage. She was so

Christ's Triumphant Appearance

overcome by all the recent events, that if hadn't have proposed, she may have saved him the trouble.

\\

CHAPTER SEVEN
THE MARRIAGE OF DAVID AND BATHSHEBA

THE CONTINUING SAGA OF DAVID & BATHSHEBA

"That Jesus would present it to himself a glorious church, not having spot, or wrinkle, or any such thing. But that the Church of Jesus Christ would be holy and without blemish." (Ephesian 5:27)

The brightness of the Coming of the Lord Jesus Christ will make all things right. The wrongs of all the injustice ever perpetrated in history will be made right. (Zechariah 14:1-4; Matthew 24:27, 30, 31; II Thessalonians 2:8; Revelation 19:11-16) At its worst, as exemplified by numerous autocratic regimes of the past, the institution of a monarchy can be synonymous with tyranny. At its best, however, a monarchy can, indeed, be seen as a repository of meaning. Kingship itself is a monarchy. Royalty, by its very nature, is the stuff of fairy tales, and fairy tales are a manifestation of myth, and myth is a creative attempt to account for reality. Underlying the concept of royalty is the principle of a dynasty. A royal marriage of a couple (a king and queen) along with the continuation of a family line romanticizes the concept of a monarchy and perpetuates the values that

Christ's Triumphant Appearance

embody a dynasty as well. A constructive, positive monarchy consists of the stuff that dreams are made of.

The purpose of a monarchy functions as a principle of duration and continuity. Both duration and continuity are important aspects of a monarchy's meaning. To the extent that it reflects duration and continuity, a monarchy can serve as a repository of meaning. And in order to maintain its status in the contemporary world, a monarchy must keep up with the times.

"Then, all the Elders of Israel gathered themselves together, and went to Samuel. And they said unto Samuel, 'Now, give us a king to judge us.' And Samuel prayed to the God of Israel. And the Lord said unto Samuel, 'Hearken unto the voice of the people in all that they ask of you. For they have not rejected you. But they have rejected me, that I shall not reign over them.' And Samuel, the Prophet of Israel, told all the words of the Lord unto the people of Israel who asked for a king. And Samuel said, 'The God of Israel is our king. This shall be the manner of the king that shall reign over you.' Nevertheless, the people refused to obey the voice of Samuel. And they said, 'No. We will have a king over us. That we may also be like all nations. And that our king will judge us, and go out before us, and fight our battles.' And the Lord said unto Samuel, 'Hearken unto their voice, and crown a king for Israel." (I Samuel 8:4-7, 10, 11, 19, 20; The Israelis wanted a king that they could see with their eyes)

Even in a modern day, the Israelis clamored for a king with a persistent outcry. And by a unanimous vote, the Restored David and Bathsheba become the King and Queen of Israel. (Ezekiel 37:25-28; Hosea 3:5)

"And the Lord preserved King David and Queen Bathsheba everywhere that they went." (II Samuel 8:14)

Bathsheba: "Am I your girl, David?"
David: "Do you want to be my girl, Bathsheba?"
Bathsheba: "I thought you'd never ask!"

David: "So, what are your plans for the future."
Bathsheba: "What's a girl to do, David?"

David: "Could you see your future with a guy like me, Bathsheba?"
Bathsheba: "If that's a marriage proposal, David, I graciously accept."

David: "Would you like a large wedding?"
Bathsheba: "It's only proper, considering that all of Israel is invited."

DR. SAMUEL GOLDSTEIN OFFICIATES THE WEDDING

Bathsheba: "For better or worse, right, David?"
David: "For better or worse, Bathsheba."

"I now pronounce you man and wife. What God has joined together, let no man put asunder ...... You may kiss your bride, David." (Dr. Goldstein)

"Ladies and Gentlemen, may I joyfully present to you our newly married bride and bridegroom, David and Bathsheba." (Dr. Samuel Goldstein)

Bathsheba: "My love for you is eternal, David."
David: "You are a hopeless romantic, Bathsheba. I've been carrying a torch for you all my life. I'd do anything for you. You'll see."
Bathsheba: "We're both hopeless romantics, smitten with each other."

"Hear, O Israel, David and Bathsheba are one."
(The Lord God of Israel)

Jonathan (David's Best Man): "A toast. To David and Bathsheba --- May your path together lead you both to everlasting peace."

THE HONEYMOONERS

"I am the man who accompanied Bathsheba to Paris, and I've thoroughly enjoyed it." (David)

DAVID AND BATHSHEBA, ON THEIR HONEYMOON, STROLLING UP AND DOWN THE SIDEWALKS OF PARIS, THE CITY OF LIGHTS

Christ's Triumphant Appearance

DAVID AND BATHSHEBA'S HONEYMOON IN PARIS, FRANCE

David: "It's rather Renaissance here in Paris, wouldn't, you say, Bathsheba?"
Bathsheba: "Perfect description. Oh, David! Let's go see the Eiffel Tower now, and then go to an Art Museum. Maybe we'll find a Rembrandt!"
David: "Your wish is my command, Bathsheba, with a slight adjustment. As your duly appointed tour guide, I just happen to know that there are several Rembrandts at the Musee Jacquemart-Andre Museum, not far from here. We'll go there first. You're somewhat of a masterpiece yourself, Bathsheba."
Bathsheba: "Somewhat?"
David: "Allow me to rephrase that, Bathsheba. You're a masterpiece."
Bathsheba: "Thanks."

David: "You're welcome."
Bathsheba: "You're plan sounds good, Commander! So, we're going there right now?"
David: "Oui ("Yes" in French), Bathsheba. You and I may arrive at the Museum fashionably late, that is, rather near to closing time. But we won't let that stop us, my dear. We'll still have some good quality time together."

Bathsheba: "You know that I like romance!"
David: "You are priceless, Bathsheba!"
Bathsheba: "We're just alike, David."
David: "Made for each other."
Bathsheba: "Exactly!"

Bathsheba: "I love it when you surprise me with flowers, David?"
David: "Every time you compliment me, Bathsheba, I pick a red rose. And when I have enough roses, I give the bouquet to you."

David: "We'll go back to Paris one day, Bathsheba."
Bathsheba: "Second Honeymoon, my Love?"
David: "Paris is our refuge."

DAVID AND BATHSHEBA - THE NEWLYWEDS

"Behold, a son shall be born unto you (David and Bathsheba), who shall be a man of rest. And I will give him rest from all his enemies round about (Israel). For his name shall be Solomon, and I will give peace and quietness unto Israel in his days. He shall build a House for my name, and I will establish the Throne of his kingdom over Israel forever." (I Chronicles 22:9, 10; The Lord God of Israel)

"And there appeared a great wonder in Heaven. A woman clothed with the sun and the moon under her feet, and upon her head a crown of twelve stars (The Twelve Tribes of Israel). And she, being pregnant with a child, cried, travailing in birth. And she was in horrible pain until her son was delivered." (Revelation 12:1, 2, referring to the Restored Bathsheba, and her son, the Restored Solomon of the last days)

"Solomon is, obviously, a Daddy's Boy." (Bathsheba)

Christ's Triumphant Appearance

"Bathsheba is my better half." (David)

"The happiest children I have ever witnessed in my life are living in the Promised Land of Israel." (Bathsheba, The Queen of Israel)

"You know, I wouldn't have an empire around this palace if it wasn't for you." (David to Bathsheba)

"I really don't know about all this king and queen stuff, Bathsheba. The only thing I know is that I worship the ground that you walk on."
(David to Bathsheba)

"You'll never be any different than the man who I've always loved, David. I know that." (Bathsheba)

Bathsheba: "Don't you think that there are definitely consolations in life, David?"
David: "The end of war for all time would be a genuine consolation, Bathsheba. But even if that miracle took place, there would still always be something left to conquer."

Bathsheba: "Who's your girl, David?"
David: "You are, Bathsheba."
Bathsheba: "I'll always be your girl."

David: "I can't always find all the right romantic lines, Bathsheba."
Bathsheba: "You manage, David."

David: "Do you love me, Bathsheba?"
Bathsheba: "Yes, David, I do love you. And I just so happen to be very much in love with you as well. Heaven is in my heart."
David: "Then, I have all that I need."
Bathsheba: "And you say that you can't find all the romantic lines, David. Those lines will do just fine until the romantic lines get here. And you're all mine!" (Jeremiah 33:11; The Joy of the Bridegroom and the Bride)

"I never believed in such a thing as unconditional love until I got to know my beloved wife, Bathsheba." (David; Song of Solomon 4:7)

Christ's Triumphant Appearance

"Thou art all fair, my Love. There is no spot in thee."
(The Israeli Messiah to the Church of Jesus Christ)

"Jesus will present a church without spot or wrinkle." (Ephesians 5:27; Revelation 19:6-9; Revelation 21:9-12)

"Forasmuch as you know that you were not redeemed with corruptible things such as silver and gold, but with the precious blood of Christ, as a Lamb without blemish and without spot, who, verily, was foreordained before the foundation of the world, but has been manifest in these last times for you." (I Peter 1:18-21)

"Looking for and hasting unto the Coming of the Day of the Lord Jesus Christ, wherein the Heavens, being on fire, shall be dissolved, and the elements shall melt with fervent heat (description of a nuclear holocaust). Nevertheless, we, according to his promise, look for new Heavens and a new Earth, wherein dwells righteousness. Wherefore, beloved, seeing you look for such things, be diligent that you may be found of him in peace, without spot or wrinkle." (II Peter 3:12-14)

"And a voice came out of the Throne, saying, 'Praise our God, all his servants, and all who fear him, both great and small. And I heard as it were the voice of a great multitude, and as the voice of many waters, and as the voice of mighty thunder, saying, 'Hallelujah! For the Lord God omnipotent reigns. Let us be glad and rejoice and give honor to Jesus. For the Marriage of the Lamb (Jesus Christ) has come, and his wife (The Church of Jesus Christ) has made herself ready.' And it was granted that the bride be arrayed in fine linen, clean and white. For fine linen is the righteousness of the saints. And the angel said unto me, 'Blessed are all they who are called unto the Marriage Supper of the Lamb (Jesus Christ; John 1:29). And the angel said unto me, 'These are the true sayings of God.'" (Revelation 19:6-9)

"And one of the seven angels talked with me, saying, 'Come hither. I will show you the bride, the Lamb's (Jesus Christ's) wife.' And he carried me away in the Spirit to a great and high mountain (The Temple Mount), and showed me that great city, the Holy Jerusalem, descending out of Heaven from God, having the glory of God. And a great and high wall, which had twelve gates, and an angel posted at each of the twelve gates, and names written thereon, which are the names of the Twelve Tribes of the children of Israel." (Revelation 21:9-12; The Church of Jesus Christ is the Holy Jerusalem!)

CHAPTER EIGHT
THE FALSE MESSIAH

Head of Gold
BABYLON
[B.C. 605 - 539]

Breast of Silver
PERSIA
[B.C. 539 - 331]

Thighs of Brass
GREECE
[B.C. 331 - 168]

Legs of Iron
ROME
[B.C. 168 - A.D. 476]

Feet of Iron & Clay
DIVIDED NATIONS OF WESTERN EUROPE

THE GREAT IMAGE/DANIEL 2:25-45
THE IMAGE OF THE BEAST/REVELATION 13:15-18

"And he (the false messiah) shall speak great words against the Most High, and wear out the saints of the Most High, and think to change times and laws." (Daniel 7:25; The Abomination of Desolation)

The false messiah will create an empire (The Modern-Day Roman Empire; The New Babylon Empire) that will be different from all other kingdoms ever devised, and he will devour the whole Earth, trampling it down and crushing it. The false messiah's desire is to unmercifully beat the people of God into the ground over and over and over again, until they are pulverized.

"There shall be a time of distress such as has not happened from the beginning of nations until then." (Daniel 12:1)

Christ's Triumphant Appearance

"I considered the horns, and behold, there came up from among them another horn, a little horn (the false messiah). And behold, in this horn were eyes like the eyes of a man, and a mouth speaking great things." (Daniel 7:8; the false messiah will speak his lies without ever stuttering)

The false messiah will be a monster, a fabrication of Satan, that is, the devil incarnate. The false messiah will be none other than Satan in human form, utterly despicable, sinister, and evil, to the extent of being void of any resemblance of good whatsoever. To encounter the false messiah in person would be equivalent to making direct contact with Satan himself, that is, shaking hands with the devil.

"And he (the false messiah) shall speak great words against the Most High (the Most High God of Israel), and wear out the saints of the Most High." (Daniel 7:25; the Abomination of Desolation)

"A stern-faced king, a master of intrigue, will arise." (Daniel 8:23)

"A contemptible person, he will invade the kingdom (Israel) when its people feel secure." (Daniel 11:21)

"I am going to raise up a shepherd over the land who will not care for the lost (of Israel). Woe to the worthless shepherd (the false messiah), who deserts the flock." (Zechariah 11:16, 17)

"And I (John, the Apostle) stood upon the sand of the sea and saw a Beast rise out of the sea having seven heads and ten horns, and upon his horns ten crowns, and upon his head the name of blasphemy." (Revelation 13:1)

"The king will do as he pleases. He will exalt and magnify himself above every god and will say unheard of things against the God of gods (Yahweh, the Eternal One). He will be successful until the time of wrath has been completed, for what has been determined must take place." (Daniel 11:36; the Abomination of Desolation perpetrated in the Tribulation Temple in Jerusalem)

"Let no man deceive you by any means. For the Day of the Coming of our Lord Jesus Christ shall not come, except there be a falling away first, and that man of sin be revealed. Who will oppose and exalt himself above God, so that he sits in God's Temple, proclaiming that he himself is God. And then, the Wicked One shall be revealed, whom the Lord shall consume with the Spirit of his mouth and shall destroy with the brightness of his coming. Even him (the false messiah), whose coming will be after the working of Satan, with all power, and signs, and lying wonders." (Christ's recompense for the Abomination of Desolation; II Thessalonians 2:3-4, 8, 9)

The fact that the Western Wall is still standing today is clear evidence that the destruction of the second Temple in 70 A.D. is not the Temple that Jesus was referring to in Matthew 24:1, 2, when he told his disciples that "there would not be left here one stone upon another (of the Temple), that shall not be thrown down." Jesus was foreseeing the absolute obliteration of the third Temple, that is, the Tribulation Temple of the Seven Year Tribulation, which will be hostilely taken over and defiled by the false messiah, resulting in a most unfortunate event referred to as the Abomination of Desolation. (Daniel 9:27; Matthew 24:15, 16)

The Abomination of Desolation would require Jesus Christ, at a critical point, to annihilate (level) the Tribulation Temple without batting an eye, with the assistance of the Israeli army that he raises up in the end time.

Biblical prophecies clearly predict the rise of the false messiah in the last days. The momentum of these futuristic days has already begun. As civilization speeds toward its final destiny, a powerful world leader will appear and move to center stage, assuming his long awaited and much-desired place.

The chaos created just prior to the Seven Year Tribulation paves the way for the rise of a new world leader, who will be able to negotiate world peace and deliver on the promise of security and harmony. This world leader will be known as the false messiah, and he will rise to the occasion as he pleases, in his own perfect timing, to mock, blaspheme, and attempt to imitate the Lamb of God, Jesus Christ.

Christ's Triumphant Appearance

The Sea Beast
(Rev. 13:1-10)
- He arises out of the Sea (society)
- He has...
  - *7 heads*
  - *10 horns*
  - *10 crowns*
  - *Blasphemous names*
- **His Body**
  - *Body Leopard*
  - *Feet Bear*
  - *Head Lion*

REVELATION 13:1-18

"These words spoke Jesus, and lifted up his eyes to Heaven, and said, 'Father the hour has come. Glorify your Son, that your Son may also glorify you. As you have given me power over all of mankind, that I should give eternal life to as many as you have given me. And this is life eternal, that they may know you, the only true God, and Jesus Christ, whom you have sent. I have come to you, holy Father. Keep, through your own name, those whom you have given me, that they may be one, as we are one. While I was with them in the world, I kept them in your name. Those who you gave me I have kept, and none of them is lost. That they all may be one, as you, Father, are in me, and I am in them, that they also may be one in us, that the world may believe that you have sent me. And the glory which you have given me I, in turn, have given unto them, that they may be one, even as we are one. I in them, and you in me, that they may be made perfect in one. And that the world may know that you have loved them, as you have loved me. Father, I will that they also whom you have given me, be with me where I am. That they may behold my glory, which you have given me. For you

Christ's Triumphant Appearance

have loved me before the foundation of the world. O, righteous Father, the world has not known you, but I have known you, and these you have given me have known that you have sent me. And I have declared unto them your name, and I will declare it. That the love wherewith you have loved me may be in them, and I in them." (John 17:1-3, 11, 12, 21-26; Jesus Christ in the Garden of Gethsemane, just prior to his Death, Resurrection, and Ascension; John 11:25)

"Where sin abounds, grace does abound much more." (Romans 5:20)

"For we have not a High Priest who cannot be touched with the feeling of our infirmities. But Jesus Christ was, in all points, tempted like we are, yet without sin. Let us, therefore, come boldly unto the Throne of grace, that we may obtain mercy, and find grace to help in time of need." (Hebrews 4:15, 16)

"If we doubt, Jesus still remains faithful, because he cannot deny himself." (II Timothy 2:13)

"For God did not send his Son into the world to condemn the world. But that the world through him might be saved. And he who believes in the Son shall not be condemned. But he who believes not is condemned already, because he has not believed in the name of the only begotten Son of God. And this is the condemnation, that light (John 9:5; Jesus is the Light of the World) has come into the world, and men loved darkness rather than light, because their deeds were evil." (Jesus Christ; John 3:17-19)

"Neither do I condemn you." (Jesus Christ; John 8:11)

"There is, therefore, now, no condemnation to them who are in Jesus Christ, those who walk not after their own inclination for self-destruction, but after the Spirit. For the law of the Spirit of life in Christ has made me free from the law of sin and death." (Romans 8:1, 2)

Jesus looked beyond our fault, and he saw our need.

Christ's Triumphant Appearance

"And when they had come to the place, which is called Calvary, they crucified Jesus Christ there. Then, Jesus said, 'Father, forgive them. For they know not what they do.'" (Luke 23:33, 34)

While the person of the false messiah desires to make himself visible in human form just prior to the beginning of the Seven Year Tribulation, the spirit of the false messiah has already been in the world throughout history, perpetrating Satan's dirty work. The war between the Israeli Messiah, Jesus, and Satan has been going on for all time in spirit. (I John 4:3)

"And this is that spirit of the false messiah, whereof ye have heard that it should come. And even, now, already is it in the world." (I John 4:3)

Satan knows the entire Bible, the Hebrew Bible and the New Testament, backwards and forwards, better than any human being. But the devil is incapable of matching wits with Jesus Christ concerning God's Word.

It is not difficult, given the current international structure and the need for a human authority figure guaranteeing a peaceful coexistence on Earth, to imagine a powerful, charismatic world leader coming on the scene in the immediate future. The greatest seducers of all had one thing in common. They could use the natural needs and instincts of other people for their own desired ends. Seduction is the most callous form of exploitation, because it tricks the victim into becoming an unwitting accomplice. The false messiah will seemingly be the most incredible leader the world has ever witnessed. The charismatic, relentless, oppressive, manipulative, constant, and incessant fashion in which this menace takes over the planet will make any-and-all of the dynamics of Adolf Hitler appear amateur in comparison. The false messiah is only interested in controlling and destroying the lives of many, many innocent people. That is what the false messiah will be all about.

While Satan does not have the power or ability to read minds, he has had full opportunity afforded him to study the fallen nature of human beings. The devil knows all too well (based upon an individual and collective observance of all men, women, and children) how to dazzle people by the attraction of power. He knows how to gratify the craving for knowledge. He can delight the ear with music and the eye with entrancing beauty. He knows

Christ's Triumphant Appearance

how to exalt people to dizzy heights of worldly power, wealth, greatness, and fame, and he knows how to control individuals to the extent that they may be used to work against God and his people.

The spirit of the false messiah is alive and well today, and this spirit is just as diabolically opposed to the Jews as much as Satan or any of his representatives have ever been (I John 4:3). The spirit of the false messiah embodies the Satan-inspired expression of lawlessness and rebellion against Yahweh, hatred for the beauty of Judaism, and a stubborn will to wipe out the memory of any-and-all Israelis, along with everyone else who loves Israel. The spirit of the false messiah has been alive since Satan slithered his way around the Garden of Eden. It has been the driving force behind the whole terrible history of the human race, producing wars, murders, mayhem, thefts, idolatry, lawlessness, and outright rebellion (shaking their fist) against the God of Israel. It is the ugly expression of the destructive nature of the great deceiver himself, Satan, who, in expert fashion, plays on man's fallen condition. The spirit of the false messiah has been active throughout all of Israel's history, expressing itself in persecutions, heresies, spiritual deceptions, false prophets, diverse religions, worship of false gods, and cruel martyrdoms. Satan has battled Israel at every turn throughout her long history (the Holocaust during World War II – WWII -, for example), waiting for the right moment to indwell the right person (the Devil Incarnate) as his final masterpiece. The spirit of the false messiah will continue to do the devil's dirty work throughout the world, cooperating fully with Satan, who will raise the person of the false messiah up to lead the new world order, waiting patiently in his own good time to ponce. And it should be stressed that evil is quite patient.

Israel is the center of all Biblical prophecy. And these prophecies are unfolding right before our very eyes.

The false messiah of the Seven Year Tribulation will be distinguished, and, eventually, identified by way of his harsh persecution of the Jewish Nation of Israel, crueler than any-and-all harassment of the past combined.

The last three-and-a-half years (1,260 days – Revelation 11:3; Daniel 9:27) of the Seven Year Tribulation are commonly referred to as the Great Tribulation ("Jacob's Trouble" --- Jeremiah 30:7). It will be at this midpoint

Christ's Triumphant Appearance

of the Seven Year Tribulation that the Israelis will come to the stark realization that they have been had, that is, deceived (duped) by the false messiah.

Satan has been accusing God's people of their sins, faults, and shortcomings before the holy God of Israel twenty-four hours a day, seven days a week, and 365 days year (24/7/365) all along in front of the very Throne of God. In the last days, during the Great Tribulation, Satan will step up that condemnation to an extremely fast pace, getting right up in the faces of God's people. (Job 1:6-12; Revelation 12:10)

"But put forth your hand, now, and touch all that Job possesses, and he will curse you to your face." (Job 1:11; Satan condemning Job before the God of Heaven)

"The accuser (Satan) of our brothers and sisters has been cast down, which accused them before God day and night." (Revelation 12:10)

"And Jesus lifted up his eyes and saw no one but the woman. And Jesus said unto her, 'Woman, where are your accusers?'" (John 8:10)

The false messiah's reign of terror will bring with it the nagging, ongoing disbelief that any single individual could possibly be so evil. That is exactly how he'll throw people and blindside them. People, after gaining awareness of the false messiah's identity, will consider that they had been totally mesmerized, if not put in a complete state of hypnosis, in an attempt to explain why they had been so oblivious. But sound reasoning will come too late. The false messiah will, by that time, have firmly gained full control, having pulled the rug out from under everyone's feet.

Concerning the Battle of Armageddon, the false messiah will arrogantly psyche himself into believing that Jerusalem will be surrounded by the armies of the world at his command, but, in all reality, it will be Yahweh calling all the shots. (Zechariah 14:1-4; Revelation 16:16)

The advent of the Great Tribulation will mark the very beginning of a world that is spiraling out of control like never before.

Christ's Triumphant Appearance

The false messiah's objective, as relegated and completely monitored carefully by Satan, is to track down anything good in the world and trample it (kill it; destroy it; annihilate it). The false messiah's allies will perpetrate many, many atrocities all over the world. Good people will be trapped and cornered by evil at every single turn.

The trademark of the false messiah's cold regime will be to impose calloused indifference upon innocent lives. After there is no mistake of the true identity of the false messiah, people will wonder how they could have possibly been so stupid as to have ignored the warning signs, and not recognized his true identity in the first place. The false messiah will be of the opinion that he is capable of convicting the entire world of sin, righteousness, and judgment, as only the Holy Spirit is qualified to do (John 16:7-11). He will become the supreme model of blasphemy against the Lord God of Israel in every possible way imaginable. And he will leave a staggering amount of human carnage (physically, emotionally, and spiritually) in his wake. He will misconstrue, misalign, and manipulate decent people at every turn intentionally to make life unbearable and totally strangled of any and all joy. Once again, this sinister imposter's chief objective will be to beat God's people down over and over and over again until they are absolutely pulverized under his metaphorical feet, with malice toward all and charity intended for none.

The false messiah will be more than happy to be the very first individual to confirm to anyone that he is, indeed, God's gift to the world.

The false messiah, as "Big Brother" on Earth, will create such desperate conditions in the world for survival that people will be maliciously killing each other over the almighty dollar, as a result of all the crossfire created by greed.

As evil world leaders, taking orders directly from the false messiah, sit in the upper echelons of society gouging people around the planet and living in the lap of luxury, they will impose their condescending tyranny upon the unfortunate, leaving "the peasants" in poverty, cold, and shivering outside in the streets. The difference between right and wrong is, now, a confusing issue.

Christ's Triumphant Appearance

"The rich and poor meet together. The Lord is the maker of them all." (Proverbs 22:2)

"But my God shall supply all your needs according to his riches in glory by Jesus Christ." (Philippians 4:19; Promise of provision to God's people)

"And, again, I say unto you. It is easier for a camel to go through the eye of a needle, than for a rich man to enter the kingdom of God." (Jesus Christ, the Israeli Messiah; Matthew 9:24)

The false messiah will be so caught up in his own self-importance that he will be oblivious to the preciousness of life.

As much as Pharaoh was a cruel taskmaster in Egypt to the children of Israel in the Hebrew Bible (in the Book of Exodus), so too will the false messiah prove himself to be an ambitious, overbearing tyrant to the entire world in the last days, many, many times over.

"The God of Israel has laid the ax to the root." (Matthew 3:10) --- In other words, John, the Baptist, is using extremely strong language to indicate that people will either have the Mark of Jesus Christ upon them (Ezekiel 9:4), or be branded with the Mark of the Devil (666; Revelation 13:16-18; the Mark of the Beast; they sold their souls to Satan), as people will be forced to make a chose whether or not to serve the true Messiah. There will be no ground in between. There is only one of two options. It will be, at this very point, when everyone will be locked into their eternal destinies. And there will be no turning back. An excellent analogy may be derived from Joshua 24:15: "Choose you this day whom you will serve."

It is interesting to note that there are 18 verses in the thirteenth chapter of the Book of Revelation, an entire chapter that concerns us specifically with the Beast in the last days. 18 divided by 3 = 6. Three 6's, hence, 666. Does that sound like a stretch? Just an observation.

"There were two men in one city. One was rich and the other was poor. The rich man had exceedingly many flocks of sheep and herds of cattle, while the poor man had nothing but one little ewe lamb, which he had bought and nourished up. The little lamb did eat the poor man's own food,

Christ's Triumphant Appearance

drank from the poor man's cup, laid in the poor man's lap, and grew up in the poor man's home with his children. One day, there came a traveler who arrived at the rich man's home. The rich man did not want to take of his own flock or herd to prepare a meal for his wayfaring guest. Instead, the rich man took the poor man's only lamb, and dressed it and cooked it as a meal for his visitor who had come unto him." (II Samuel 12:2-4)

From this parable of II Samuel 12:2-4, we may derive the rich man, by way of an analogy, to be the false messiah, who seeks to maliciously deprive all of Christ's chosen people, who are depicted by the poor man. The false messiah's desire is to cheat everyone who loves Israel out their God given blessings and rights in life (i.e., life, liberty, and the pursuit of happiness). The false messiah desires to oppress God's people to the extent that there is absolutely nothing remaining, especially the joy of living.

The false messiah will prove himself to be an expert on developing complex problems for the world that didn't exist in the first place. To sum it all up, the false messiah is a creep, a deviant, and a menace to society.

The fact that people will so easily follow someone like the false messiah is a statement that attests to the fact that people will blindly follow after anyone for guidance. This pitiful affirmation reflects a very sad state of affairs. This serves as a reality check and vivid reminder of Jesus comparing people to sheep, who will naively follow after anyone and anything in the absence of a caring shepherd (John 10:1-18). Jesus Christ himself is the good Shepherd. And his sheep hear and recognize his voice. Not only that, but Jesus Christ also willingly laid down his own life for the sheep. (John 10:3, 14, 18)

In the middle of the Seven Year Tribulation, when the Great Tribulation begins, and the false messiah breaks his treaty with Israel, there will just be one thing all good people on Earth will be saying to themselves: "Who does this guy think he is?"

"And when they bring you unto the synagogues, and unto magistrates, and powers, take no thought how or what thing you shall answer, or what you shall say. For the Holy Spirit shall teach you in the same hour what you ought to say." (Jesus Christ, the Israeli Messiah; Luke 12:11, 12)

Christ's Triumphant Appearance

People will discover themselves waking up more and more and more to a world where no one cares about anyone else but themselves. No one, with the exception of God's chosen, will have the best interests of another person at heart. You will be able to cut the indifference in the air with a knife. People will not be overcoming evil with good. People will be overcoming good with evil. (Romans 12:21)

Peace or utter destruction! It is up to the Israelis and their allies to make the difference. They are the only hope of standing in the gap.

It is a terrifying thought to know that something as sinister as the false messiah is lurking somewhere out there in the world.

"We do not want another committee. We have too many already. What we want is a man of sufficient stature to hold the allegiance of all the people, and to lift us out of the economic morass in which we are sinking. Send us such a man, and be he God or be he the devil, we will receive him." (Paul Henri Spaak, Former Prime Minister of Belgium)

"When Moses saw it, he wondered at the sight (The Burning Bush). And as he drew near to behold it, the voice of the Lord God of Israel came unto him, saying, 'I am the God of your fathers, the God of Abraham, and the God of Isaac, and the God of Jacob.' Then, Moses trembled. And the Lord said to Moses, 'Put off your shoes from your feet. For the place where you're standing is holy ground. Surely, I have seen the affliction of my people, and I have heard their groaning, and I have heard their cry by reason of their taskmasters, and I have come to deliver them, for I know their sorrows.'" (Exodus 3:1-14; Acts 7:31-34; Yahweh, "I AM THAT I AM")

The false messiah will make a concerted, serious, determined effort to manipulate the Ark of the Covenant into the Tribulation Temple for the single focus, objective, and motive of defiling it in the Holy of Holies within the Temple.

And at the same time, he will be doing everything in his power to thwart the Restored David's efforts to bring the Ark of the Covenant to its final resting place in the Holy of Holies in the Millennial Temple.

Christ's Triumphant Appearance

And yet despite all the thwarting, manipulative efforts of the false messiah to prevent the fourth Israeli Temple from materializing, the Ark of the Covenant is anticipated to be miraculously restored to the Millennial Temple at the end of the Seven Year Tribulation/the beginning of the Millennial Kingdom, just in time for the Millennial Reign of Jesus Christ.

"'And it shall come to pass, when you are multiplied and increased in the land (The Eternal Promised Land of Israel), in those days,' says the Lord, 'they shall say no more, the Ark of the Covenant of the Lord, neither shall it come to mind, neither shall they remember it, neither shall they visit it, neither shall that be done any more. At that time, they shall call Jerusalem, 'The Throne of the Lord.' And all nations shall gather unto it, to the name of the Lord, to Jerusalem. In those days, the House of Judah shall walk with the House of Israel. And they shall come together out of the land of the north to the land that I have given for an inheritance unto your fathers.'" (Jeremiah 3:16-18)

Very poetically, Jesus Christ is expected to use the Restored David of the last days to restore the Ark of the Covenant to the Temple, that is, the Millennial Temple. The Restored David will, certainly, know better than to risk divulging any information regarding the Ark of The Covenant's whereabouts. That's a given. David would not dare take the chance of the false messiah satisfying his determined desire of defiling the Ark in the Holy of Holies inside the Tribulation Temple.

"David danced before the Lord with all his might. So, David and all of the House of Israel brought up the Ark of the Covenant with shouting, and with the sound of the trumpet. And the Ark came into the City of David, and David was leaping and dancing before the Lord. And they brought the Ark of the Lord and set it in the midst of the Tabernacle."
(II Samuel 6:14-17)

This time, in the latter days, David, by God's grace, will have his golden opportunity to bring the Ark of the Covenant to rest for good in the Temple, that is, the Millennial Temple, a place of everlasting peace (Shalom).

"And they shall dwell in the land (The Eternal Promised Land) that I have given unto Jacob, my servant, wherein your fathers have dwelt. And

Christ's Triumphant Appearance

they shall dwell therein, even they, and their children, and their children's children forever. And, my servant, David shall be their prince forever. Moreover, I will make a Covenant of peace (everlasting peace) with them. It shall be an everlasting Covenant with them. And I will multiply them and set my Sanctuary (The Millennial Temple) in the midst of them forevermore." (Ezekiel 37:25, 26)

God's chosen people are sealed in Christ with the Holy Spirit of promise. And the Mark of God upon their foreheads is the name of Jesus Christ. (Ephesians 1:12, 13; Ezekiel 9:4; Revelation 7:2, 3; Revelation 22:4)

"And the Seraphim, each with six wings, cried one to another in the Temple, and said, 'Holy, holy, holy, Lord God Almighty, which was, and is, and is to come.'" (Isaiah 6:1-3; Revelation 4:8)

In these last days that we are living in, you don't have to be a prophet, like Daniel, to see the handwriting on the wall (the fifth chapter of Daniel in the Hebrew Bible; Deuteronomy 9:10, 11), and discern that we are teetering on the very brink (the very edge) of witnessing the coming of the Great and Terrible Day of the Lord Jesus Christ firsthand.

"And I beheld and heard an angel flying through the midst of Heaven, saying, 'WOE, WOE, WOE UNTO THE INHABITANTS OF THE EARTH by reason of the other voices of the trumpet of the three angels, which are yet to sound!'" (Revelation 8:13)

"One woe is past. And behold, there come two woes more hereafter." (Revelation 9:12)

"And when the Two Witnesses (The Restored David and Jonathan) shall have finished their testimony, the Beast that ascended out of the Bottomless Pit shall make war against them, and shall overcome them, and kill them. And their dead bodies shall lie in the street of Jerusalem, where our Lord, Jesus Christ, was crucified. And they of the people and tongues and nations shall see their dead bodies three-and-a-half days, and their mockers shall not suffer their dead bodies to be put in graves. And they that dwell upon the Earth shall rejoice over them, and make merry, and shall send gifts to one another, because these Two Prophets tormented them that dwelt upon

Christ's Triumphant Appearance

the Earth. And after three-and-a-half days, the Spirit of life from God entered into them, and they stood upon their feet. And great fear fell upon them which saw them. And they heard a great voice from Heaven, saying unto them, 'Come up hither.' And they ascended up to Heaven in a cloud. And their enemies beheld them. The second woe is past. And behold, the third woe comes quickly. (Revelation 11:7-14)

"WOE UNTO THE INHABITANTS OF THE EARTH and the sea! For the devil has come down unto you, having great wrath, because he knows that he has but a short time." (Revelation 12:12; The Third Woe)

"If the world hates you, you know that it hated me first." (John 15;18; Jesus Christ speaking to his disciples)

"Sufficient for the day is the evil thereof. Behold, I come quickly. My reward is with me. I am Alpha and Omega, the Beginning and the End, the First and the Last. I, Jesus, have sent my angel to testify unto you these things. I am the root and the offspring of David, and the Bright and Morning Star. Surely, I come quickly." (Jesus Christ; Matthew 6:34; Revelation 22:12-21)

Christ's Triumphant Appearance

"The god of this world (Satan) has blinded the minds of them who do not believe (in Jesus Christ), lest the light of the glorious Gospel of Christ, who is the image of God, should shine unto them." (II Corinthians 4:4)

The last days will reflect a period when people will be riddled with the love of money, the root of all evil. Money is not the root of all evil. The love of money is the root of all evil. The love of money and materialism will prove to be a powerful playing card representing which side someone may be fighting on this precarious, subtle spiritual battlefield. (I Timothy 6:10)

What exactly is the light of the Gospel of Jesus Christ? It's that Jesus was born of a virgin without sin, that he lived a pure, holy life, never yielding to the temptations of Satan, that he is a man of great compassion, that he willingly laid down his life as a sacrifice for the sins of mankind, and rose from the dead in victory over sin and death, ascending to the right hand of the Father, to make intercession for all of his saints. And this glorious Gospel of Jesus Christ is exactly what firmly establishes the purpose of human lives.

Genuine truth is not found in a doctrine. It's found only in the person of Jesus Christ. Jesus is the very embodiment of truth. (John 8:32; John 14:6)

"For unto us a child (The Israeli Messiah, Jesus Christ) is born, unto us a Son is given. And the government shall be upon his shoulder. And his name shall be called Wonderful, Counselor, the Mighty God, the everlasting Father, the Prince of Peace. Of the increase of his government and peace there shall be no end, upon the Throne of David (The Restoration of the Throne of David), and upon his kingdom, to order it and to establish it with judgment and with justice from henceforth even forever. The zeal of the Lord of hosts will perform this." (Isaiah 9:6, 7; The Restoration of the Throne of David procured in the powerful name of Jesus Christ)

"Whereby, the Lord Jesus Christ has given unto us exceeding great and precious promises. That by these promises you may be partakers of his divine nature, escaping the corruption in the world." (II Peter 1:4)

Christ's Triumphant Appearance

Perhaps, it's just too much to ask that people behave themselves like human beings. It, apparently, is just not that simple to have a heart. There's little wonder why Jesus said: "Without me, you can do nothing." (Jesus Christ - John 15:5)

"Therefore, endure hardness, as a good soldier of the Lord Jesus Christ." (II Timothy 2:3)

And, so, it begins…

CHAPTER NINE

THE BATTLE OF ARMAGEDDON --- REVELATION 16:16

"And the Lord Jesus Christ gathered them together into a place called, in the Hebrew tongue, Armageddon."
(Revelation 16:16)

"Multitudes, multitudes in the Valley of Decision. For the Day of the Lord is near in the Valley of Decision. The sun and the moon shall be darkened, and the stars shall withdraw their shining. The Lord also shall roar out of Zion and utter his voice from Jerusalem. And the Heavens and the Earth shall shake. But the Lord will be the hope of his people, and the strength of the children of Israel. So shall you know that I am the Lord, your God, dwelling in Zion (Jerusalem), my holy mountain (Mount Moriah; The Temple Mount). Then, shall Jerusalem be holy, and no strangers shall pass through there anymore. And it shall come to pass in that day, that the mountains shall drop down new wine, and the hills shall flow with milk, and all the rivers of Judah shall flow with waters, and a fountain shall come forth out of the House of the Lord (The Millennial Temple; The fourth

Christ's Triumphant Appearance

Israeli Temple on Earth). Judah shall dwell forever, and Jerusalem from generation to generation. For the Lord will dwell in Zion." (Joel 3:14-18, 20, 21)

"And white robes were given unto every one of the saints. And, lo, there was a great earthquake. And, the sun became black, and the moon became as blood. And the stars of Heaven fell unto the Earth. And Heaven departed as a scroll when it is rolled together. And every mountain and island moved out of their places. And the kings of Earth, and the great men, and the rich men, and the chief captains, and the mighty men, and the slaves, and every free man hid themselves in the dens and in the rocks of the mountains. And they said to the mountains and rocks, 'Fall on us, and hide us from the face of him who sits on the Throne, and from the wrath of the Lamb (Jesus Christ). For the great day of his wrath has come. And who shall be able to stand?'" (Revelation 6:11-17)

"And Jesus went out, and departed from the Temple (the second Temple). And his disciples came to Jesus to show him the buildings of the Temple. And Jesus said unto them, 'Do you see all these things? Verily, I say unto you, there shall not be left one stone here upon another, that shall not be thrown down.'" (Jesus Christ referring to the Tribulation Temple being obliterated toward the end of the Battle of Armageddon; Matthew 24:1, 2)

Obviously, since the Western Wall (The Wailing Wall) of the second Temple is still standing, Jesus was not referring to the destruction of the second Temple by the Romans in 70 A.D. Jesus said, "There shall not be left here one (single, last) stone upon another, that shall not be thrown down." Jesus was referring to the complete and utter annihilation of the Tribulation Temple, that will take place at his glorious coming toward the end of the Battle of Armageddon. It's the only thing that makes sense. And leveled right to the ground the Tribulation Temple shall be, as a direct result of the Abomination of Desolation. Needless to say, this will be a clear indication that Jesus Christ is done with Satan and the false messiah. The wrath of God will have spoken loud and clear, to say the least. (Daniel 9:27; Matthew 24:15, 16)

Christ's Triumphant Appearance

The destruction of the first and second Temples have forced the advocates of Judaism to assess the cause of their calamity and see what lessons can be learned. The first Temple was destroyed by the Babylonians, and the second Temple was destroyed by the Romans. A third Jewish Temple must be built to make way for the Millennial Temple. And, the Tribulation Temple will be destroyed by the Jews, quite intentionally.

The discovery that the first two Temples were both destroyed on the very same day of the year (The Ninth of Av) is proof to Israeli rabbis that even the destruction of the Temples had been part of God's predetermined plan, rather than a historical coincidence. The lesson and conclusion that emerged is that Yahweh was just as much in control of the destruction of the Temples as he had been in control of their construction. So shall it be concerning the absolute and total destruction (obliteration) of the Tribulation Temple at the end of the Seven Year Tribulation. God has already given us a sneak preview that Israel's third Temple will be annihilated to make way for the Millennial Temple, that is, the 4th Israeli Temple. It will be very interesting to note whether or not the Tribulation Temple happens to meet its fate of destruction on the Ninth of Av. But whether or not the Tribulation Temple is leveled on the Ninth of Av, we can all still be quite certain that it was the God of Israel who called the shot.

The third Temple will be destroyed at the command and will of Almighty God in his own perfect timing. The desecration of the Tribulation Temple by the false messiah will demand that Solomon's Temple Rebuilt be blasted to smithereens in the last of the last days, at the end of the Seven Year Tribulation. (Daniel 7:25)

The Queen of Israel (The Restored Bathsheba; The woman of war mentioned in Song of Solomon 6:10 and Revelation 12:1-17) is the focus of the devil's hatred. Satan attempts to counteract and discredit God's favor upon the Restored Bathsheba in the end time by producing a flood of lies, deceit, terror, confusion, and utter chaos that the devil manipulates in the woman's direction. (Revelation 12:13-17)

"But thou, O, Daniel, shut up the words, and seal the book, even to the time of the end. Many shall run to and fro, and knowledge shall be increased." (Daniel 12:4)

Christ's Triumphant Appearance

"But of the times and the seasons, brothers and sisters, you have no need that I write unto you. For you know perfectly that the Day of the Lord Jesus Christ so comes as a thief in the night. For when they shall say, 'Peace and safety,' then, sudden destruction shall come upon them. And they shall not escape." (Paul, the Apostle, I Thessalonians 5:1-3)

"But the Day of the Lord will come as a thief in the night, in which the Heavens shall pass away with a great noise, and the elements shall melt with fervent heat. The Earth also and the works that are therein shall be burned up." (II Peter 3:10)

In view of the fact that the Coming of the Lord Jesus Christ shall be accompanied by a great outpouring of God's Spirit (Joel 2:28, 29; Acts 2:17, 18), the possibility should be considered that the Great and Terrible Day of the Lord Jesus Christ will be an invisible event, that is, "as a thief in the night." The prophecies of the Holy Bible may be referring to a manifestation of the Holy Spirit. On the other hand, the appearance of Jesus Christ with his angels and saints could be as optical as watching the most visual, 3-D, high-drama, technicolor, real-life movie you could ever imagine witnessing. No one is an expert on this matter but Jesus Christ himself. He knows the end from the beginning and the beginning from the end. One thing is quite certain: It will be the most awesome main event to ever take place up to this point in time. The end time drama of the last days is unfolding dramatically.

"Alas, for the great day! For the Day of the Lord is at hand, and as a destruction from the Almighty shall it come!" (Joel 1:15)

"A wonderful and horrible thing is committed in the land." (Jeremiah 5:30)

We are racing headlong, further and further, into the last days. We, indeed, are moving toward a cataclysmic situation, beyond our wildest imaginations.

A worldwide computer will be established in the last days, contributing to the enforcement of absolute, total conformity to the new world order.

Christ's Triumphant Appearance

"And no man will be able to buy or sell unless he/she has the Mark of the name of the Beast or the number of his name." (Revelation 13:17; 666)

In the last days, those who are proponents of the one world order won't have the Mark of God upon them (Ezekiel 9:4). They will be branded with the imprinted Mark of the Devil (666; Revelation 13:18). And all those who receive the false messiah's mark will be irreparably doomed. They will find no place to get back to the living God. All hopes for an optimistic future will be dashed. During the Seven Year Tribulation, it will seem like most men, women, and children will be totally out for themselves. Utter indifference and distrust will abound. There will be a Catch 22 at every turn in life. Every aspect of the tyranny of the one world order will be a constant, grinding source of irritation, emotional suffering, and pain. The lack of love on the planet of Earth will bring about a slow, agonizing torture to mankind. All of this will serve as the trademark and mantra of the Seven Year Tribulation and the false messiah, the Devil Incarnate, who will rule with an iron fist during this period.

"Choose you this day whom you will serve. But as for me and my house, we will serve the Lord God of Israel." (Joshua 24:15)

Eventually, the false messiah, who will be dominated and controlled by Satan, the god of this world (The Angel of Light; II Corinthians 11:14; II Corinthians 4:4), will gain control of this expanding empire, spreading the influence of European conglomerate in an attempt to rule the entire world. Daniel 2:31-35 predicts such a development in a prophecy referred to as the Great Image, in which the two legs mentioned represent the east (Greek) and the west (Latin) divisions of the new Roman Empire, and the ten toes (ten nations initially) represent the kingdom of the false messiah.

Daniel's vision of the ten modern-day Roman nations was given to him after Israel was exiled to Babylon. Daniel was taken captive to ancient Babylon by King Nebuchadnezzar and his army. The Babylonians had utterly destroyed Solomon's Temple (the first Israeli Temple) and Jerusalem. Daniel stood before Nebuchadnezzar to interpret a dream for the king. Daniel told the king that the God of Israel was revealing what will happen in days to come (Daniel 2:25-45; Revelation 13:15-18). Nebuchadnezzar's dream, which brought tremendous fear upon him, was

Christ's Triumphant Appearance

about a Great Image (the Image of the Beast) having a head of gold with ten horns, arms of silver, a belly of brass, legs of iron, and feet of iron and clay. In the king's dream, the statute was obliterated by a rock (Daniel 2:31-35). Daniel proceeded to tell Nebuchadnezzar that the head of gold was Babylon, which would rise to power only to be crushed. The ten horns are identified as the ten kings who will come from modern-day Rome. Afterwards, another king (the false messiah) will arise, that is, an eleventh king. This impostor and imitator of the Israeli Messiah will eventually show his true colors, blaspheming God in the Tribulation Temple (the Abomination of Desolation; Daniel 7:25; Daniel 9:24-27) and persecuting the Israelis. Daniel is clearly pointing to Europe as the new Roman Empire of the last days. The future design of the European union will lead to the vision of the United States of Europe.

We already have world currency in the form of credit cards. When you take your credit card and travel to any part of the world, you can, instantaneously, buy virtually anything in any currency. We do not have to wait for a one world financial system to appear in the world, because it is already right now in place at this moment. The world already functions as a global community. Now, credit cards have chips in them to process transactions. Possibly, the next step will be for those chips to be implanted somewhere in the physical body of consumers, in order to make monetary purchases more convenient, and serve as a quick identification of all those who are mandated to comply with the new world order. But God's Mark upon his people (Ezekiel 9:4; Revelation 9:1-10) will insure Yahweh's protection and provision (Manna from Heaven; Exodus 16:15, 31, 35). Obviously, more merit and significance should be rendered to God's Mark than the Mark of the Beast. (Ezekiel 9:4; Ephesians 1:12, 13; Revelation 9:3, 4; Revelation 13:16-18; Revelation 22:3, 4)

"Ho, everyone that thirsts, come ye to the waters, and he that has no money, come, buy, and eat. Yes, come, buy wine and milk without money and without price." (Isaiah 55:1; God's Provision to his People)

The Hebrew Prophet, Daniel, was told by the God of Israel about a ruler (prince; Satan), who would encourage the rebuilding of Solomon's Temple in the latter days, because this fiend's plot is to overtake and ransack the third Israeli Temple, in order to perpetrate the prophesied Abomination of

Christ's Triumphant Appearance

Desolation in the Holy of Holies of the Temple, the ultimate expression of blaspheming God and his Sanctuary. The devil has every intention of preventing Christ, by way of manipulation, from building the Millennial Temple, the Temple intended to usher in everlasting peace. All during the Seven Year Tribulation, the Rebuilt Solomon's Temple will stand. At the end of the Seven Year Tribulation, the defiled Tribulation Temple will be leveled by the army of Jesus Christ (Revelation 19:11-21; Revelation 20:1-15; Ezekiel 37:10). Then, the sanctified, that is, the set apart and declared holy Millennial Temple (built ONLY by the Israeli Messiah, Jesus Christ; Zechariah 6:12, 13) will stand in its place.

The building of Solomon's Temple will not come without a fight just prior to its manifestation. The Battle of Gog and Magog must occur first. The shofar has sounded to all Israelis and all those who love Israel, indicating that this intense spiritual warfare is imminent.

As the world is speeding toward its ultimate date with destiny, we are caught between the balance of our present responsibilities and our future expectations. As the clock of time ticks away, mankind comes closer and closer to Earth's final hour. A showdown is forthcoming. Based on biblical prophecy, it is only a matter of time before our planet will experience the most devastating catastrophes imaginable. The end of the world, as we know it, is near. There will come a point when no prophetic event remains to be fulfilled before the appearance of the Jewish Messiah takes place. This is an imminent reality, and it will occur suddenly and without warning. God's timetable is not our timetable. One-thousand years to the God of Israel is as a day to him, and a day is as one-thousand years (I Peter 3:8). Time is relative to Yahweh (The Eternal One). The Lord does not wear a wristwatch. A literal interpretation of biblical prophecy concerning the people of Israel returning to the Promised Land has been fulfilled, that is, the State of Israel being established on May 14th, 1948. Solomon's Temple is to be built and become the Tribulation Temple. Solomon's Temple will be built prior to the beginning of the Seven Year Tribulation. The false messiah will endorse the building of the 3rd Temple for narcissistic purposes, that is, having the full intention of taking over the new Temple to make it his headquarters. Hence, the Tribulation Temple will have become manifested. Therefore, the glorious appearing of the genuine Israeli Messiah, Jesus Christ, must occur for Israel to secure peace. Jerusalem will

Christ's Triumphant Appearance

be surrounded on all sides by armies of the adversaries of Israel (Zechariah 14:1-4). The Battle of Armageddon (in the figurative Valley of Megiddo, representing the entire world) will take place as a showdown of force between good and evil at "the Worldwide O.K. Corral." And with the defeat of the false messiah comes the defeat of Satan. In fact, the disposal of the false messiah, conclusively, is a direct correlation to the end of the devil's career and existence. The fourth Jewish Temple on Earth, the Millennial Temple, will be built only by Jesus Christ, and the Millennial Reign (1,000 Year Reign) of Jesus will follow, radiating the comfort of everlasting peace.

The Coming of Jesus Christ will be sudden, instantaneous, and without warning, catching everyone by surprise. No one knows the hour when the Israeli Messiah will appear (Matthew 24:36; Jesus Christ). It will occur quickly and suddenly. In the twinkling of an eye, like a thief in the night, the Jewish Messiah is going to gallantly come out of nowhere. This is an event whose time has come (Zechariah 14:1-4; Malachi 3:1-4; Matthew 24:27; II Thessalonians 2:1-4, 8; II Peter 3:2-13).

In the meantime, Satan's unrelenting, evil wrath will break completely loose upon human beings. He will be in a race against time, yet at the same time, he will be in self-denial that his time is short (Revelation 12:12). The devil's spiritual darkness is right on the verge of engulfing the entire world. It will be a total eclipse.

A godless, worldwide state will become the environment that is successful in justifying war for the common good of the state only, with total disregard for the decent citizens of Earth. As our culture continues to become more secularized, the stage will be set for the endorsement of war against all those who oppose the will of the state. Israel will have a central role in confronting and colliding with this world state. And the God of Israel will set the stage for what should be considered as the Battle of Armageddon in the figurative Valley of Megiddo (which represents the entire world; Zechariah 14:10-3).

"In that day, there shall be a great mourning in Jerusalem, as the mourning in the Valley of Megiddo (Armageddon)." (Zechariah 12:11)

While Satan's influence in society worldwide will be great, Yahweh (The Eternal One), through it all, remains sovereign. God has everything

Christ's Triumphant Appearance

under control, despite how bleak the adverse events inflicted upon God's people may appear, and despite the doom and gloom reports we observe when watching the evening news on television every night.

People can take comfort in the fact that in the midst of all the despondency, God has a firm hand in all matters of life. On the surface, it may not appear to be apparent.

Only God knows his timetable.

"Declare in Judah and publish in Jerusalem. And say, 'Blow the trumpet (shofar) in the land. Cry, gather together, and say, Assemble yourselves, and let us go into the cities that are defended. Set up the standard toward Zion.'" (Jeremiah 4:5, 6)

"Blow the trumpet in Zion and sound an alarm in my holy mountain. Let all the inhabitants of the land tremble. For the Day of the Lord has come, for it is near at hand." (Joel 2:1)

"Awake, awake. Stand up, O Jerusalem!" (Isaiah 51:17)

"Awake, awake. Put on thy strength, O, Zion. Put on your beautiful garments, O, Jerusalem, the holy city!" (Jerusalem: The City of David; Isaiah 52:1)

Albert Einstein warned that the atomic age would propel the world toward unprecedented catastrophe. Robert Oppenheimer, the father of the atomic bomb, called for the urgency of international controls on nuclear weapons, as he famously stated: "Now, I have become Death, the destroyer of the world."

We are all witnessing a quantum leap toward the fulfillment of the Biblical prophecies of the last days. The final climatic acts predicted will bring this human drama that mankind has endured to a final conclusion. Current events could not be more ideally in place (positioned) for the fulfillment of these last remaining Biblical prophecies concerning the latter days. We are being swept down the corridor of time to an inevitable date

Christ's Triumphant Appearance

with destiny. The book of recorded time has been turned to the final chapter of human history.

Nothing marks today's moment in history more strikingly than the acceleration of change. As stated in the Book of Daniel concerning the end time: Many shall run to and fro, and knowledge shall be increased."

"For the Lord has opened his armory and has brought forth the weapons of his indignation. For this is the work of the Lord God of hosts." (Jeremiah 50:25)

In this intense battle against spiritual oppression, the struggle for world dominion is, ultimately, between the power of the Israeli Messiah, Jesus Christ, and the forces of Satan.

Israel is the third strongest military power on Earth.

"But thou, O, Daniel, shut up the words, and seal the book, even to the time of the end. Many shall run to and fro, and knowledge shall be increased." (Daniel 12:4)

Eventually, the false messiah, who will be dominated and controlled by Satan, the god of this world (The Angel of Light; II Corinthians 11:14; II Corinthians 4:4), will gain control of this expanding empire, spreading the influence of European conglomerate in an attempt to rule the entire world. Daniel 2:31-35 predicts such a development in a prophecy referred to as the Great Image, in which the two legs mentioned represent the east (Greek) and the west (Latin) divisions of the new Roman Empire, and the ten toes (ten nations initially) represent the kingdom of the false messiah.

Daniel's vision of the ten modern-day Roman nations was given to him after Israel was exiled to Babylon. Daniel was taken captive to ancient Babylon by King Nebuchadnezzar and his army. The Babylonians had utterly destroyed Solomon's Temple (the first Israeli Temple) and Jerusalem. Daniel stood before Nebuchadnezzar to interpret a dream for the king. Daniel told the king that the God of Israel was revealing what will happen in days to come (Daniel 2:25-45; Revelation 13:15-18). Nebuchadnezzar's dream, which brought tremendous fear upon him, was

Christ's Triumphant Appearance

about a Great Image (the Image of the Beast) having a head of gold with ten horns, arms of silver, a belly of brass, legs of iron, and feet of iron and clay. In the king's dream, the statute was obliterated by a rock (Daniel 2:31-35). Daniel proceeded to tell Nebuchadnezzar that the head of gold was Babylon, which would rise to power only to be crushed. The ten horns are identified as the ten kings who will come from modern-day Rome. Afterwards, another king (the false messiah) will arise, that is, an eleventh king. This impostor and imitator of the Israeli Messiah will eventually show his true colors, blaspheming God in the Tribulation Temple (the Abomination of Desolation; Daniel 7:25; Daniel 9:24-27) and persecuting the Israelis. Daniel is clearly pointing to Europe as the new Roman Empire of the last days. The future design of the European union will lead to the vision of the United States of Europe.

We already have world currency in the form of credit cards. When you take your credit card and travel to any part of the world, you can, instantaneously, buy virtually anything in any currency. We do not have to wait for a one world financial system to appear in the world, because it is already right now in place at this moment. The world already functions as a global community. Now, credit cards have chips in them to process transactions. Possibly, the next step will be for those chips to be implanted somewhere in the physical body of consumers, in order to make monetary purchases more convenient, and serve as a quick identification of all those who are mandated to comply with the new world order. But God's Mark upon his people (Ezekiel 9:4; Revelation 9:1-10) will insure Yahweh's protection and provision (Manna from Heaven; Exodus 16:15, 31, 35). Obviously, more merit and significance should be rendered to God's Mark than the Mark of the Beast. (Ezekiel 9:4; Ephesians 1:12, 13; Revelation 9:3, 4; Revelation 13:16-18; Revelation 22:3, 4)

"Ho, everyone that thirsts, come ye to the waters, and he that has no money, come, buy, and eat. Yes, come, buy wine and milk without money and without price." (Isaiah 55:1; God's Provision to his People)

The Hebrew Prophet, Daniel, was told by the God of Israel about a ruler (prince; Satan), who would encourage the rebuilding of Solomon's Temple in the latter days, because this fiend's plot is to overtake and ransack the third Israeli Temple, in order to perpetrate the prophesied Abomination of

Christ's Triumphant Appearance

Desolation in the Holy of Holies of the Temple, the ultimate expression of blaspheming God and his Sanctuary. The devil has every intention of preventing Christ, by way of manipulation, from building the Millennial Temple, the Temple intended to usher in everlasting peace. All during the Seven Year Tribulation, the Rebuilt Solomon's Temple will stand. At the end of the Seven Year Tribulation, the defiled Tribulation Temple will be leveled by the army of Jesus Christ (Revelation 19:11-21; Revelation 20:1-15; Ezekiel 37:10). Then, the sanctified, that is, the set apart and declared holy Millennial Temple (built ONLY by the Israeli Messiah, Jesus Christ; Zechariah 6:12, 13) will stand in its place.

The building of Solomon's Temple will not come without a fight just prior to its manifestation. The Battle of Gog and Magog must occur first. The shofar has sounded to all Israelis and all those who love Israel, indicating that this intense spiritual warfare is imminent.

As the world is speeding toward its ultimate date with destiny, we are caught between the balance of our present responsibilities and our future expectations. As the clock of time ticks away, mankind comes closer and closer to Earth's final hour. A showdown is forthcoming. Based on biblical prophecy, it is only a matter of time before our planet will experience the most devastating catastrophes imaginable. The end of the world, as we know it, is near. There will come a point when no prophetic event remains to be fulfilled before the appearance of the Jewish Messiah takes place. This is an imminent reality, and it will occur suddenly and without warning. God's timetable is not our timetable. One-thousand years to the God of Israel is as a day to him, and a day is as one-thousand years (I Peter 3:8). Time is relative to Yahweh (The Eternal One). The Lord does not wear a wristwatch. A literal interpretation of biblical prophecy concerning the people of Israel returning to the Promised Land has been fulfilled, that is, the State of Israel being established on May 14th, 1948. Solomon's Temple is to be built and become the Tribulation Temple. Solomon's Temple will be built prior to the beginning of the Seven Year Tribulation. The false messiah will endorse the building of the 3rd Temple for narcissistic purposes, that is, having the full intention of taking over the new Temple to make it his headquarters. Hence, the Tribulation Temple will have become manifested. Therefore, the glorious appearing of the genuine Israeli Messiah, Jesus Christ, must occur for Israel to secure peace. Jerusalem will

Christ's Triumphant Appearance

be surrounded on all sides by armies of the adversaries of Israel (Zechariah 14:1-4). The Battle of Armageddon (in the figurative Valley of Megiddo, representing the entire world) will take place as a showdown of force between good and evil at "the Worldwide O.K. Corral." And with the defeat of the false messiah comes the defeat of Satan. In fact, the disposal of the false messiah, conclusively, is a direct correlation to the end of the devil's career and existence. The fourth Jewish Temple on Earth, the Millennial Temple, will be built only by Jesus Christ, and the Millennial Reign (1,000 Year Reign) of Jesus will follow, radiating the comfort of everlasting peace.

The Coming of Jesus Christ will be sudden, instantaneous, and without warning, catching everyone by surprise. No one knows the hour when the Israeli Messiah will appear (Matthew 24:36; Jesus Christ). It will occur quickly and suddenly. In the twinkling of an eye, like a thief in the night, the Jewish Messiah is going to gallantly come out of nowhere. This is an event whose time has come (Zechariah 14:1-4; Malachi 3:1-4; Matthew 24:27; II Thessalonians 2:1-4, 8; II Peter 3:2-13).

In the meantime, Satan's unrelenting, evil wrath will break completely loose upon human beings. He will be in a race against time, yet at the same time, he will be in self-denial that his time is short (Revelation 12:12). The devil's spiritual darkness is right on the verge of engulfing the entire world. It will be a total eclipse.

People can take comfort in the fact that in the midst of all the despondency, God has a firm hand in all matters of life. On the surface, it may not appear to be apparent.

Only God knows his timetable.

"Declare in Judah and publish in Jerusalem. And say, 'Blow the trumpet (shofar) in the land. Cry, gather together, and say, Assemble yourselves, and let us go into the cities that are defended. Set up the standard toward Zion.'" (Jeremiah 4:5, 6)

"Blow the trumpet in Zion and sound an alarm in my holy mountain. Let all the inhabitants of the land tremble. For the Day of the Lord has come, for it is near at hand." (Joel 2:1)

Christ's Triumphant Appearance

"Awake, awake. Stand up, O Jerusalem!" (Isaiah 51:17)

"Awake, awake. Put on thy strength, O, Zion. Put on your beautiful garments, O, Jerusalem, the holy city!" (Jerusalem: The City of David; Isaiah 52:1)

The Coming of Jesus Christ cannot be predicted or manipulated.

"And if it seems evil unto you to serve the Lord God of Israel, choose you this day whom you will serve." *** (Joshua 24:15) ***

Satan himself has been left guessing when Jesus Christ will arrive on the scene. Satan is always left to wait on God's perfect timing.

The Battle of Gog and Magog takes place just prior to the Seven Year Tribulation. At the end of this war, Satan will devise his own agenda to successfully seize Solomon's Temple to use as his headquarters.

The Battle of Armageddon takes place at the end of the Seven Year Tribulation. It will, by no means, be an overnight war.

The world has obviously come to a great crossroads. We have all come full circle. It is time to get the world back into alignment and make way for the Restored Jerusalem. Surely, Jesus, the Israeli Messiah, will come quickly.

"Behold, the Day of the Lord will come. For I will gather all nations against Jerusalem to battle. Then, shall the Lord Jesus Christ go forth and fight against those nations, as when he fought in the day of battle. And then, his feet shall stand in that day upon the Mount of Olives, which is before Jerusalem in the east." (Zechariah 14:1-4; The Battle of Armageddon and the Coming of the Lord Jesus Christ)

A clear indicator of the Battle of Armageddon will be that Jerusalem will be surrounded by the armies of all the nations of Earth (friends and foes alike) to do battle. (Zechariah 14:1-4)

Christ's Triumphant Appearance

There are certain verses in the Bible that express empathy for the havoc his people endure:

"Are not two sparrows sold for a farthing? And one of them shall not fall on the ground without your Father in Heaven knowing. But the very hairs of your head are numbered. Do not fear, therefore. For you are of much more value than many sparrows. There shall not one hair of your head perish." (The Lord Jesus Christ; Matthew 10:29-31; Luke 21:18)

"Surely, I have seen the affliction of my people." (The God of Israel; Exodus 3:7; The Heavenly Father is a doting father to his children) The loss of innocent lives throughout all time, attributed to the overall sources of tragedy, is absolutely heartbreaking to Jesus Christ.

"Pray for the peace of Jerusalem. All they who love her shall prosper." (David; Psalm 122:6)

"And then, shall that wicked one be revealed, whom the Lord Jesus Christ shall consume with the spirit of his mouth, and shall destroy with the brightness of his coming." (II Thessalonians 2:8)

"That you may be mindful of the words which were spoken before by the holy prophets of Israel and of the commandment of us, the apostles of our Lord and Savior: Knowing this first, that there shall come scoffers in the last days, saying, 'Where is the promise of the Coming of the Lord Jesus Christ? For since our forefathers passed away, all things have continued as they were since the beginning of creation.'" (II Peter 3:2-4)

"Even so, come quickly, Lord Jesus!" (Revelation 22:20)

The Coming of Jesus Christ cannot be predicted or manipulated.

"And if it seems evil unto you to serve the Lord God of Israel, choose you this day whom you will serve." *** (Joshua 24:15) ***)

Satan himself has been left guessing when Jesus Christ will arrive on the scene. Satan is always left to wait on God's perfect timing.

Christ's Triumphant Appearance

The Battle of Gog and Magog takes place just prior to the Seven Year Tribulation. At the end of this war, Satan will devise his own agenda to successfully seize Solomon's Temple to use as his headquarters.

The Battle of Armageddon takes place at the end of the Seven Year Tribulation. It will, by no means, be an overnight war.

Satan is the common enemy (archnemesis) of every man, woman, and child who have ever lived. Every last one of us have an everyday foe in Satan, who is causing us to fight and bicker among ourselves. The devil is the culprit who has been creating all the crossfire (throughout history and all time) in our midst. Destroy Satan, and everything else will fall into place. That is, cut off the head, and the tail dies.

Ultimately, the entire Israeli fleet, made up of men and women sworn to protect Israel at any cost with modern-day weaponry, is battling against Satan and all those who are, to their misfortune, under his control. Satan is the condemner, the accuser, and the fault finder of all those who have put their faith (Habakkuk 2:4) in Jesus Christ, the Messiah.

From the very outset of Israel becoming a State in 1948, the doomsday clock has measured in minutes the time it would take for the apocalypse to take place. Ever since, Satan's been convincing us that abuse is the norm.

"And there was a war in Heaven. Michael, the archangel, and all the angels of God chose to do battle against the Red Dragon." (Revelation 12:3, 4, 7)

The world has obviously come to a great crossroads. We have all come full circle. It is time to get the world back into alignment and make way for the Restored Jerusalem. Surely, Jesus, the Israeli Messiah, will come quickly.

"Behold, the Day of the Lord will come. For I will gather all nations against Jerusalem to battle. Then, shall the Lord Jesus Christ go forth and fight against those nations, as when he fought in the day of battle. And then, his feet shall stand in that day upon the Mount of Olives, which is before

Christ's Triumphant Appearance

Jerusalem in the east." (Zechariah 14:1-4; The Battle of Armageddon and the Coming of the Lord Jesus Christ

The only person who qualifies to be the Israeli Messiah is Jesus Christ. The life of Jesus provides all the evidence we need to safely come to that verdict. And when he suddenly appears (Malachi 3:1, 2), no one is going to have the composure to dare dispute that Jesus is King of kings and Lord of lords.

"And then, shall that wicked one be revealed, whom the Lord Jesus Christ shall consume with the spirit of his mouth, and shall destroy with the brightness of his coming." (II Thessalonians 2:8)

"That you may be mindful of the words which were spoken before by the holy prophets of Israel and of the commandment of us, the apostles of our Lord and Savior: Knowing this first, that there shall come scoffers in the last days, saying, 'Where is the promise of the Coming of the Lord Jesus Christ? For since our forefathers passed away, all things have continued as they were since the beginning of creation.'" (II Peter 3:2-4)

"Even so, come quickly, Lord Jesus!" (Revelation 22:20)

"Fear, and the pit, and the snare, are upon you, O, inhabitants of Earth. And it shall come to pass, that he who flees from the noise of the fear shall fall into the pit. And he that comes up out of the midst of the pit shall be taken in the snare. For the windows from on high are open, and the foundations of the Earth do shake. The Earth is utterly broken down. The Earth is split open. The Earth is moved exceedingly. The Earth shall reel to and fro like a drunkard, and sway like a hut." (Isaiah 24:17-20)

Air raid sirens were blaring all over Israel. David was suited up to board his F-22 Raptor. Bathsheba came to send David off at Jerusalem Air Force Base, that David established as king years ago. Military personnel scurried all over the base, preparing for the war to end all wars. The two were embraced just outside a hanger. Bathsheba had no idea if she was saying farewell to David for the last time. It was reminiscent of the final scene in the movie, "Casablanca," starring Humphrey Bogart and Ingrid Bergman.

Christ's Triumphant Appearance

Bathsheba: "You cheat death, don't you, David? You approach death like a Poker Game with high stakes. And even though the deck of cards is stacked against you, you insist on playing to win."

David: "Yes, Bathsheba. I cheat death."

Bathsheba: "You've played your last card quite a few times, haven't you, David?"

David: "That's perhaps a good way of putting it, Bathsheba. War is the trade of all kings."

Bathsheba: "No one knows you the way I do, David! I wish I could be with you when you're fighting in combat up there in the not quite so blue sky."

David: "You are, Bathsheba."

Bathsheba: "When you're in battle, David, I contact Israeli Command every day and ask the Commander on Duty where you are and what you're doing. So, fly placidly, my Love, amidst the noise and confusion. You and I are so involved. You come back to me safe. I will be right here waiting for you. You left me standing here a long, long time ago. Good things come to those who wait. When will we meet again, David?"

David: "I look forward to seeing you again when the Israeli war is over!!!"

Bathsheba: "Until then."

Commander David Hartman: "Soaring Eagle airborne."

Commander Jonathan Diamond: "Joshua, Greased Lightning airborne."

Christ's Triumphant Appearance

Israeli Command --- Code Name: Joshua: "Received and understood, Greased Lightning. You're a man on the go."
Commander Ariel Rosenberg (Chief Israeli Defense Forces Commander at Israeli Command): "Who's up there right now?"
Israeli Operations Officer: "Eagle and Lightning, Commander."
Commander Rosenberg: "Eagle and Lightning. Chances are that it won't be a boring day."
Israeli Operations Officer: "All bets are off, Commander."

David: "It's getting to the place where we've seen just about everything together in battle, right, Lightning?"
Jonathan: "That's why they call us 'partners in crime.' We've been through thick and thick. But don't speak too soon, Eagle. Your total focus needs to be staying out of trouble."
David: "It's a full-time job for me, Lightning. You know that. But everyone knows that you're the hardest working Israeli TOP GUN Fighter Pilot in the business."
Jonathan: "Yeah. I'm the hardest working Israeli TOP GUN Fighter Pilot in the business because covering your back requires total focus, Chief."
David: "That's why you're an all-round swell guy and an award-winning Wingman, Greased Lightning."
Jonathan: "You know something, Soaring Eagle. I can't wait for tomorrow, because I get better looking every day."
David: "LOL on that, Lightning."

Jonathan and David's fighter jets are in a parallel 45-degree tactical turn together in space, riding the wave, and going for the gusto.

"This is very peculiar." (David at the helm of Soaring Eagle)

David: "Lightning, are you picking up some odd activity on radar?"
Jonathan: "Yeah. How intense can you get? It's an all-out invasion!"
David: "They're, obviously, attempting to jam radar."

Jonathan: "We don't have to look for trouble, do we, Eagle?"
David: "No, if we stick around long enough in one place, the trouble, eventually, finds us. We'll surprise them, Lightning. They're not aware yet that we're on to their approach."

Christ's Triumphant Appearance

David: "Jerusalem, we officially have a problem!"
Jonathan: "Joshua, all airborne fighter pilots and those in the fleet covering our perimeter are getting red flags. Battle lines are officially being drawn. This is not a drill!"
Joshua: "We're assessing the overall situation now, Lightning. Do not fire unless you are fired upon. That is an order to TOP GUN and the entire Israeli fleet at this bearing. Stand by."
Jonathan: "Roger that. Greased Lightning standing by."

David: "It's quite apparent Satan is directly behind all this activity. It's the trademark of his direct commands. I can see his wheels turning now."
Jonathan: "Heads up, Eagle! Joshua, Soaring Eagle is under fire! Man, that was close!"
David: "Horseshoes and grenades."

Jonathan: "Joshua, these bandits are coming at us like World War II Kamikaze Zeros. I repeat: They're approaching all of us like suicide bombers."
Joshua: "We read you, Lightning. We're alerting the entire fleet to take their positions and stand by for offensive action. The order to not fire unless fired upon, obviously, does not apply to you and Soaring Eagle. You've been fired upon."
Jonathan: "Received, Joshua. Greased Lightning standing by."

Israeli Command (Joshua): "The official alert status is Major Red Alert."

Jonathan: "Looks like the big picture assessment is turning into one gigantic super puzzle. Talk to me, Eagle."
David: "Lightning, I'm tracking hostile bandits inbound, Vector 090. And that's just to mention the enemy aircrafts coming from that heading!"
Jonathan. "Roger. I'll take the one at Contact 20, left at 30 miles,
with nine minutes closure. I'm going for my guns to start."

Mulholland Drive: "Joshua, we have bandits like fireflies all over the sky. Clouds of them."

David: "Joshua, this is Soaring Eagle. I have inbound bandits heading 2,7,0 at 10 miles, approximately 3 minutes closure! I have a visual I.D."

Christ's Triumphant Appearance

Joshua: "Roger that, Eagle. We have radar contact. These bandits are coming in from all directions! That is confirmed."
Israeli Operations Officer: "We, certainly, weren't expecting this much activity today, Commander!"
Commander Aerial Rosenberg: "That's why they call it Armageddon, Captain."

Sky Hawk: "Okay. Let's see how many of these things come out of the woodwork. Can you see any trailers?"
David: "I'm getting radar data, clearly showing a supernatural phenomenon that's working on our behalf, against these bandits. They're commanded only to attack anyone without the seal of God in their foreheads." (Revelation 9:1-12)
Ezekiel: "They appear to be V/STOL Helicopters, like Boeing AH-64 Apache Attack Helicopters.
Geronimo: "You mean they look like a swarm of locusts coming in from all points west. Courtesy of Moses, I'd say! It definitely looks like his style, all right." (The Tenth Chapter of Exodus)
Ezekiel: "No complaints from me. We'll gladly take the assistance."

David: "Lightning, I'm going head-to-head with these bandits to see how much company they've got! I'm going to break high and right and try to get a glimpse of how much backup these frontrunners have."
Jonathan: "They're nose-to-nose with us at four minutes closure, Eagle!"

Commander Rosenberg: "Keep doing the math until we get an exact number of how many bandits are moving in. And let's get an exact position on every last one of them."
Operations Officer: "We're working on it, Commander. Sensors are reading and calculating data to the quantum computer now for an overall assessment. We'll have complete computations very shortly, just a few seconds."
Commander Rosenberg: "Let's get the stats on any and all the various computations as quickly as they come in, and then, prioritize those scenarios."

David: "Lightning, you take Black Angel One. I'm going after Black Angel Two. I'll catch you on down the road."

Christ's Triumphant Appearance

Jonathan: "Sounds like a plan to me. And I'll be in Jerusalem before you. Wait a minute! I lost Black Angel One in the sun, Eagle! Hold on. There he is. He made a 360 degree turn, and he's right on our tail! This bandit is all over us! Joshua, we are under missile lock from the rear courtesy of the enemy, but we've got a course of action."

Joshua: "Go with the flow, Eagle and Lightning. Focus your energy. You guys know the drill. Push the envelope."

David: "Acknowledged, Joshua. Greased Lightning and I are working on a Bracket now.

Jonathan: "You bet your shekels we know the drill. The Split worked, Eagle. Let's turn the tables and get them in a Bracket."

Commander Ariel Rosenberg: "Launch the Alert Six Aircrafts, Captain!"
Operations Officer: "Yes, sir!"
Jonathan: "Go get him, Eagle."
David: "I'm going for missile lock on Black Angel Two. Come on, Baby. I've got a lock on him! Bingo! He didn't even know what hit him."
Jonathan: "You got him, all right, Eagle! No shortage of work ahead."
David: "It sure is nice to know that our weapons are in direct sync with the Holy Bible. Nothing but technicolor! We're on the cutting edge."
Jonathan: "We're definitely earning our paychecks today."

Commander Rosenberg: "Where are Eagle and Lightning right now?"
Operations Officer: "They're at heading 0, 6, 7 in a 45-degree tactical turn in parallel, Commander Rosenberg."
Commander Rosenberg: "Armageddon simply enhances their acrobatics, Captain!"

Jonathan: "I've got some new trouble now. If I reversed on yet another hard cross, Eagle, I could, immediately, go to laser guns on him."
David: "You're definitely in proper range for laser guns, Lightning."
Jonathan: "Done deal! That bandit is past tense now, Eagle."
David: "Gutsiest move I ever saw, Greased Lightning."

David: "Joshua, we have bandits, left, at 10 o'clock. We're still incognito at this bearing."
Jonathan: "Eagle, you've got the lead. You're covered! Break now."

Christ's Triumphant Appearance

David: "He's too close for missiles, Lighting. I'm switching to laser guns. That bandit is history!"

Joshua: "All right, gentlemen. You're in the World Series. It's the bottom of the ninth, and the score is tied. The enemy fighter jets that you're up against right now are smaller, faster and more maneuverable than what you've ever been up against in the past. Stand your ground, gentlemen. Armageddon is officially impending."

David: "Lightning, you've got a bandit right on your tail. He's riding your back. It's your old nemesis, Black Angel One once again."
Jonathan: "Yeah. I got him in my rear sight. It's Black Angel One, all right. I'd recognize that demon anywhere. Eagle, I'm gonna hit the brakes, and he'll fly right by. Here it goes."

Jonathan slowed down to draw the bandit in closer. Then, he did an abrupt pull up to slow down rapidly, which forced the bandit to overshoot and fly right in front of Jonathan, where a missile shot from Greased Lightning's fighter jet quickly nipped the fight in the bud.

Jonathan: "As promised, Black Angel One was all mine. That demon is washed up now, Eagle! Thanks for the heads up."
David: "You are one cool cucumber, Greased Lightning."
Jonathan: "It was butter. Just like that, Eagle. I hit the high note."
David: "Smooth, Lightning. Like margarine. What a game changer!"

"We are officially at battle stations, all the way around. Assume your firing positions. All Israeli TOP GUN Fighter Jet Pilots will adhere to details and directives coming only from the Israeli Messiah, Joshua, and Israeli Air Traffic Controllers. We are all in this together. And as for you, Soaring Eagle and Greased Lightning: Keep your head about you, Mates." (Command Ariel Rosenberg; Israeli Command --- Joshua)

"Therefore, you also be ready. For in such an hour when you think not, I will come." (Jesus Christ; Matthew 24:44)

"For I came from Heaven, not to do my own will, but to do the will of the Father who sent me. And the Father has sent me so that out of all who

Christ's Triumphant Appearance

he has given me, I should not lose anyone. But that I should raise them all up at the last day. And this is the will of the Father who has sent me, that everyone who sees the Son and believes on him may have everlasting life. And I will raise them up at the last day." (John 6:38-40)

Suddenly, as an unprecedented event, and at the sound of a trumpet, Jesus Christ, the Israeli Messiah, came forth in the clouds with a host of angels and saints behind him, causing all the inhabitants of the nations of Earth to be in absolute awe of the sight. And Jesus opened his mouth, and the Word of God continually came out in great power, destroying all those who had brought harm and injustice upon his people.

"And they shall look upon the Israeli Messiah, Jesus Christ, whom they have pierced." (Zechariah 12:10; Revelation 1:7)

"Comfort ye, comfort ye my people,' says the Lord God of Israel. 'Speak ye comfortably to Jerusalem, and cry unto her, that her welfare is accomplished." (Jesus Christ; Isaiah 40:1, 2)

"For, then, shall be the Great Tribulation, as there never has been since the beginning of the world to this time, no, nor ever shall be. And except those days be shortened, there will be no human being to save. But for the elect's sake, those days shall be shortened. For as the lightning comes out of the east, and shines even unto the west, even also the Coming of the Son of God shall be. Immediately after the Seven Year Tribulation of those days

Christ's Triumphant Appearance

shall the sun be darkened, and the moon shall not give her light, and the stars shall fall from Heaven, and the powers and the Heavens shall be shaken. And then, shall appear the sign of the Son of God in Heaven. And the tribes of the Earth mourn, and they shall see the Son of God coming in the clouds of Heaven with power and great glory. And I shall send my angels with the great sound of a trumpet. And they shall gather together my elect from the four corners of the wind, from one end of Heaven to another. Verily, I say unto you, This generation will not pass away, until all these things are fulfilled. Heaven and Earth shall pass away, but my words shall not pass away. But of that day and hour no man knows, no, not even the angels of Heaven, but my Father only." (Jesus Christ; Matthew 24:21, 22, 27-31, 34-36)

"And I saw Heaven open, and behold, a white horse. And he (Jesus Christ, the Israeli Messiah) who sat upon the white horse was called, 'Faithful and True.' And in righteousness did he judge and make war. His eyes were as a flame of fire, and on his head were many crowns. And he had a name written, that no man knew, but he himself. And he was clothed with a vesture dipped in blood. And his name is called, 'The Word of God.' (John 1:1) And the armies which were in Heaven followed him upon white horses, clothed in fine linen, white and clean. And out of his mouth went a sharp Sword (Hebrews 4:12), that with it he could suddenly attack the nations. And he shall rule them with a rod of iron, as he treads the winepress of the fierceness and wrath of Almighty God. And he had on his vesture a name written, 'KING OF KINGS, AND LORD OF LORDS.' And the Remnant of Israel was empowered with the Sword of him who sat upon the horse, that is, the Sword that proceeds out of his mouth." (Revelation 19: 11-16, 21; (By the testimony of John, the Apostle; The Coming of The Lord Jesus Christ; The Great and Terrible Day of the Lord; Who can abide it?)

"So shall my Word be that goes forth out of my mouth. It shall not return void. But it shall accomplish that which I please, and it shall prosper in the thing whereunto I sent it." (Jesus Christ; Isaiah 55:11)

"In the beginning was the Word. And the Word was with God, and the Word was God." (John 1:1; Revelation 19:11-13; Jesus Christ is the Word of God)

Christ's Triumphant Appearance

"For the Word of God is quick and powerful, and sharper than any two-edged Sword, piercing even to the dividing asunder of soul and spirit, and of the joints and marrow, and is a discerner of the thoughts and intents of the heart." (Hebrews 4:12)

As Jesus and his entourage of angels and saints approached the Earth, the impact of his words struck the Earth like incredibly powerful bolts of lightning. Loud and clear, everyone understood Jesus in their own language.

"And I looked, and, lo, a Lamb (Jesus Christ) stood on Mount Zion, and with him all the Remnant of Israel, having his Father's name written in their foreheads." (Revelation 14:1; The Mark of God; Revelation 22:3, 4)

"I am the Pearl of Great Price." (Jesus, Matthew 13:45, 46)

CHAPTER TEN
THE PRESIDENT OF THE UNITED STATES' ADDRESS
TO THE NATIONS OF THE WORLD

"Good evening, my fellow citizens of the United States, and all allies of America on the planet of Earth. The United States Government, as promised, has maintained the closest surveillance of a military build-up in our world. Unmistakable evidence has established the fact that a series of ongoing offensive nuclear attacks is now in preparation, endangering all of mankind.

The purpose of these unrelenting, unyielding strategies can be none other than to provide further nuclear strikes from certain evil forces, attempting to undermine any and all safety that we cherish in our world. It has become quite apparent to everyone around the entire world that we all, at this present moment, are being faced with a devastating crisis of unparalleled proportion. The United States is currently on a MILITARY DEFCON ONE ALERT STATUS to the degree of being unprecedented in the history of our country, indicating that we are at maximum readiness and that an all-out nuclear war is imminent. As evidence of this build-up was already in my

Christ's Triumphant Appearance

hand, it was all too apparent that every last nation of Earth is preparing for a war in which no man, woman, and child will be unaffected.

Those who are in opposition with each other on Earth can be divided into two distinct factions: The forces of good and the forces of evil. The opponents of good confront us on a battlefield composed of many confusing elements, mixed signals, and demoralizing crossfire. This conflict, provoking the proponents of good, has existed throughout all time. It has been an ultimate tragedy for all generations from the beginning of history leading up to our generation.

Ladies and gentlemen, we all stand at a critical, devastating crossroads at this very moment. I am speaking in no uncertain terms. We are all, now, at this very point in time, witnessing the unfolding of whether the forces of good or the forces of evil, with dyer and eternal consequences, will, ultimately, prevail and dominate the world, as we know it, once and for all.

It is the position and intention of the United States of America, in reacting to these clandestine, underhanded, treacherous assaults that have been perpetrated upon us all, to bring about an unwavering, ultimate victory, resulting in conclusive freedom from the tyranny of our enemies.

Therefore, acting in the defense of the security of the United States and all of our allies around the entire world, under the authority entrusted to me by the U. S. Constitution, as endorsed by Congress, and supported by the United Nations, the Joint Chiefs of Staff of the NATO member nations, and top-level supportive military leaders here in our country and throughout our globe, we will unanimously and officially remain at our highest military alert level as an integral part of our strategy to maintain protection from all of our adversaries, out of sheer self-preservation. In addition, I have directed that the following recommendations be taken immediately:

The United States is making an appeal, with a sense of urgency, that all of our allies around the world join forces with us to ultimately seek peace among each other on a global basis, in a bond of unity. We implore the nations of Earth, who are committed to the good, common values that keep us content, prosperous, and safe, to set aside conflicting political differences and perspectives long enough to connect with each other. I would consider

Christ's Triumphant Appearance

it imperative that we take any and all opportunities to rally together as one in a unified effort to eradicate, once and for all, the evil that has plagued our world and inflicted pain upon the lives of so many harmless, innocent people.

It shall be the policy of this nation to regard any offensive attack launched by our opponents upon our allies, especially Israel, as an attack on the United States, requiring a full retaliatory response.

Let there be no misunderstanding to anyone concerned within the sound of my voice. We are engaged in a campaign in which the outcome will result in either total victory or utter defeat. May the human race be allowed to experience a future of peace, not doom. And may our prize, therein, be life, liberty, and the eternal pursuit of happiness.

I look forward to a great future for America. A future in which our country will match its military strength with our moral restraint. Its wealth with our wisdom. Its power with our purpose. I look forward to an America which will not be afraid of grace and beauty, which will protect the beauty of our natural environment. And I look forward to a world which will be safe, not only for democracy and diversity, but also for personal distinction.

It is the sincere hope of the United States of America that all nations committed with us as participants in this precarious endeavor will triumph in what should be considered to be the Battle of Armageddon."

"But they shall serve the Lord, their God, and David, their king, whom I will raise up unto them." (Jeremiah 30:9)

Israeli Commander Ariel Rosenberg to all Israeli TOP GUN Fighter Jet Pilots: "All right, gentlemen. We have had enough time to calculate the severity of this campaign that we're currently engaged in. The forces of evil have pulled out all the stops. This is the big one. In each combat sequence, you're going to continually be met with yet another original, different challenge. Each and every new encounter is going to get even more and more difficult. We will be guiding you in this battle to fly right to the cutting edge of the envelope, faster and more dangerously than you've ever flown before. Israeli TOP GUN Fighter Jet Pilot Rules of Engagement exist for

Christ's Triumphant Appearance

your safety, gentlemen, and for that of your team. They are not flexible, nor is Israeli Command. You are the elite. You are all the best of the best. And at this very crossroads, you are going to have to be even better. This is the real thing. This is what you've been trained for. You are Israel's hope for peace, with the Israeli Messiah's blessing upon you all. The code name for this colossal operation is officially: "Crossing over the Jordan River." That code name has been encrypted into your quantum computers onboard your fighter jets. Needless to say, this will be the colossal operation of all colossal operations for Israel. It will be an immense endeavor. This is Armageddon unfolding right before our very eyes, that is, Israeli biblical prophecy in the making. And we need to ensure that this War of Armageddon, gripping our world, is the war to end all future wars, giving us the advantage. Blood may come up to the horse's bridle in this battle (Revelation 14:14-20). That's what we're up against. Let's make sure that the blood being shed in this particular theater is not the blood of any Israeli or that of our allies. Keep in mind that you are God's chosen in battle, and you are his anointed. And as the God of Israel's anointed, you cannot be touched by your adversaries (Psalm 89:20-23; Psalm 105:15; Isaiah 54:17). You are filled with God's Spirit, endued with his power, and baptized with fire. Just like the Israeli Messiah, Jesus Christ, you are all lions of the Tribe of Judah, whether it be by heritage or an honor bestowed upon you. Nevertheless, you are all the warriors of Israel. And the lion is not bothered by the thoughts of the leopard. You all have your assignments, gentlemen. Show us what you've got and make us proud."

"Mankind must put an end to war, or war will put an end to mankind." (President John Fitzgerald Kennedy; JFK; The 35th President of the United States of America; May 29th, 1917 – November 22nd, 1963)

"The weapons of war must be abolished before they abolish us." (United States President John F. Kennedy)

"But they that wait upon the Lord shall renew their strength. They shall mount up with wings of eagles. They shall run, and not be weary. And they shall walk, and not faint." (Isaiah 40:31; Israeli TOP GUN)

Elijah, the Prophet, was surrounded by four hundred and fifty prophets of Baal, and he only had invisible spiritual forces to rely on. (I Kings 18:21-

39; Israeli TOP GUN Fighter Jet Pilots have been outnumbered in every single battle that they've ever been up against)

"Then, shall there enter, into the gates of Jerusalem, kings and princes sitting upon the Throne of David, riding in chariots and on horses, and the men of Judah, and the inhabitants of Jerusalem. And the City of David, Jerusalem, shall remain forever." (Jeremiah 17:25)

"Move in and take your positions!" (Israeli Command --- Joshua)

"And, Israel said, 'It is enough.'" (Genesis 45:28)

"And, Elijah said, 'It is enough, now, O, Lord.'"
(I Kings 19:4)

Shimma (David's third oldest brother): "Looks like a modern-day Holy Crusade, all right!"

David: "Duty calls. Watch out, Lightning. Metaphorically speaking, Satan has a gun in his Bible! That devil always speaks with a forked tongue. And he doesn't have any hang-ups about hitting below the belt."
Jonathan: "O.K., I see them! You've got the lead. I'll cover you. Break now, Eagle!"
David: "Received."
Jonathan: "Joshua, we have multiple bandits. 1, 6, 5, Two miles out. They're heading away from us. Wait a minute. They're turning around. They're boomeranging and coming right at us! Those demons just cut me off! Where did these bandits learn how to drive? I've just been sideswiped! I'm not going to let any of them get in my face like that again! You take your pick of the litter of bandits, Eagle, and that one will be all yours."
David: "Don't let em' yank your chain, Lightning. I can't take the shot from here. That's the Big Kahuna, you know? The false messiah himself in true form. The international incident from hell waiting to happen. We have an official I.D. on Satan. Looking as hideous as ever, I see."
Jonathan: "Yeah. Bad hair day, for sure. That's the legend in his own mind, all right. I've seen that look in his eyes in every Alfred Hitchcock movie. Absolute power corrupts absolutely. Eagle, go with him on a hard right. Get in there, and then, engage."

Christ's Triumphant Appearance

David: "Cover me, Lightning."
Jonathan: "Not a problem, Eagle! I'm your Wingman. I'm right behind you, and I'm not going anywhere. I'm sworn to protect your back, and, right now, I've got you're back covered better than ever."
David: "That's comforting to know. These demons are nothing but a bunch of Control Freaks! I'm telling ya: 'Satan's strategy has been to irritate us all to death.'"
Jonathan: "Looks like blue sky for you at this bearing, Eagle."
David: "I'm playing this one out, Lightning, my friend."
Jonathan: "You call all your Israeli comrades your friends, Soaring Eagle."
David: "Roger that, Greased Lightning. But I don't call all of them 'my best friend.'"
Jonathan: "Back at ya, Soaring Eagle."

"And David said unto his men, 'Gird ye on every man his sword.' So, every man girded on his sword, and David also girded on his sword." (I Samuel 25:13)

The entire army (fleet) of Israel is right behind David when he does battle with Goliath. (I Samuel 17:1-58; Ezekiel 37:9, 10)

"Then, said the Lord God of Israel unto me, 'Prophesy unto the wind, prophesy, Son of man, and say to the wind, Thus says the Lord God of Israel. Come from the four winds, O, breath, and breathe upon these slain, that they may live.' So, I prophesied as he commanded me. And, they lived, and stood up upon their feet, an exceeding great army." (Ezekiel 37:9, 10; Israeli TOP GUN, the entire Israeli fleet, all their warrior allies, and the Twelve Tribes of Israel)

The army of Israel, in the last days, is totally under the command of the God of Israel (Yahweh, the Eternal One; The Heavenly Father) and the Israeli Messiah (Jesus Christ), who are both one in the same. (I John 5:7)

"Hear, O, Israel. The Lord our God is one Lord. And you shall love the Lord your God with all your heart, and with all your mind, and with all your soul, and with all your strength." (Deuteronomy 6:4, 5; I John 5:7)

Christ's Triumphant Appearance

"I alone have the key to the House of David. What I open, no man can shut. And what I close, no man can open." (Jesus – Isaiah 22:22; Revelation 3:7)

Satan: "From hell's heart, I stab at thee."

"Woe unto them that call evil good, and good evil. That put darkness for light, and light for darkness. That put bitter for sweet, and sweet for bitter." (Isaiah 5:20)

IAI Arava VII: "It's high time that we rebuked Satan once and for all."

"Yet Michael, the archangel, in contending with the devil, said, 'The Lord rebuke you." (Jude 1:9)

Jonathan: "They're coming, all right. They're coming in droves!"
David: "Wait for the volley."
Jonathan: "Joshua, send in the rest of the regiment."

"Fire at will. You may engage at any time. Fire when ready."
(Israeli Command; Joshua)

Joshua: "Clear or fire, Soaring Eagle!"

"Put on the whole armor of God, that you may be able to stand against the wiles of the devil. For we wrestle not against flesh-and-blood enemies, but against principalities, against powers, against the rulers of the darkness of this world, against spiritual wickedness in high places. Wherefore, take unto you the whole armor of God, that you may be able to withstand in the evil day, and having done all to stand. Stand firm, therefore, having the belt of truth buckled around your waist, with the breastplate of righteousness in place. And your feet clothed with the readiness of the Gospel of peace. Above all, taking the shield of faith, wherewith you shall be able to quench all the fiery darts of the wicked. And take the helmet of salvation, and the Sword of the Spirit, which is the Word of God. Praying always with all prayer and supplication in the Spirit, and watching thereunto, with all perseverance and exhortation for all the saints." (Ephesians 6:10-18)

Christ's Triumphant Appearance

"Fight the good fight of faith. Lay hold on eternal life. I charge you in the sight of God, that you keep this commandment, until the appearing of our Lord, Jesus Christ." (II Timothy 6:12-14)

"I am crucified with Christ, nevertheless, I live. Yet not I. But Christ lives in me. And the life which I, now, live, I live by the faith of the Son of God, who loves me, and gave his life for me." (Galatians 2:20)

David: "Let's see if we can get this world back into proper alignment. Joshua, I have the Chief Bandit in my pipper. I'm in hot pursuit of him for a six o'clock rear attack."
Israeli Command (Joshua): "You're no mystery to us, Eagle. Keep in mind the definition of happiness according to the Greeks, Commander: 'The full use of your powers along the lines of excellence.'"
David: "Well received, Joshua."

"Prepare to fire." (Israeli Command --- Joshua)

David: "Could I make a quick statement, off the record, to you, Lightning?"
Jonathan: "Whatcha got?"
David: "More than anything, you know my main inspiration for getting through all of this is Bathsheba, because her and I mean so much to each other. I want to see her again. My kingdom for Bathsheba!"
Jonathan: "Received, Eagle. I follow you. You'll see Bathsheba soon. You are right on the verge. I know you well enough to know that you're not going to allow anything to jeopardize her slipping through your fingers. And because of that fact, it's all just a walk in the park, Buddy."
David: "God knows my heart (I Samuel 13:14), Lightning."
Jonathan: "No truer words have ever been spoken, Eagle. I'm counting on that fact."
David: "This whole thing started out as a Lark. But now, it's turned into a Holy Grail."

"For God, who commanded the light to shine out of darkness, has shined in our hearts, to give the light of the knowledge of the glory of God in the face of Jesus Christ. We are troubled on every side, yet not distressed. We are perplexed, but not in despair. Persecuted, but not forsaken. Cast down, but not destroyed." (II Corinthians 4:6-9)

Christ's Triumphant Appearance

"I have made a Covenant with my chosen. I have sworn unto David, my servant. Your seed will I establish forever and build up your Throne to all generations. Selah. I have exalted one chosen out of the people. I have found David, my servant. With my holy oil have I anointed him. With whom my hand shall be established. My arm also shall strengthen him. The enemy shall not exact upon him, nor the son of wickedness afflict him. And I will beat down his foes before his face, and plague them that hate him. My Covenant will I not break, nor alter the thing that has gone out of my lips. Once I have sworn by my holiness that I will not lie unto David. His seed will endure forever, and his Throne as the sun (David) before me. It shall be established forever as the moon (Bathsheba) as a faithful witness in Heaven." (Psalm 89:3, 4, 19-23, 34-27; Acts 13:22, 23)

"Blow ye the trumpet in Zion (Jerusalem, Israel), and sound an alarm in my holy mountain (The Temple Mount). Let all the inhabitants of the land tremble. For the Day of the Lord has come, for it is at hand, a day as there has never been the likes of it. A fire devours before God's people, and behind them a flame burns. The land (The Eternal Promised Land of Israel) is as the Garden of Eden before them, and behind them desolate wilderness. Yea, and nothing can escape them. The appearance of them is as the appearance of horses. And as horses, so shall they run. Like the noise of chariots on top of the mountains shall they leap, like the noise of a flame of fire that devours the stubble, as a strong people set in battle array. They shall run like mighty men. They shall climb the wall like men of war. And they shall march everyone on his ways, and they shall not break their ranks. Neither shall they thrust one another, and everyone shall walk in their path. And when they fall upon the sword, they shall not be wounded. The Earth shall quake before them. The Heavens shall tremble. The sun and the moon shall withdraw their shining. And the Lord shall utter his voice before his army. For his camp is very great. For he is strong who executes his Word. For the Day of the Lord is great and terrible. And who can abide it?" (Joel 2:1-11)

Christ's Triumphant Appearance

CHAPTER ELEVEN
PRAY FOR OUR TROOPS

"And when the Lamb (Jesus Christ; John 1:29) had opened the third seal, I heard the third beast say, 'Come and see. And I beheld, and, lo, a black horse. And he who sat upon the horse had a pair of balances in his hand. And I heard a voice in the midst of the four beasts (Revelation 4:6-9; Isaiah 6:1-3) say, 'A measure of wheat for a penny, and three measures of barley for a penny. And see that you not hurt the oil and the wine.' And when the Lamb (Jesus Christ; John 1:29) had opened the fourth seal, I heard the voice of the fourth beast say, 'Come and see. And I looked, and behold, a pale horse. And his name that sat upon the horse was Death, and Hell followed with him. And power was given unto them over the fourth part of the Earth, to kill with the sword, and with hunger, and with death, and with the beasts

Christ's Triumphant Appearance

of the Earth. And when the Lamb (Jesus Christ; John 1:29) had opened the fifth seal, I saw under the altar all the souls of them that were slain for the Word of God, and for the testimony which they held. And they cried with a loud voice, saying, 'How long, O, Lord, holy and true, do you not judge and avenge our blood on them that dwell on the Earth?' And white robes were given unto each one of them. And it was said unto them, that they should rest for a little season, until their fellow servants were also killed, as it was fulfilled that they were (Revelation 12:11). And I beheld when the Lamb (Jesus Christ; John 1:29) had opened the sixth seal, and, lo, there was a great earthquake. And the sun became black as sackcloth, and the moon became as blood. And Heaven departed as a scroll when it is rolled together. And every mountain and island were moved out of their places. And the kings of the Earth, and the great men, and the rich men, and the chief captains, and the mighty men, and every bondman, and every free man hid themselves in the dens and in the rocks of the mountains. And they said to the mountains and rocks, 'Fall on us, and hide us from the face of him that sits on the Throne, and from the wrath of the Lamb (Jesus Christ; John 1:29). For the great day of Jesus Christ's wrath has come. And who shall be able to stand?" (Revelation 6:5-17)

"The Lord has sought him a man after his own heart, and the Lord has commanded him to be Captain over his people, Israel." (Samuel, the Hebrew Prophet; I Samuel 13:14; Acts 13:22, 23)

"And I will restore (The Restoration of the Israelis; The Restoration of the Throne of David; The Restoration of The Garden of Eden) unto you the years that the locusts have eaten, the cankerworms, and the caterpillars, and the palmerworms by my great army which I send among you. And you shall eat in plenty, and be satisfied, and praise the name of the Lord your God, who has dealt wondrously with you. And my people shall never be ashamed. And you shall know that I am in the midst of Israel, and that I am the Lord your God, and none else. And my people shall never be ashamed. And it shall come to pass, afterward, that I will pour out my Spirit upon all of mankind. In those days, I will pour out my Spirit." (Jesus Christ; Joel 2:25-29)

David: "Lightning, do you remember what happened at General George Custer's last stand?"

Christ's Triumphant Appearance

Jonathan: "Dead to the last man." (Revelation 12:11)

"So be it, Lord." (David)

"Then, said David to the Philistine (Goliath), 'You come to me with a sword, and a spear, and with a shield. But I come to you in the name of the Lord of hosts, the God of the armies of Israel, whom you have defied. This very day will the Lord deliver you into my hand. And I will defeat you, that all the Earth may know that there is a God in Israel. For the battle is the Lord's, and he will give you into our hands.'" (I Samuel 17:45-47)

The Israeli Messiah, Jesus Christ, has come to restore Israel, and seek justice for God's anointed! (Psalm 105:15; Joel 2:25-32; Romans 12:19)

"Put yourselves in array against Babylon (The Modern-Day Babylon; The New Roman Empire) round about. All you who bend the bow, shout at Babylon, spare no arrows. For Babylon has offended the Lord God of Israel. Shout against her round about. Her foundations are fallen, her walls are thrown down. For it is the vengeance of the Lord. Take vengeance upon Babylon. All she has done, do unto her." (Deuteronomy 19:21; Jeremiah 50:14, 15)

These are official orders from the Lord in combat to utterly wipe out Babylon, coming directly from the Israeli Messiah, Jesus Christ, to the entire army of Israel, which includes: All TOP GUN Fighter Jet Pilots, the entire Israeli fleet, and every single ally of Israel.

"The Lord God of Israel has brought forth our righteousness (holiness). Come, and let us declare in Zion (Jerusalem) the work of the Lord our God. Make bright the arrows and gather the shields. The Lord has raised up the spirit of the kings. For his device is against Babylon (The Modern-Day Babylonian Empire; The New Roman Empire) to destroy it. Because it is the vengeance of the Lord, the vengeance of his Temple."
(Jeremiah 51:10, 11)

"'Vengeance is mine. I will repay.' says the Lord." (The Lord Jesus Christ, the Israeli Messiah; Romans 12:19; Hebrews 10:30, 31)

Christ's Triumphant Appearance

"For it is the day of the Lord's vengeance, and the year of recompences of the controversy of Zion (Jerusalem)." (Isaiah 34:8)

"Look unto me, and be saved, all ends of the Earth. For I am God, and there is none else. (Isaiah 45:22)

"I am the Lord your God, who brought you out of the land of Egypt, out of the house of bondage. You shall have no other gods before me." (Exodus 20:2, 3).

"I have sworn by myself, the Word is gone out of my mouth in righteousness (holiness) and shall not return. That unto me every knee shall bow, and every tongue shall confess that I am Lord. In the Lord shall all the seed of Israel be justified and shall glory." (Jesus Christ, the Israeli Messiah; Isaiah 45:23, 25; Philippian 2:9-11)

"Wherefore, God also has highly exalted him, and given him a name which is above every name. That at the name of Jesus every knee should bow, of things in Heaven, and of things in Earth, and things under the Earth. And that every tongue should confess that Jesus Christ is Lord to the glory of the Father." (Philippians 2:9-11; Isaiah 45:22, 23, 25)

"Jesus said unto her, 'I am the Resurrection, and the Life. He who believes in me, though he were dead, yet shall he live. And whosoever lives and believes in me shall never die.'" (Jesus Christ; John 11:25,26)

"He who has an ear, let him hear what the Spirit says unto the churches: 'To him who overcomes I will give to eat of the Tree of Life, which is in the midst of the Paradise of God." (Jesus Christ referring to eternal Paradise; Revelation 2:7)

"The Sun of Righteousness (The Son of God; The Israeli Messiah; Jesus Christ) shall arise with healing in his wings." (Malachi 4:2)

"Our Father in Heaven gives good gifts unto them who ask him?" (Jesus - Matthew 7:11; Luke 11:13)

Christ's Triumphant Appearance

"Heaven and Earth shall pass away, but my words shall not pass away." (The Lord Jesus Christ; Matthew 24:35)

"'No weapon that is formed against you shall prosper. And every tongue that shall rise against you in judgment you shall condemn. This is the heritage of the servants of the Lord God of Israel, and their righteousness is of me,' says the Lord." (The Lord Jesus Christ; Isaiah 54:17)

"I hate them with a perfect hated. I count them my enemies." (David; Psalm 139:22; The God of Israel's enemies are David's enemies, and David's enemies are the God of Israel's enemies.)

"I have made a Covenant with my chosen. I have sworn unto David. Your seed will I establish forever and build up your Throne to all generations. I have found David, my servant. With my holy oil have I anointed him. With whom my hand shall be established. My arm also shall strengthen him. Once I have sworn by my holiness that I will not lie unto David, his seed shall endure forever." (Psalm 89:3, 4, 20, 21, 35, 36)

"This is Eagle at the helm, and we're coming in!!!"
(David)

Jonathan: "Ready. Don't let anything rob you of your peace. Satan and his cronies are going down fast, Eagle."
David: "Our custom-made coup d'etat is about to be implemented with deadly accuracy. It's our turn to torment the devil."

Target and Position

"I've got that Red Dragon in my scope, and I'm about to lock in on him right now!" (Soaring Eagle)

Christ's Triumphant Appearance

REVELATION 12:3, 4

David: "You're going down, Satan! You went a different way, Stranger. The Ark of the Covenant is against you!!!"
Satan: "I couldn't quite hear you. Pausing for effect, David?"
David: "I didn't stutter, big shot. --- Satan, I'm laughing at the superior intellect."
Satan: "All troops full speed ahead! Stand by for collective fire at my orders only."
Jonathan: "I'll say one thing for Satan, Eagle..."
David: "What's that, Lightning?"
Jonathan: "He's consistent. You drew fire on him, for sure and totally!"
David: "Yeah. Creature of habit. That's what I was counting on."

"Touch not mine anointed of Israel!!!" (The Lord Jesus Christ, the Israeli Messiah; I Chronicles 16:22; Psalm 105:15)

"We're firing on all cylinders, Joshua! Quantum physics. We're straining every gasket." (David reporting to Israeli Command)

Christ's Triumphant Appearance

"Rev up your engines, Israeli TOP GUN. You're all collectively a unit of machines. Shove it into overdrive. Fire only upon the Israeli Messiah's Command. We're not alone. He has assigned angels, with gossamer wings, to be posted all over Earth." (Commander Ariel Rosenberg; Israeli Command --- Code Name: Joshua)

David: "Lightning, get as high as you can go, to get the edge, my trusty Wingman. Looks like I spoke too soon about having seen it all in combat."
Jonathan: "The entire Israeli fleet is on the same wavelength, Eagle. And I can hear the collective roar of Israeli TOP GUN Fighter Jets revving, and you're on red line overload. I can feel the power!"
David: "Israel's waited a long, long time for this moment, Lightning."

"Steady. God's speed, Soaring Eagle. It's lonely at the top time. We're just about to set the world on fire with firepower." (Jonathan to David)

"And I, the Lord God of Israel, will give power unto my Two Witnesses." (Revelation 11:3)

"These are the Two Olive Trees, and the Two Candlesticks standing before the God of the Earth." (Revelation 11:4)

"Because the Two Prophets tormented them that dwell on the Earth. (Revelation 11:10)

"And the Two Olive Trees." (Zechariah 4:3, 11)

"These are the Two Anointed Ones that stand by the Lord of the whole Earth." (Zechariah 4:14)

The Two Anointed Ones, the Two Olive Trees, the Two Olive Branches (Zechariah 4:12), the Two Prophets, the Two Candlesticks, and the Two Witnesses are none other than the Restored David and Jonathan of the end time, empowered by Jesus Christ, Moses, and Elijah.

"I will build my Church. And the gates of hell shall not prevail against the kingdom of God." (Jesus Christ, the Israeli Messiah; Matthew 16:18)

Christ's Triumphant Appearance

"Fire!!!" (Commander David Hartman)

"And David gave a commandment, and they were burned with fire!!!" (I Chronicles 14:12)

THE BATTLE OF ARMAGEDDON
Apocalyptic Warfare in the End Times

"And Jonathan said to David, 'Go in peace, forasmuch as we have sworn both of us in the name of the Lord God of Israel, saying, The Lord is between us, and between my seed and your seed forever.'" (I Samuel 20:42; The fruition of the prophecy of an eternal relationship of purpose between David and Jonathan, ordained by the God of Israel)

Christ's Triumphant Appearance

"The Lord's oath that was between David and Jonathan." (II Samuel 21:7)

"And I will give power unto my Two Witnesses, and they shall prophesy a thousand two hundred and threescore days (1,260 days equals 3 ½ years; The last half of the Seven Year Tribulation; the Great Tribulation; "Jacob's Trouble" --- Jeremiah 30:7), clothed in sackcloth." (Revelation 11:3)

"'The burden of the word of the Lord for Israel,' says the Lord, 'who stretched forth the Heavens, and laid the foundations of the Earth, and formed the spirit of man within him. Behold, I make Jerusalem a cup of trembling unto all the people round about, when they shall be in the siege both against Judah and against Jerusalem. And in that day, I will make Jerusalem a burdensome stone for all people. All that burden themselves with it shall be cut in pieces, though all the people of Earth be gathered together against it. In that day,' says the Lord God of Israel, 'I will smite every horse with astonishment, and his rider with madness. And I will open my eyes upon the House of Judah, and I will smite every horse of the people with blindness. And the Governors of Judah shall say in their heart, the inhabitants of Jerusalem have found strength in the Lord of hosts, their God. In that day, I will make the Governors of Judah like a hearth of fire among the wood, and like a torch of fire in a sheaf. And they shall devour all the people round about, on the right hand and on the left. And Jerusalem shall be inhabited again in her own place, even in Jerusalem. In that day, the Lord will defend the inhabitants of Jerusalem. And the House of David shall be as God. And it shall come to pass, in that day, that I will seek to destroy all the nations that come against Jerusalem. And I will pour upon the House of David and upon the inhabitants of Jerusalem the Spirit of grace and supplications.'" (Zechariah 12:1-6, 8-10)

"'And it shall come to pass afterward,' says the Lord, 'that I will pour out my Spirit upon all of mankind." (Joel 2:28; The Hebrew Bible)

"'And it shall come to pass in the last days,' says the God of Israel, 'I will pour out my Spirit upon all of mankind.'" (Acts 2:17; The New Testament)

Christ's Triumphant Appearance

"And there shall come forth a rod out of the stem of Jesse, and a Branch (The Lord Jesus Christ, the Israeli Messiah; Zechariah 6:12, 13) shall grow out of his roots. And the Spirit of the Lord God of Israel shall rest upon him, and the Spirit of wisdom and understanding, the Spirit of counsel and might, the Spirit of knowledge and of the fear of the Lord. And make him quick of understanding in the fear of the Lord." (Isaiah 11:1-3)

Joshua: "Soaring Eagle. You, Jonathan, and Israeli TOP GUN are under strict orders, at this very bearing, to destroy the Tribulation Temple. Repeat, Eagle. Level the Temple in Jerusalem to a parking lot by direct order of Jesus Christ. That is official. The Messiah will be with you on an assist. Look sharp. Don't break your momentum. Every last Israeli citizen is secure in the bomb shelters that you ordered to have built, Commander."
David: "Received and clearly understood, Joshua. On our way to the designated target now."

David: "Gloriosky, Lightning!"
Jonathan: "No love lost at this bearing, Eagle."

"And during the final One Week of Years (The Seven Year Tribulation) of the Seventy Weeks of Years (Daniel 9:24-27), the Abomination of Desolation shall take place, resulting in the wrath of God being poured out, and leading to the fulfillment and ultimate end of the defiled Tribulation Temple." (Daniel 9:27)

"The Day of Christ is at hand. That man of sin has been revealed, who opposed and exalted himself above God, so that he sat in the Temple showing himself to be God. Whom the Lord Jesus Christ shall consume with the Spirit of his mouth and shall destroy Satan with the brightness of his coming." (II Thessalonians 2:2-4, 8)

"Then, shall they begin to say to the mountains, 'Fall on us.' And to the hills, 'Cover us.'" (A quote of Jesus Christ; Luke 23:30)

"And I will give power unto my Two Witnesses. These are the Two Olive Trees and the Two Candlesticks standing before the God of the Earth. And if any man hurt them, fire will proceed out of their mouth, and devour

Christ's Triumphant Appearance

their enemies. And if any man shall hurt them, he must in this manner be killed." (The Restored David and Jonathan; Revelation 11:3-5)

"And David put his hand in his bag, and took thence a stone, and slung it, and smote the Philistine (Goliath) in his forehead. And the Philistine fell upon his face to the Earth. So, David prevailed over the Philistine with a slingshot and with a stone, and smote the Philistine, and slew him. But there was no sword in the hand of David." (I Samuel 17:49, 50)

Jonathan: "Joshua, The Tribulation Temple is leveled and in flames. Repeat, Joshua. Mission accomplished. The Tribulation Temple is totally thrown down. We couldn't have done it without the Messiah. Trust me. And right now, as a direct result, we are in hot pursuit of a retreating devil. What's left of Satan's buddies can be seen fleeing in his direction directly behind him."

"And Jesus went out of the (2nd) Temple. And his disciples came to him concerning the Temple. And Jesus said unto them, 'There shall not be left one stone upon another of the Temple that shall not be thrown down." (Matthew 24:1, 2; Jesus' prophecy is totally fulfilled in regard to the Tribulation Temple being obliterated at his command and through his participation). Jesus had said that the Tribulation Temple would be destroyed ("every stone thrown down") as the sign of his coming and the end of the world (Matthew 24:3).

Christ's Triumphant Appearance

Joshua: "Cease fire! We've made some progress. Now, we're getting somewhere. These ballistic nuts could dish it out, but they just couldn't take it."
David: "Joshua, this is Soaring Eagle. These demons are all going so berserk right now that they are turning against each other."
Commander Ariel Rosenberg: "Eagle, that's the best news that I've heard all day!"

Jonathan: "All of these bandits are sweating bullets! Every last one of them."

Eliab (David's oldest brother): "Do you think you used enough fire power there, Soaring Eagle?"
David: "I must have been holding my mouth right. There's been enough push and pull to go around for all of us. Our victory at Armageddon is going be the ticket for Israel's admission into the Millennial Kingdom, Eliab"

Mulholland Drive: "Joshua, the Israeli Messiah is officially out in front, coercing Satan and his good time buddies into the Bottomless Pit, as only he can do."

"For the time has come that judgment must begin in the House of God." Jesus Christ – I Peter 4:17

Michael, the Archangel: "Do you yield, Satan?" (Revelation 12:7; Revelation 20:1-10)
Satan: "I yield."

"It is finished!!!" (Jesus Christ; The Israeli Messiah; John 19:30)

"And after these things, I saw another angel come down from Heaven, having great power. And he cried mightily with a strong voice, saying, 'Babylon the great has fallen, and has become the habitation of devils.'" (Revelation 18:1, 2)

"Alas, alas. That great city, Babylon, that mighty city! For in one hour your judgment has come." (Revelation 18:10)

Christ's Triumphant Appearance

"How art thou fallen from Heaven, O Lucifer! How art thou cut down to the ground, you who did weaken the nations! For you have said in your heart, I will ascend into Heaven, I will exalt my throne above the stars of God. I will sit also upon the Mount (i.e., Mount Moriah; The Temple site in Jerusalem; The Temple Mount) of the congregation. I will ascend above the heights of the clouds. I will be like the Most High (God). Yet you have been brought down to hell, to the sides of the pit. And they that see you shall consider you, saying, 'Is this the one that made the Earth to tremble, that did shake the nations?'" (The God of Israel; Isaiah 14:12-16)

In Zechariah 14:4, when Jesus Christ's feet stand upon the Mount of Olives, it will "cleave" ("baqa" in Hebrew, which means "split") the Mount from the east to the west. This is the same verb (in Hebrew) used for the first and most famous of Israel's deliverances at the hand of the God of Israel, when he "split" the Red Sea (Exodus 14:16, 17, 21, 22; Nehemiah 9:11; Psalm 78:13) to provide a ticket for the Israelites to be released from the bondage of the Egyptians and the tyranny of Pharaoh. No other place in the Bible than Zechariah 14:4 is the Hebrew word "baqa" used with the exception of God parting the Red Sea to insure the Israelites freedom. Just as the children of Israel were cornered by the armies of Pharaoh, so here the Israelis of our modern-day world were surrounded by all of the armies of Satan. Just as the situation in Exodus seemed hopeless, so it has seemed utterly bleak for the Twelve Tribes of the Remnant. And yet the Israeli Messiah, Jesus Christ, intervenes and leads the entire Remnant of Israel to safety, delivering people once and for all from the snares of an unmerciful devil (Satan), just as the Lord God of Israel had promised in the Bible that not one of the Israelis would be lost. And just as God successfully blocked the Egyptian's attempt of preventing the Israelites' escape from Egypt via the Rea Sea, so it came to pass that the Israeli Messiah's feet touched down on the Mount of Olives and opened a gateway of freedom for Israel, securing the long awaited ultimate, triumphant victory that has been so very much coveted by God's anointed. Jesus, somehow, managed to find a way to bring freedom to all those who were held captive by the devil (Romans 8:1, 2). Indeed, the Battle of Armageddon has proven itself to be the final war to end all wars for good. Hence, Jesus Christ proclaims the triumphant words of confirmation: "It is finished!!!" (John 19:30) The Israeli Messiah, who knows the beginning from the end and the end from the beginning, has proven himself to be the greatest warrior of all time and eternity (Zechariah

Christ's Triumphant Appearance

14:3). And now, he will rule the world throughout the Millennial Age (The Israeli Messiah's 1,000 Year Reign; the Millennium).

A fascinating observation that needs to be made is pointing out that just as Jesus left the Earth by way of the Mount of Olives, ascending to Heaven after his Resurrection, so too, in a most poetic fashion, he descends upon the Mount of Olives on Earth from Heaven on the day of the coming of the Lord. (Matthew 24:27)

"And Jesus said, 'For John (the Baptist) truly baptized with water. But you shall be baptized with the Holy Spirit not many days hence. You shall receive power after the Holy Spirit has come upon you.' And when Jesus had spoken these things, while his disciples beheld, he was taken up (ascended), and a cloud received him out of their sight. And while the disciples loyally looked towards Heaven as Jesus went up, behold, two angels stood by them in white apparel. And they said to the disciples, 'You men of Galilee, Why do you stand gazing into Heaven? This same Jesus, who is taken up from you into Heaven, shall so come in like manner as you have seen him go into Heaven.' Then, the disciples returned to Jerusalem from the Mount of Olivet (The Mount of Olives)." (Christ ascending to Heaven after his Resurrection; Acts 1:5, 8, 9-12)

"Behold, the Day of the Lord has come. And the Israel Messiah's feet shall stand in that day upon the Mount of Olives." (Christ descending from Heaven at the end of the Seven Year Tribulation; Zechariah 14:1, 4)

"For as the lightning comes out of the east, and shines even unto the west, so shall also the coming of the Son of God be." (The Lord Jesus Christ; Matthew 24:27)

The false messiah along with the Tribulation Temple have been utterly destroyed at the hand of Jesus Christ, to make way for the Millennial Temple, and the Messiah's Millennial Reign. (Matthew 24:1-3; Jesus predicted that every last stone of the third Temple would be thrown down)

"The modern-day Babylon (The New Great Roman Empire) has suddenly fallen and been destroyed." (Jeremiah 51:8; Revelation 18:1, 2, 10)

Christ's Triumphant Appearance

The false messiah arrogantly believed that Jerusalem was surrounded by the armies of the world at his command, but it was Jesus Christ, the Messiah, calling every single shot all along. (Zechariah 14:1-4)

Satan and his demons have been tried, judged, convicted, and sentenced in Jesus Christ's courtroom, and supreme justice has been established. All wrongs have been made right. All the innocent people throughout history, who have been treated unjustly, have finally received overwhelming justice, along with the gift of everlasting peace. While man's justice has proven to be limited, Jesus has demonstrated that his justice is not.

"And death and hell were cast into the Lake of Fire. This is the Second Death. And whosoever was not found in the Book of Life was cast into the Lake of Fire." (Revelation 20:14,15)

"Justice and judgment are the Habitation of your Throne. Mercy and truth shall go before your face. Blessed are the people that know the joyful sound. They shall walk, O, Lord, in the light of your countenance." (David; Psalm 89:14, 15)

"Thou hast brought us out with a mighty hand, O, Lord."
(King Solomon, the son of David)

"Thus, the Lord saved Israel (The Eternal Promised Land) that day." (Exodus 14:30; In the midst of very difficult problems and issues that all of God's people were up against)

"And the Lord wrought a great victory that day."
(II Samuel 23:10)

And not a single one of the Israelis was lost, as the Lord God of Israel had promised. (Ezekiel 34:11-16; Ezekiel 37:22, 24-28; John 17:12)

"For thus says the Lord God of Israel, 'Behold, I, even I, will both search for my sheep, and seek them out. As a shepherd seeks out his flock in the day that he is among his sheep that were scattered, so will I seek out my sheep, and will deliver them out of all places where they have been scattered in the cloudy and dark day. And I will bring them out from the people, and gather them from the countries, and will bring them to their own land (Israel) and feed them upon the mountains of Israel by the rivers, and in all inhabited places of the country. I will feed them in a good pasture, and upon the high mountains of Israel shall their fold be. There they shall lie in a good fold, and in a fat pasture shall they feed upon the mountains of Israel. I will feed my flock, and I will cause them to lie down,' says the Lord God of Israel. 'I will seek that which was lost and bring back again that which was driven away.'" (Ezekiel 34:11-16; The Eternal Promised Land)

"And I will make them one nation in the land (The Eternal Promised Land of Israel) upon the mountains of Israel. And one king shall be king to them all. And David, my servant, shall be king over them. And they shall have one shepherd. And they shall also walk in my judgments, and observe my statutes, and do them. And they shall dwell in the land (The Eternal Promised Land of Israel) that I have given unto Jacob, my servant, wherein your fathers have dwelt. And they, and their children, and their children's children forever. And my servant, David, shall be prince forever. Moreover, I will make an everlasting Covenant with them. And I will place them, and multiply them, and I will set my Sanctuary (The Millennial Temple) in the midst of them forevermore. Yea, I will be their God, and they shall be my people. And the heathen shall know that I, the Lord God of Israel, do sanctify Israel, when my Sanctuary (The Millennial Temple) shall be in the midst of them forevermore." (Ezekiel 37:22, 24-28)

"Being an Israeli is not what you do. It's what you are." (David)

"And David gathered all Israel together and passed over Jordan." (II Samuel 10:17; I Chronicles 13:5; I Chronicles 19:17; The Israeli TOP GUN Operation, "Passing over the Jordan River," has successfully been accomplished)

"Then, David arose, and all the people that were with him, and they crossed over Jordan. By the morning light at daybreak, there was no one left who had not crossed over the Jordan River." (II Samuel 17:22)

"Then, David and the people that were with him lifted up their voice and wept, until they had no more power to weep." (I Samuel 30:4)

Christ's Triumphant Appearance

"So, David and all the people returned unto Jerusalem."
(II Samuel 12:31)

"And David went up by the ascent of the Mount of Olives and wept as he went up. And all the people that were with David went up, weeping as they went up." (II Samuel 15:30)

"And the fame of David spread throughout all the lands. And the Lord God of Israel brought awe of David upon all the nations."
(I Chronicles 14:17)

"And the devil who deceived them was cast into the Lake of Fire and Brimstone to be tormented day and night forever and ever."
(Revelation 20: 9, 10)

"Be still and know that I am God." (Psalm 46:10; The God of Israel)

"And Jesus arose, and rebuked the wind, and said unto the sea, 'Peace, be still.' And the wind ceased, and there was a great calm." (John 4:39)

The finish of the war to end all wars, the Battle of Armageddon, signals the beginning of the Millennial Reign of Jesus Christ, ushering in his kingdom of everlasting peace.

"A new heart also will I give you, and a new spirit will I put within you. And I will take the stony heart out of your flesh, and I will give you a heart of flesh. And I will put my Spirit within you and cause you to walk in my statutes. And you shall keep my judgments and do them. And you shall dwell in the land that I gave to your fathers. And you shall be my people. And I will be your God." (The God of Israel; Ezekiel 36:26-28; Jeremiah 31:31-33; Hebrews 8:8-10)

"Your Word is a lamp unto my feet and a light unto my path."
(David; Psalm 119:105)

"This is the First Resurrection. Blessed is he/she who has part in the First Resurrection." (Revelation 20:5, 6)

Christ's Triumphant Appearance

"Awake, awake. Put on your strength, O, Zion. Put on your beautiful garments, O, Jerusalem, the holy city." (Isaiah 52:1)

Jesus has managed to cause the power of good to prevail over the power of evil eternally, once and for all. No small feat. (Romans 12:21)

"And I, John (the Apostle), saw the Holy City, New Jerusalem, coming down from God out of Heaven, prepared as a bride (The Church of Jesus Christ) adorned for her husband (Jesus Christ). (Revelation 21:2)

"And there was a pure river of water of life, clear as crystal, proceeding out of the Throne of God and of the Lamb (Jesus Christ; John 1:29). In the midst of the street of it, and on either side of the river, there was the Tree of Life, bearing twelve manner of fruits, and yielding her fruit every month. And the leaves of the tree were for the healing of the nations. And there was no more curse. But the Throne of God and the Lamb shall be in it. And his servants shall serve him. And they shall see the face of Jesus Christ. And his name shall be in their foreheads forever." (Revelation 22:1-4)

Israel managed to become one of the world's strongest military powers, often victorious in battles against insurmountable odds. And the victory in the Battle of Armageddon that Israel has procured in a show of strength has been nothing short of miraculous.

"For other foundation can no man lay than that is laid, which is Jesus Christ." (I Corinthians 3:11)

Christ's Triumphant Appearance

CHAPTER TWELVE
"I"VE BEEN TO THE MOUNTAINTOP"
A Speech Delivered by Dr. Martin Luther King Jr.

"Well, I don't know what will happen now. We've got some difficult days ahead. But it really doesn't matter with me now. Because I've been to the mountaintop! And I don't mind. Like anybody, I would like to live a long life. Longevity has its place. But I'm not concerned about that now. I just want to do God's will. And he's allowed me to go up to the mountain! And I've looked over! And I've seen the Promised Land! I may not get there with you. But I want you to know tonight that we, as a people, will get to the Promised Land! And so I'm happy tonight! I'm not worried about anything! I'm not fearing any man! Mine eyes have seen the glory of the coming of the Lord!!!"

THE MILLENNIAL TEMPLE BUILT BY JESUS CHRIST
ZECHARIAH 6:12, 13 --- MALACHI 3:1-4

The appearing of Jesus Christ on the Great and Terrible Day of the Lord has occurred suddenly and without warning.

Jesus, purely out of compassion for his people, has brought the entire world back into "proper alignment" in a dramatic fashion.

"And Jesus went forth, and saw a great multitude of people, and was moved with compassion." (Matthew 14:14)

Christ's Triumphant Appearance

"Behold, one like the Son of God came with the clouds of Heaven. And there was given the Israeli Messiah dominion, and glory, and a kingdom that all people, nations, and languages should serve him. His dominion is an everlasting dominion, which shall not pass away, and his kingdom shall not be destroyed." (Daniel 7:13, 14; 1,000 Year Reign of Christ)

"And from Jesus Christ, who is the faithful witness, and the first begotten of the dead, and the prince of the kings of the Earth. Unto Him who loved us and washed us from our sins in his own blood. And has made us kings and priests unto God, his Father. To him be glory and dominion forever and ever." (Revelation 1:5, 6)

"And the saints of God overcame Satan by the blood of the Lamb (Jesus Christ; John 1:29; I John 1:7), and by the word of their testimony, and they loved not their lives even unto the death." (Revelation 12:11)

"Of the increase of the Israeli Messiah's government and peace there shall be no end, upon the Throne of David, and upon his kingdom, to order it, and establish it with judgment and with justice from henceforth even forever." (Isaiah 9:7; The Restoration of The Throne of David)

At this point, Jesus Christ alone has built the Millennial Temple. (Zechariah 6:12, 13)

"Except the Lord Jesus Christ build the House (The Millennial Temple), they labor in vain that build it." (Psalm 127:1)

"Thus speaks the Lord of hosts, saying, 'Behold the man whose name is 'THE BRANCH' (Jesus Christ, the Jewish Messiah). And he shall grow out of his place, and he shall build the Temple of the Lord (The Millennial Temple). Even he shall build the Temple of the Lord. And he shall bear the glory and shall sit and rule upon his Throne.'" (Zechariah 6:12, 13; The Millennial Kingdom has become established by the Messiah)

"'Behold, I will send my messenger, and he shall prepare the way before me. And the Lord (Jesus Christ), whom ye seek, shall suddenly come to his Temple, even the Messenger of the Covenant, whom you delight in. Behold, he shall come,' says the Lord of hosts." (Malachi 3:1)

Christ's Triumphant Appearance

"I can hear the distant voice of ancestors whispering by the night fire. Or a big, bold choir shouting, 'I woke up with my mind stayed on freedom.' All their voices, roaming for centuries, have finally found their home here, in this great monument to our pain, our suffering, and our victory." (United States Congressman John Lewis)

The Millennial Temple and the Shekinah Glory of God will be the center focal points of worldwide blessing. The Temple will serve as the eternal dwelling place on Earth of the God of Israel's glory. (Ezekiel 43:1-7)

"My dwelling place (The Millennial Temple; "mishkan" in Hebrew) also will be with them. And I will be their God, and they will be my people." (Ezekiel 37:27)

"'And I will shake all nations, and the desire of all nations shall come. And I will fill this House (The Millennial Temple) with glory,' says the Lord of hosts. 'The silver is mine, and the gold is mine,' says the Lord of hosts. 'The glory of this House shall be greater than the former,' says the Lord of hosts. 'And in this place will I give peace,' says the Lord of hosts." (Haggai 2:7-9)

"'Who has heard such a thing? Who has seen such things? Shall the Earth be made to bring forth in one day? Or a nation be born at once? For as soon as Zion travailed, she brought forth children. Rejoice with Jerusalem, and be glad with her, all of you who love her. Rejoice for joy with her, all of you who mourn for her.' For thus says the Lord God of Israel, 'Behold, I will extend peace to her like a river. As one whom his mother comforts, so will I comfort you. And you shall be comforted in Jerusalem. And when you see this, your heart shall rejoice, and the hand of the Lord shall be known toward his servants. They shall be sanctified and purified in the Garden (of Eden) with one tree (The Tree of Life) in the midst, and they shall declare my glory in my holy mountain (The Temple Mount), Jerusalem, and in the House of the Lord (The Millennial Temple). For as the new Heaven and the new Earth, which I will make, shall remain before me' says the Lord, 'so shall your seed and your name remain.'" (Isaiah 66:8, 10, 12, 13-20, 21)

Christ's Triumphant Appearance

"'So, will I make my holy name known in the midst of my people, Israel. And the heathen shall know that I am the Lord, the holy one of Israel. Behold, it has come! And it is done' says the Lord God of Israel; 'This is the day whereof I have spoken.'" (Ezekiel 39:7, 8)

Ultimately, supreme justice and everlasting peace are procured by Jesus Christ in the Millennial Kingdom, as he rules and reigns upon his Throne forever.

From the end of the Battle of Armageddon and the beginning of the Millennial Kingdom, Christ will rule and reign forever and ever. At this point, there is nothing left to detour Israel from a well-deserved, sublime eternity, that is, never-ending eternal life. Jesus Christ, the Israeli Messiah, who is the Resurrection and the Life (John 5:21, 24-29; John 11:25, 26) has secured and resurrected (raised; restored) many, many mortal Israelis and mortal allies of Israel to immortality. (I Corinthians 15:52-54)

The Battle of Armageddon and the cataclysmic events that accompanied this war have, obviously, been the signs of time to indicate that Jesus Christ was close to appearing. And his arrival has, now, put an end to the devil's evil reign of terror upon mankind once and for all, allowing the Millennial Kingdom and the reign of the Jewish Messiah to be ushered in upon Earth. (Isaiah 9:6, 7; The Restoration of the Throne of David)

"Thus says the Lord God of Israel, 'I am returned unto Zion, and I will dwell in the midst of Jerusalem. And Jerusalem shall be called a city of truth. And the mountain of the Lord of hosts (The Temple Mount; Mount Moriah) shall be called the holy mountain'" (Zechariah 8:3)

Jesus Christ, the Jewish Messiah (who is not the Restored David or the Restored Solomon), is now the undisputed, unchallenged king over the newly restored Earth and the newly restored Heavens. His 1,000 Year Messianic Reign provides all of God's folks with a taste of Heaven, the Tree of Life bearing twelve kinds of fruit to heal the nations, the eternal Temple with its pearly gates, streets of gold, mansions to accommodate everyone (John 14:2, 3), the cessation of tears and sorrow, and the eternal Jerusalem (The Holy Jerusalem; The Bride of Jesus Christ; Revelation 21:1-3)

Christ's Triumphant Appearance

"In my Father's House are many mansions. I go to prepare a place for you. And if I go to prepare a place for you, I will come again, and receive you unto myself. That where I am, there you may be also." (John 14:2, 3)

"The word that Isaiah, the Prophet, saw concerning Judah and Jerusalem. And it shall come to pass in the last days that the mountain of the Lord's House (The Millennial Temple) shall be established in the top of the mountains and shall be exalted above the hills. And all the nations shall flow unto it. And many people shall go and say, 'Come ye, and let us go up to the mountain of the Lord, to the House of the God of Jacob. And he will teach us of his ways, and we will walk in his paths. For out of Zion shall go forth the law, and the Word of the Lord (Jesus Christ, the Israeli Messiah) from Jerusalem. And he shall judge among the nations and shall rebuke many people. And they shall beat their swords into plowshares, and their spears into pruninghooks. Nation shall not lift up sword against nation, neither shall they learn war anymore. O, House of Jacob, come, and let us walk in the light of the Lord. For all people will walk everyone in the name of his God (The God of Israel), and we will walk in the name of the Lord, our God, forever and ever." (Isaiah 2:1-5; Micah 4:1-3, 5)

"And the Lion shall lay down with the Lamb." (Isaiah 11:6

Christ's Triumphant Appearance

ALL THE ARMAMENTS OF WAR, ESPECIALLY NUCLEAR WEAPONS AND EVERY DESTRUCTIVE DEVICE THAT MANKIND HAS EVER UTILIZED, WILL BE DISMANTLED AND DESTROYED. AND WORLDWIDE PEACE WILL PREVAIL FOR ALL ON EARTH.

THE SONG OF MOSES (EXODUS 15:1-19)

"Then, sang Moses and the children of Israel this song unto the God of Israel, singing, 'I will sing unto the Lord, for he has triumphed gloriously. He has thrown the horse and the rider into the sea. You shall bring your people in, and plant them in the mountain of your inheritance (the Temple Mount), in the place, O, Lord, that you made where you may dwell, in the Sanctuary (the Millennial Temple), O, Lord, which your hands have established. The Lord shall reign forever and ever."
(Exodus 15:1, 17, 18)

"AND A LITTLE CHILD SHALL LEAD THEM." ISAIAH 11:6

THE NEW EARTH BECOMES THE ETERNAL PROMISED LAND, FLOWING WITH MILK AND HONEY

"And that you may prolong your days in the land (The Eternal Promised Land of Israel), which the Lord swore unto your fathers to give them and to their seed, a land that flows with milk and honey." (Deuteronomy 11:9)

"Ah, Lord God! Behold, you have made the Heaven and Earth by your great power and stretched out your arm, and there is nothing too hard for you. You have made a name for yourself, at this day. And you have brought forth your people, Israel, out with a stretched arm and great terror. And you have given them this land (The Eternal Promised Land of Israel), a land flowing with milk and honey." (Jeremiah 32:17, 20, 21, 22)

The new Heaven, the new Earth, and God's Sanctuary ("Mikdash" in Hebrew; The Millennial Temple) are all perfectly created and ultimate in every respect.

"For, behold, I create new Heavens and a new Earth. And the former shall not be remembered, nor come to mind. But be glad and rejoice forever in that which I create. For, behold, I create Jerusalem a rejoicing, and her people a joy. And I will rejoice in Jerusalem, and joy in my people. And the voice of weeping shall be no more heard in her, nor the voice of crying." (Isaiah 65:17-19)

"And God shall wipe away all tears from their eyes. And there shall be no more death, neither sorrow, nor crying, neither shall there be any more pain. For the former things are all passed away." (Revelation 21:4)

With the new Heaven and the new Earth having been created, every aspect of God's promise to his people, (the Israelis and their allies) will have been fully performed. (I Kings 8:56; Jeremiah 33:14)

"Blessed be the Lord, who has given rest to his people according to his promise. There has not failed one word of his good promise." (I Kings 8:56; Hebrews 4:9)

Christ's Triumphant Appearance

One of the most distinguishing aspects of the Millennium is that the Millennial Temple, of which Ezekiel, the Prophet, wrote of in vast detail (Ezekiel chapters 40-48; The Millennial Temple), will be the source of restoration (revitalization) for the landscape of Israel. The verses of the Hebrew Bible, Ezekiel 47:1, 9, 12, 13 and Joel 3:18, show that fructuous waters will flow from beneath the Sanctuary (The Millennial Temple), transforming the Dead Sea into a body of water teeming with aquatic life, and renewing the land so that it becomes like the Garden of Eden. (Ezekiel 36:35)

The Dead Sea, currently 1,350 feet below sea level, will be turned into fresh water by a river that flows from beneath the altar in the Millennial Temple. (Ezekiel 47:1-14; Genesis 2:8-14) The territorial boundaries of Israel have been significantly expanded. These changes, of course, provide plenty of room for the greatly enlarged Millennial City of Jerusalem and the Millennial Temple.

The Dead Sea in Israel currently possesses no aquatic life, because it is consumed with salt. As a result, it is impossible to sink in the Dead Sea. The Dead Sea of the Millennium, in stark contrast, will become a living body of water as a direct result of Jesus Christ's Millennial Reign.

"On that day, a fountain will be opened to the House of David and the inhabitants of Jerusalem." (Zechariah 13:1)

There is a direct correlation between the Restoration of the Throne of David and the Restoration of the Garden of Eden.

"A fire devours before them. And behind them a flame burns. The Land of Promise (The Eternal Land of Promise, Israel) is as the Garden of Eden before them." (Joel 2:3)

"This land (The Eternal Promised Land of Israel) that was desolate has become like the Garden of Eden." (Ezekiel 36:35)

"For the Lord God of Israel shall comfort Zion. He will comfort all her waste places. And he will make her wilderness like Eden, and her desert like the Garden of the Lord. Joy and gladness shall be found therein, thanksgiving, and the voice of melody." (Isaiah 51:3)

"'Behold, I will bring it health and cure, and I will cure them, and I will reveal unto them the abundance of peace and truth. And I will cause the captivity of Judah and the captivity of Israel to return, and will build them, AS AT THE FIRST. The voice of joy, and the voice of gladness, the voice of the bridegroom (Jesus Christ), and the voice of the bride (The Church of Jesus Christ), the voice of them that shall say, 'Praise the Lord of hosts. For the Lord is good. For his mercy endures forever.' And of them that shall bring the sacrifice of praise into the House of the Lord. For I will cause to return the captivity of the land (The Eternal Promised Land of Israel), AS AT THE FIRST,' says the Lord God of Israel. 'Behold, the days come,' says the Lord, 'that I will perform that good thing which I have promised unto the House of Israel and to the House of Judah. In those days, and at that time, will I cause the Branch of righteousness to grow up unto David. And he (Jesus Christ; The Jewish Messiah) shall execute judgment and righteousness in the land. In those days shall Judah be saved, and Jerusalem shall dwell safely. And this is the name wherewith she shall be called, 'THE LORD OUR RIGHTEOUSNESS.' For thus says the Lord, 'David shall never lack a man to sit upon the Throne of the House of Israel.'" (Jeremiah 33:6, 7, 11, 14-17; I Kings 2:4; I Kings 8:25; Kings 9:5)

THE ISRAELI MESSIAH PREPARES A LAVISH CELEBRATION BANQUET

"The Lord of hosts will prepare a lavish banquet for all people on this mountain. A banquet of delightful food, with choice pieces of meat and refined aged wine. And he will destroy in this mountain the face of the covering that is cast over all the people, even the veil which spread over all nations. The Lord will swallow up death in victory for all time, and the Lord God of Israel will wipe tears away from all faces, and he will remove the reproach of his people from all the Earth. For the Lord has spoken. And it will be said in that day, 'Behold, this is our God for whom we waited that he might save us. Let us rejoice and be glad in his salvation. For the hand of the Lord will rest on this mountain.'" (Isaiah 25:6-10)

Christ's Triumphant Appearance

THE LAST SUPPER
MATTHEW 26:26-30 – MARK 14:22-26 – LUKE 22:7-20

"And when the hour had come, Jesus sat down, and the twelve Apostles with him in a large upper room. And Jesus said unto them, 'With desire I have desired to eat this Passover with you before I suffer. For I say unto you, I will not eat any more thereof, until it be fulfilled in the kingdom of God.' And he took the cup, and gave thanks, and said, 'Take this and divide it among yourselves. For I say unto you, I will not drink of the fruit of the vine, until the kingdom of God has come. And he took the bread, and gave thanks, and broke it, and gave it unto them, saying, 'This is my body which is given for you. 'This do in remembrance of me.' Likewise also he took the cup, saying, 'This cup is the New Testament in my blood, which is shed for you.'" (Luke 22:14-20)

Jesus desired that his disciples honor partaking of the Communion of the Last Supper until the kingdom of God had come. Of course, this would come to be a regular practice of the Church of Jesus Christ until the day of Christ's coming on the Great and Terrible Day of the Lord. In a great respect, there was an element of sorrow in regard to the Last Supper, because it was signal event pointing to the suffering that lied directly ahead for Jesus, and his departure after he resurrected. But upon the Coming of Jesus Christ in the latter days, and the subsequent Marriage Supper of the Lamb, a time of great celebration would commence, that would bring so much joy to the hearts of the people. Even Jesus, at this point, is comfortable in participating with everyone at the feast, eating, drinking, and reveling in

Christ's Triumphant Appearance

the victory that he has so charismatically procured. And the happiness will be unending. And the celebrating will never cease. Because the kingdom of God has come to its rightful place. The Marriage Supper of the Lamb is the clearest indication that Christ's kingdom has come. Therefore, the Last Supper is in direct relation to the Marriage Supper of the Lamb.

"He (Jesus Christ, the Israeli Messiah) brought me into his banqueting house, and his banner over me is love." (Song of Solomon 2:4; Jesus is the master of ceremonies and the official host for the Marriage Supper of the Lamb (John 1:29), keeping the celebration agenda flowing smoothly)

"Let us be glad and rejoice and give honor to Jesus. For the Marriage Supper of the Lamb has come. Blessed are all they who are called unto the Marriage Supper of the Lamb. Come and gather yourselves together unto the supper of the great God." (Revelation 19:7, 9, 17)

"And I appoint unto you a kingdom, as my Father has appointed unto me. That you may eat and drink at my table in my kingdom and sit on Thrones judging the Twelve Tribes of Israel." (Luke 22:29, 30; Jesus)

The setting for the Messianic Banquet in the Messianic Kingdom will be taking place on Mount Zion (The Temple Mount; Mount Moriah).

Passover (Pesach) will be the Jewish holiday of focus in the Messianic kingdom. (Exodus 12:1-13; Numbers 9:1-4)

Eating and drinking merrily in the kingdom of God will take place continually once the Jewish Messiah has come to take up his reign in the Millennial Temple on the Temple Mount.

There will be a restoration of the Levitical priesthood in the Millennial Temple.

Now, the Tribe of Levi will resume their function as the God of Israel's priests in the Temple (an everlasting priesthood; the Melchizedek and Aaronic Priesthoods; Genesis 14:18, 19; Exodus 28:1-4; Hebrews 7:11).

"Even them will I bring to my holy mountain and make them joyful in my House of Prayer. Their burnt offerings and their sacrifices shall be accepted upon my altar (The Levitical Priesthood is restored in the Millennial Temple). For my House shall be called a House of Prayer for all the people of Israel." (Isaiah 56:7)

"And I will raise me up a faithful priest (Jesus Christ, the Israeli Messiah; After the Order of Melchizedek; The Great High Priest; Genesis 14:18, 19; Hebrews 7:20-22), who shall do according to that which is in my heart and mind. And I will build him a sure House (The Millennial Temple). And he shall walk before my anointed forever." (I Samuel 2:35)

"You are a priest after the Order of Melchizedek. By so much was Jesus made a surety of a better testament." (Genesis 14:18-20; Psalm 110:4; Hebrews 7:21, 22)

"But Christ will come as a High Priest of good things to come, by a greater and more perfect Temple, not made with hands." (Hebrews 9:11)

"And Jesus said unto them, 'It is written, my House is the House of Prayer.'" (Luke 19:46)

Jesus is the Great High Priest, after the Order of Melchizedek. (Genesis 14:18, 19; Hebrews 7:14-17, 21, 24-27)

THE NEW COVENANT IS FULFILLED BY JESUS CHRIST, THE ISRAELI MESSIAH

God's Covenant with the House of David is a perpetual, unconditional, everlasting promise of his favor. The Covenant between the Lord and David is founded upon the sure mercies of David. (II Chronicles 6:42; Isaiah 55:3, 4; Acts 13:33, 34)

"Howbeit, the Lord would not destroy the House of David, because of the Covenant that he had made with David, and as he promised to give a light to him and his sons forever." (II Chronicles 21:7)

Christ's Triumphant Appearance

"I will not break my Covenant, nor alter the thing that is gone out of my lips. Once I have sworn by my holiness that I will not lie unto David. His seed shall endure forever, and his Throne as the sun before me." (The Lord has sworn by the highest possible standard: his holiness; Psalm 89:34-36)

"As the host of Heaven cannot be numbered, neither the sand of the sea be measured. So will I multiply the seed of David, my servant." (Jeremiah 33:22)

The Covenant made by Yahweh (The Eternal One) to Israel, in respect to the Millennium, is a Covenant of peace ("Shalom" means peace in Hebrew).

"'Behold, the days come,' says the Lord, 'that I make a new Covenant with the House of Israel, and with the House of Judah. Not according to the Covenant that I made with their fathers in the day that I took them by the hand to bring them out of Egypt' says the Lord. 'But this shall be the Covenant that I will make with the House of Israel. After those days,' says the Lord, 'I will put my law in their inward parts and write it in their hearts. And I will be their God, and they shall be my people.'" (Jeremiah 31:31-33; stated in the Hebrew Bible, along with Ezekiel 36:26-28)

"'Behold, the days come,' says the Lord God of Israel, 'when I will make a new Covenant with the House of Israel and the House of Judah. Not according to the Covenant that I made with their fathers in the day when I took them by the hand to lead them out of the land of Egypt, because they continued not in my Covenant, and I regarded them not. For this is the Covenant that I will make with the House of Israel after those days,' says the Lord: 'I will put my laws into their minds and write them in their hearts. And I will be their God, and they shall be my people.'" (Hebrews 8:8-10; stated in the New Testament of the Holy Bible)

"'And I shall put my Spirit in you, and you shall live, and I shall place you in your own land (Israel). Then, you shall know that I, the Lord, have spoken it, and performed it,' says the Lord God of Israel. 'Behold, I will take the children of Israel from among the heathen, whither they be gone, and I will gather them on every side, and bring them into their own land. And I will make them one nation in the land upon the mountains of Israel.

Christ's Triumphant Appearance

And one king shall be king to them all. And David, my servant, shall be king over them. And they all shall have one shepherd. And they shall dwell in the land that I have given unto Jacob, my servant, wherein your fathers have dwelt. And they shall dwell therein, even they, and their children, and their children's children forever. And my servant, David, shall be their prince forever. Moreover, I will make a Covenant of peace with them. It shall be an everlasting Covenant with them. And I will place them, and multiply them, and will set my Sanctuary in the midst of them forevermore. My Temple shall be with them. Yea, I will be their God, and they shall be my people. And the heathen shall know that I, the Lord, do sanctify Israel, when my Sanctuary (The Millennial Temple) shall be in the midst of them forevermore.'" (Ezekiel 37:14, 21, 22, 24-28)

"The God of Israel is not the God of the dead, but the God of the living." (Jesus Christ; Matthew 22:32)

THE ARK OF THE COVENANT IS BROUGHT INTO THE MILLENNIAL TEMPLE

KING DAVID BRINGING THE ARK OF THE COVENANT INTO JERUSALEM

And most appropriately and poetically, it will be the Restored David who will have the distinct honor of supervising the Ark of the Covenant being brought into the Millennial Temple.

Christ's Triumphant Appearance

The God of Israel would not allow the Ark of the Covenant to rest in the Holy of Holies in the Tribulation Temple when the Abomination of Desolation took place. Yet in the most glorious fashion imaginable, the Ark of the Covenant will have its proper place in the Millennial Temple. The Ark of the Covenant had not rested in the Temple since the days of Solomon's Temple in the Hebrew Bible, when Jerusalem was destroyed by the Babylonians.

"They carried the Ark of the Covenant of God again to Jerusalem. And David went up by the ascent of Mount Olivet (The Mount of Olives) and wept. And all the people that were with David wept as they went up. And it came to pass that when David was come to the top of the Mount, he worshipped God." (II Samuel 15:29, 30, 32)

"Lord, remember David, and all his afflictions. How he swore unto the Lord God of Israel and vowed unto the mighty God of Jacob. Surely, I will not come into the comfort of my house, nor go up into my bed. I will not give sleep to my eyes, or slumber to my eyelids, until I find a place for the Lord, a Habitation (The Millennial Temple) for the mighty God of Israel." (Psalm 132:1-5)

The Ark of the Covenant will be present in the Holy of Holies in the Millennial Temple forever. (Jeremiah 3:16-18; Psalm 132:1-5)

"Put the Holy Ark in the House that the Lord Jesus Christ did build." (II Chronicles 35:3)

Shekinah is the manifest presence of God's everlasting peace, that is, the glory of God upon the mercy seat of the Ark of the Covenant.

There is absolutely no doubt that the Ark of the Covenant has found its eternal place on Earth in the Millennial Temple.

At long last, David has fulfilled his vow to restore the Ark of the Covenant to the Habitation of the Lord, and on an eternal basis. The Ark has a resting place in the Millennial Temple forever.

"So, the king and all the children of Israel dedicated the House of the Lord (The Millennial Temple). (I Kings 8:63)

JERUSALEM, ISRAEL AND THE ENTIRE WORLD ARE ENGULFED IN EVERLASTING PEACE
(Psalm 122:6)

"So, there was great joy in Jerusalem. For since the time of Solomon, the son of David, the king of Israel, was not the like in Jerusalem." (II Chronicles 30:26)

The restored Jerusalem will saturate the entire world in an unhindered manner with the Shekinah Glory of Yahweh, the Eternal One. The boundaries of Israel will have expanded to embrace all the nations of Earth. Also, purity will permeate every atom and molecule of space on Earth. The new mountain of the Lord God of Israel will have been formed. And there will be no more war ever again, only everlasting peace. (Isaiah 2:2-4; Micah 4:1-3; Zechariah 8:3)

"For I will defend Jerusalem to save it for mine own sake, and for the sake of David, my servant." (Isaiah 37:35; The God of Israel)

"For David said, 'The Lord God of Israel has given rest unto his people, that they may dwell in Jerusalem forever.'" (I Chronicles 23:25)

Jerusalem, Israel is the City of David.

"The God of Israel's Habitation is in Jerusalem." (Ezra 7:15)

"And the name of the city (the restored Jerusalem) shall be, 'THE LORD IS THERE.'" (Ezekiel 48:35; Yahweh, the Eternal One)

The Coming of the Lord Jesus Christ will usher in the power of the Holy Spirit in full force, completely unhindered and never-ending in gaining continuous momentum. (Ezekiel 39:29; Joel 2:28, 29; Zechariah 12:8-10; Acts 2:17, 18)

Christ's Triumphant Appearance

Jerusalem will serve as an international capital, and the government of the Millennial Kingdom will be centered around the Throne of the Israeli Messiah, Jesus Christ. (Isaiah 6:6, 7; Jeremiah 3:17, 18)

"Pray for the peace of Jerusalem. All they who love her shall prosper." (Psalm 122:6; David)

Psalm 122:6 is an appropriate prayer for the City of Jerusalem, whose very name means peace (Shalom).

ISRAEL IS ENCOURAGED BY YAHWEH, THE ETERNAL ONE

"You are children of the Lord, your God. For you are a holy people unto the Lord your God, and the Lord has chosen you to be a peculiar people unto himself, above all the nations that are upon the Earth." (Deuteronomy 14:1, 2)

"For you are a holy people unto the Lord, your God. The Lord God of Israel has chosen you to be a special people unto himself, above all people that are upon the face of the Earth. The Lord did not set his love upon you, nor choose you, because you were more in number than any people. For you are the fewest of all people." (Deuteronomy 7:6, 7)

"Great deliverance the God of Israel gives to his king. And he shows mercy to his anointed, David, and to his seed forevermore." (Psalm 18:50)

"The Lord God of Israel gave the kingdom of Israel over to David forever." (II Chronicles 13:5)

"I will extol you, O, Lord. For you have lifted me up and have not made my foes to rejoice over me. O, Lord, my God, I cried unto you, and you have healed me." (David; Psalm 30:1, 2)

"Fear thou not, for I am with you. Be not dismayed, for I am your God. I will strengthen you. Yea, I will help you. Yea, I will uphold you with the right hand of my righteousness." (The God of Israel; Isaiah 41:10)

Christ's Triumphant Appearance

All Israelis and their allies in the Twelve Tribes of the Remnant of Israel are celebrities (superstars) in the sight of the Lord. (David; Psalm 147:4)

"The God of Israel tells the number of the stars. He calls them all by their names." (Psalm 147:4)

The constellation making up the chosen people of Jesus Christ, that is, the Israelis and all those who love Israel, can be charted as the Twelve Tribes of Israel.

"I have chosen, Israel, my servant,' says the Lord. 'You are the seed of Abraham, my friend.'" (Isaiah 41:8; James 2:23)

"'For I know the thoughts that I think toward the Israelis,' says the Lord God of Israel, 'thoughts of peace, and not of evil, to give you an expected end.'" (Jeremiah 29:11)

"For the Lord's portion is his people. Israel is the lot of his inheritance. He found Israel in the desert land, and in the wilderness. He led Israel about, and instructed Israel. The Lord kept Israel as the apple of his eye." (Deuteronomy 32:9, 10)

"They that trust in the Lord shall be as Mount Zion, which cannot be moved, but abides forever, As the mountains are round about Jerusalem, so the Lord is round about his people (Israel) from henceforth even forever." (Psalm 125;1, 2)

The chosen people of Israel are safe at last for eternity! Some wondrous factor has brought divine protection to all of God's anointed people representing all dispensations of time in history, preserving them for this glorious day of ultimate deliverance. That omnipotent and all-powerful quality of the God of Israel, who's motive all along was to embrace his people on Earth as his own, has more than passed the test for all time and eternity.

"If my people, which are called by my name, shall humble themselves, and pray, and seek my face, and turn from their wicked ways, then, I will

Christ's Triumphant Appearance

hear from Heaven, and will forgive their sin, and heal their land." (The Lord God of Israel; II Chronicles 7:14)

"And Jesus said unto them, 'Verily, I say unto you, That you who have followed me, in the regeneration when the Son of God shall sit in the Throne of his glory, you also shall sit upon twelve Thrones, judging the Twelve Tribes of Israel. And everyone who has forsaken houses, or brothers, or sisters, or father, or mother, or wife, or children, or lands for my sake, shall receive a hundredfold, and shall inherit everlasting life."
(Matthew 19:28, 29)

"And I (John, the Apostle) saw Thrones, and they sat upon them, and judgment was given unto them. And I saw the souls of them who were martyred for the witness of Jesus, and for the Word of God. And they reigned with Christ a thousand years. This is the First Resurrection. Blessed and holy is he/she who has part in the First Resurrection. On such the second death has no power. But they shall reign with him a thousand years."
(Revelation 20:4-6)

"For the Son of God has come to seek and save that which was lost. What do you think? If a shepherd has a hundred sheep, and one of them has gone astray, does he not leave the ninety-nine, and go into the mountains, and seek after that sheep which has gone astray? Even so it is not the will of your Father who is in Heaven that one of these little ones should perish."
(Luke 19:11, 12, 14)

The best three words to describe Jesus are compassionate, caring, and understanding.

One thing was quite certain: Jesus is here on Earth to stay.

"In my Father's House are many mansions. And if I go and prepare a place for you, I will come again, and receive you unto myself. That where I am, there you may be also." (Jesus Christ; John 14:2, 3)

Christ's Triumphant Appearance

"Suffer the little children to come unto me. For of such is the kingdom of Heaven." (Jesus Christ; Matthew 19:14; Mark 10:14; Luke 16:18)

"Well done, my good and faithful servant. You have been faithful over a few things. I will make you ruler over many things. Enter into the joy of the Lord." (The Lord Jesus Christ; Matthew 25:21, 23)

CHAPTER THIRTEEN
THE RESTORATION OF THE THRONE OF DAVID

THE SYMBOL OF JERUSALEM – PSALM 122:6

"And David, my servant, shall be king over them. And they shall have one shepherd. And they shall dwell in the land that I have given unto Jacob, my servant, wherein your fathers have dwelt. And they shall dwell therein, even they, and their children, and their children's children forever. And my servant, David, shall be their prince forever. Moreover, I will make a Covenant of peace with them. It shall be an everlasting Covenant. And I will place them, and multiply them, and will set my Sanctuary (The Millennial Temple) in the midst of them forevermore. And the dwelling place shall be with them. Yea, I will be their God, and they shall be my people." (Ezekiel 37: 24-27; The Restoration of the Throne of David)

"For unto us the Israeli Messiah (Jesus Christ) is born, unto us a Son is given. And the government shall be upon his shoulder. And his name shall be Wonderful, Counselor, the mighty God, the everlasting Father, the Prince of Peace. Of the increase of his government and peace there shall be no end, upon the Throne of David, and upon his kingdom, to order it, and establish it with judgment and with justice from henceforth even forever." (The Millennial Kingdom and Government of Jesus Christ; Isaiah 9:6, 7)

Christ's Triumphant Appearance

"And I have restored unto you the years that the locusts have eaten." (The God of Israel; Joel 2:25)

When United States President John F. Kennedy stated with confidence, on June 26th, 1963 in West Berlin, Germany, that we all one day would, as free people, join to make Earth a peaceful, hopeful globe, and proclaimed: "When that finally day comes, AS IT WILL," little did he realize that he was referring directly to the Great and Terrible Day of the Coming of the Lord Jesus Christ. May the Prince of Peace, Jesus Christ, who is the Israeli Messiah, bring everlasting peace to his Millennial Temple and the entire world quickly. The Coming of the Lord Jesus Christ will surely make it all happen.

"And this is the promise that the Son of God (Jesus Christ) has promised unto us, even eternal life." (I John 2:25)

"Out of Jerusalem, the perfection of beauty, God has shined." (Psalm 50:2)

"As the mountains are round about Jerusalem, so the Lord is round about his people from henceforth even forever." (Psalm 125:2)

"'For a small moment have I forsaken you. But with great mercies will I gather you. In a little wrath, I hid my face from you for a moment, but with everlasting kindness will I have mercy on you,' says the Lord your redeemer." (Isaiah 54:7, 8)

The Hebrew Bible continually focuses on God's Covenantal promises to Israel, the nation that descended from Abraham, Isaac, and Jacob, the three fathers (patriarchs) of Israel.

"I will put my Spirit in you, and you will live, and I will settle you in your own land. Then, you will know that I, the Lord, have spoken and performed it." (Ezekiel 37:14)

"'And it shall come to pass in the last days' says the Lord God of Israel. 'I will pour out my Spirit upon all of mankind.'" (Joel 2:28-32; Acts 2:17)

Christ's Triumphant Appearance

"'And I will plant them (the Israelis) upon their land (The Holy Land; The Promised Land of Israel), and they shall no more be pulled up out of their land which I have given them,' says the Lord God of Israel." (Amos 9:15)

"For God so loved the world that he gave his only begotten Son (Jesus Christ), that whosoever believes in him shall not perish, but have eternal life." (John 3:16)

"Verily, verily, I say unto you, he that hears my Word, and believes on him that sent me (The Heavenly Father) has everlasting life, and shall not come into condemnation, but shall be passed from death unto life. Verily, verily, I say unto you, The hour has come, and now is, when the dead shall hear the voice of the Son of God (Jesus Christ), and they that hear shall live." (Jesus Christ; John 5:24, 25)

"And now also the ax has been laid to the root. I, indeed, baptize you with water unto repentance, but he who shall come after me is mightier than I, and I am not even worthy to wear his shoes. He shall baptize you with the Holy Spirit and with fire." (Matthew 3:10, 11; John, the Baptist, referring to Jesus, the Messiah; Luke 24:49 --- The promise of the Father)

"These words Jesus spoke, and lifted up his eyes to Heaven, and said, 'Father, the hour has come. Glorify your Son, that your Son may also glorify you. As you have given me power over all of mankind, that I should give eternal life to as many as you have given me.'" (John 17:1, 2)

"The gift of God is eternal life." (Romans 6:23)

"To everything there is a season, and a time to every purpose under Heaven. A time to be born, and a time to die. A time to plant, and a time to pluck up that which has been planted. A time to kill, and a time to heal. A time to break down, and a time to build up. A time to weep, and a time to laugh. A time to mourn, and a time to dance. A time to cast away stones, and a time to gather stones together. A time to embrace, and a time to refrain from embracing. A time to get, and a time to lose. A time to keep, and a time to cast away. A time to reap, and a time to sow. A time to keep silence, and a time to speak. A time to love, and a time to hate. A time of war, and

Christ's Triumphant Appearance

a time of peace. THE GOD OF ISRAEL HAS MADE EVERYTHING BEAUTIFUL IN HIS TIME. ISRAEL IS THE VERY HEART OF GOD. Nothing can be added or be taken from what God has made from the beginning to the end. That which has been is now. And that which is to be has already been. And God requires that which is past." (Ecclesiastes 3:1-8, 11, 15; King Solomon)

"'For I have poured out my Spirit upon the House of Israel,' says the Lord God of Israel." (Ezekiel 39:29; Joel 2:28, 29; Acts 2:17, 18)

"'Not by might, nor by power, but by my Spirit,' says the Lord of hosts." (Zechariah 4:6)

"But you are holy, O, Lord, who inhabits the praises of Israel!" (Psalm 22:3; David and the Twelve Tribes of Israel)

"Not unto us, O, Lord, not unto us, but unto your name we give glory, for your mercy and your truth's sake." (Psalm 115:1)

To Jesus Christ alone be the glory.

"Worthy is the Lamb who was slain (Jesus Christ) to receive power, and riches, and wisdom, and strength, and honor, and glory, and blessing." (Revelation 5:12)

The Millennial Temple was of particular significance to Isaiah, the Prophet, because it was in the Temple where he received a great vision of God's glory. (Isaiah 6:1-9)

The supernatural illumination of the restored Jerusalem is the result of the glory of Yahweh, the Eternal One.

God, the Father, and Jesus Christ, the Messiah, are one in the same. (Deuteronomy 6:4, 5' John 17:11, 21-23; I John 5:7)

"And the glory which you have given me I have given them. That they be one, even as we are one." (Jesus praying in the Garden of Gethsemane to his heavenly Father; John 17:22)

Christ's Triumphant Appearance

In the restored Jerusalem, God is able to dwell with his people face to face. (Genesis 32:24-30; Exodus 33:11, 18, 20; Psalm 67:1; Psalm 119:135)

"And Moses said, 'I urgently beg of you, Lord, show me your glory.'" (Exodus 33:18)

"As for me, I will behold your face in righteousness. I shall be satisfied when I awake with your likeness."
(David; Psalm 17:15)

"When you say, 'Seek my face, my heart said unto you, 'Your face, Lord, will I seek.'" (David; Psalm 27:8)

"Seek the Lord, and his strength. Seek his face evermore."
(David; Psalm 105:4)

"The Lord God of Israel bless you and keep you. The Lord make his face shine upon you and be gracious unto you. The Lord lift up his countenance upon you and give you peace." (Numbers 6:24-26; a Hebrew prayer of blessing)

"Wherefore, David blessed the Lord before all the congregation. And David said, 'Blessed are you, Lord God of Israel, our Father, forever and ever.'" (I Chronicles 29:10)

"Then, shall the children of Judah and the children of Israel be gathered together." (Hosea 1:11)

"And Solomon loved the Lord God of Israel, walking in the statutes of David, his father." (I Kings 3:3)

Now that Jesus Christ has come, there is no need to sort out the proponents of what is right and wrong. For all wrong has been dispelled and replaced with good. Therefore, it's no longer necessary to make distinctions between what is right and wrong. Because only right remains on an eternal basis. All wrongs have been made right. And that will never change.

Christ's Triumphant Appearance

"Blessed be the Lord, your God, who delights in you, to set you on the Throne of Israel. Because the Lord loved Israel, to establish the people forever. Therefore, he made you king, to do judgment and justice." (The Queen of Sheba speaking to King Solomon; The Queen of Sheba is the love of King Solomon's life; I Kings 10:9, 10; II Chronicles 9:8)

"And Judah and Israel dwelt safely all the days of Solomon." (I Kings 4:25)

"And King Solomon shall be blessed, and the Throne of David shall be established before the Lord God of Israel forever." (I Kings 2:45)

Jesus Christ's kingdom shall have no end. (Isaiah 9:7)

"Therefore, the redeemed of the Lord shall return, and come with singing unto Zion. And everlasting joy shall be upon their heads. They shall obtain gladness and joy. And sorrow and mourning shall flee away." (Isaiah 51:11)

"Weeping may endure for the night, but joy comes in the morning." (Psalm 30:5)

"For the joy of the Lord is your strength." (Nehemiah 8:10)

"For a small moment, I have forsaken you. But with great mercies I have gathered you." (Isaiah 54:7; The Lord God of Israel to his people, Israel)

"May the Lord establish his kingdom in your lifetime, in your days." (a Hebrew prayer)

"So, the House of Israel shall know that I am the Lord, their God, from this day forward." (Ezekiel 39:22)

"And David sang unto the Lord God of Israel the words of a song in the day that the Lord had delivered him out of the hand of all his enemies." (II Samuel 22:1-51; Psalm 18:1-50)

Christ's Triumphant Appearance

"I am a part of all that I have met. Too much is taken. Much abides. That which we are, we are. One equal temper of heroic hearts. Strong in will to strive, to seek, to find, and not to yield." (Lord Alfred Tennyson)

"Many waters cannot quench love." (Song of Solomon 8:7)

"And the Lord gave unto Israel all the land which he swore to give unto their fathers. And they possessed it and dwelt therein. And the Lord gave them rest round about, according to all that he swore unto their fathers. And there stood not a man of all their enemies before them. The Lord delivered all their enemies into their hand. There failed not aught of any good thing which the Lord had spoken unto the House of Israel. All came to pass." (Joshua 21:43-45)

People are created by God as body, soul, and spirit. Ever since the fall of mankind took place, people have been born with mortal bodies. But now, since the Great and Terrible Day of the Coming of the Lord Jesus Christ has taken place, everything in the world has been restored (Isaiah 9:6, 7; Joel 2:25-31; Matthew 24:27, 30, 31), and all of God's people have immortal bodies. And the spirit of the people, which God created to be eternal, has been united with God's Holy Spirit forever and ever. And this will serve as a far higher blessing than that which was lost by Adam and Eve as a result of the fall. The Coming of Christ has blotted out sin and death.

Not until the reign of David does the Hebrew Bible state the probability that the kingdom of Israel will actually secure its promised imperial dimensions.

David reinvented the army, government, and religion (Judaism) of Israel, freeing his people from their primitive tribal existence and showing them how a modern cosmopolitan nation ought to function. David turned the Twelve Nomadic Tribes of Israel into a single unbeatable superpower.

"And David, my servant, shall be king over them (the Remnant of Israel). And they all shall have one shepherd." (Ezekiel 37:24)

Christ's Triumphant Appearance

SO, DAVID MOVED ON, AND HIS ARMY FOLLOWED HIM

"In that day, the Lord shall defend the inhabitants of Jerusalem. And he that was feeble among them at that day shall be as David. And the House of David shall be as God, as the angel of the Lord before them. And it shall come to pass in that day that I will seek to destroy all the nations that come against Jerusalem. And I will pour upon the House of David, and upon the inhabitants of Jerusalem, the Spirit of grace and of supplications." (Zechariah 12:8-10)

THE SOVEREIGNTY OF GOD
by David
Dedicated to my wife, Bathsheba
Psalm 122:6

God looks down from his Throne in Heaven, and he sees the entire parade of history (past, present, and future) before him. God sees it all from the beginning to the end and from the end back to the beginning. God sees everything in infinite detail, and he considers all the ramifications from his unique point of view (perspective). God has created all the characters on the stage, and God knows the entire script by heart. God is the Supreme Director of all the good matters in life that, ultimately, lead to a positive conclusion.

Christ's Triumphant Appearance

We cannot comprehend this glorious concept, but God, ultimately, and in his own perfect timing, demonstrates that he alone is sovereign forever.

"He who dwells in the secret place of the Most High shall abide under the shadow of the Almighty." (Psalm 91:1)

"The Earth is the Lord's, and the fullness thereof. The world, and they that dwell therein. Lift up your heads, O, you gates. And be lifted up, you everlasting doors. And the king of glory shall come in. Who is this king of glory? The Lord God of Israel, strong and mighty, is the king of glory. For the Lord is mighty in battle. The Lord of hosts, he is the king of glory." (Psalm 24:1, 7, 8, 10; Jesus Christ is the King of Kings and the King of Glory - Selah)

"Then, went King David in, and sat before the Lord God of Israel, and he said, 'Who am I, O, Lord God? And what is my house, that you have brought me hitherto? And this was yet a small thing in your sight, O, Lord God. But you have spoken also of thy servant's house for a great while to come. And you have regarded me according to the estate of a man of high degree, O, Lord God. And what can David say more unto you for the honor of your servant? For you, O, Lord God, know your servant. For your servant's sake, and according to your own heart, you have done all these great things to make your servant know them. Wherefore, you are great, O, Lord God. For there is none like you, neither is there any God beside you, according to all that we have heard with our ears. And what one nation in the Earth is like your people, even like Israel, whom God went to redeem for a people unto himself, and to do for you great things, whom you brought out of Egypt, from the nations and their gods? For you have confirmed to yourself your people, Israel, to be a people unto you forever. And you, Lord, have become their God. Therefore, now, Lord, let this thing that you have spoken concerning your servant and concerning his house be established forever, and do as you have said. Let it even be established that your name be magnified forever, saying, The Lord of hosts is the God of Israel. And let the house of David, your servant, be established before you. For you, O, Lord of hosts, God of Israel, have revealed to your servant, saying, 'I will build you a House' Therefore, your servant has found in his heart to pray this prayer unto you. And now, O, Lord God, you are God, and your words are true, and you have promised this goodness to your servant. Therefore,

Christ's Triumphant Appearance

now, let it please you to bless the house of your servant, that it may continue forever before you. For you, O, Lord God, have spoken it. And with your blessing let the house of your servant be blessed forever." (II Samuel 7:18-29; I Chronicles 17:16-27; David)

"Except the Lord God of Israel (Yahweh, the Eternal One) build the House, they labor in vain that build it." (Psalm 127:1; Zechariah 6:12, 13; Jesus Christ alone built the Millennial Temple)

"Some men see things as they are, and ask: 'Why?' I dream things that never were, and ask: 'Why not?'" (Robert Francis Kennedy; 1925-1968)

"The Lord God of Israel has sought him a man after his own heart (David), and the Lord has commanded him to be Captain over his people." (I Samuel 13:14; Acts 13:22, 23)

David's single passion in life was to abide in the eternal Temple where he could behold the Lord God of Israel in all of his beauty and glory.

"One thing have I desired of the Lord, that will I seek after. That I may dwell in the House of the Lord God of Israel all the days of my life, to behold the beauty of the Lord, and to enquire in his Temple. For in the time of trouble, he shall hide me in his pavilion. In the secret place of his Temple shall he hide me. He shall set me up as a rock." (David; Psalm 27:4, 5)

"Behold, a whirlwind of the Lord God of Israel has gone forth in fury, even grievously upon the head of the wicked. The anger of the Lord shall not return, until he has executed and performed the thoughts of his heart. In the latter days, you shall consider it perfectly." (Jeremiah 23:19, 20)

"Blessed be the Lord, who has given rest unto his people, Israel, according to all that that he promised. There has not failed one word of all his good promise." (I Kings 8:56)

"We enjoy sharing all the stories about David and Bathsheba!" (Charity; The daughter of the Restored David and Bathsheba; Charity is the absolute embodiment of pure love; I Corinthians 13:1-13)

Christ's Triumphant Appearance

Harvard University Rhodes Scholars (David and Bathsheba)

And, so, the days of the Israeli war to end all wars had ended. Nations like men, it is sometimes said, have their own destiny. As for the Israeli Captain (I Samuel 13:14), no one knows what became of him after the war was finally over. Some say that he that died of his wounds. Others, that he returned to his own country, Israel, with his wife, Bathsheba. But we'd like to think that he may have, at last, found some small measure of peace, that we all seek, but few of us ever find. (Psalm 89:18-23, 34-37; Isaiah 55:3, 4)

THE MOST GLORIOUS RENDEZVOUS OF ALL TIME

WHEN WE LAST LEFT DAVID & BATHSHEBA...

Christ's Triumphant Appearance

"'I will not break my Covenant once I have sworn unto David,' says the God of Israel. 'His seed shall endure forever, and his Throne as the sun before me. It shall be established forever as the moon, and as a faithful witness in Heaven.'" (David, the King of Israel; Psalm 89:34-37)

"Who is she that looks forth as the morning, fair as the moon, and clear as the sun, and terrible as an army with banners?" (Bathsheba, the Queen of Israel; Song of Solomon 6:10)

It was a glorious rendezvous between King David and Queen Bathsheba after the Battle of Armageddon. You could easily say that it was the single most glorious reunion of all time. And the people of the Earth reveled in witnessing the King and Queen of Israel, Prince Solomon, Princess Charity, and even the palace German Shepherd, Shalom, all brought back together again, especially in view of everyone, now, living in such a new, novel world. The family dynasty of Israel dazzled the entire globe, and David and Bathsheba were the talk of the town. Everyone, it seemed, desired to hear all the stories covering the King and Queen of Israel.

While the people of Israel fell in love with the couple eternally, David and Bathsheba decided to get away from the limelight to spend some quality time with each other and chose to go to what use to be the Dead Sea. But following suit with the newly restored planet of Earth, the body of water there had become perfectly pure and pristine, teeming with robust life, and was, now, appropriately dubbed as the Sea of Living Water.

The couple traveled to a spot they were familiar with and slipped chest-deep into the non-threatening water together. They were under a full moon that shimmered a beautiful reflection upon the Sea of Living Water. The light of the moon upon the water traveled all the way up to where the happy couple were embracing each other.

"Hope springs eternal, David." Bathsheba pointed out.

David looked Bathsheba deep into her eyes, and said, "I'd take another chance, take a fall, take a shot for you, Bathsheba."

Christ's Triumphant Appearance

"Looks like there really are consolations in life, huh, David?" Bathsheba asked, fishing for an appropriate response.

"You are eternally luminous, Bathsheba. I'll settle for that consolation." David stated in all sincerity. "The only mystery I could never solve is why my heart could never let go of you. You're the only one who ever really knew me at all."

"There goes that disarming charm of yours again, David, accompanied by that infectious smile." Bathsheba joyfully remarked. "We're both just a couple of hopeless romantics."

David and Bathsheba embraced each other even closer and kissed in a most passionate manner.

"How's that for verifiable data, Commander?" Bathsheba asked, staring David directly in his eyes with a laser beam focus.

"Millennium! We may have just concluded the war to end all wars, but there's always something left to conquer, Bathsheba." David responded, referring to the endless pursuit of his wife. "Here's to World War None!!!"

"Love gives not but itself and takes not from itself. Love possesses not nor would it be possessed. For love is sufficient unto love, my Love." Bathsheba recited to the love of her life. "Isn't the moon beautiful tonight, David?"

"That's not the moon in the sky, Bathsheba. That's a reflection of the moon. You're the beautiful moon, causing that reflection." David clarified.

"And should I be the moon, then, you are the sun who gives me light, David." Bathsheba added.

"I bet you're hard to get over, Bathsheba. I bet the moon just doesn't shine," David said, as tears streamed from Bathsheba's eyes down her cheeks.

CHAPTER FOURTEEN
THE ARK OF THE COVENANT REMAINS SIGNIFICANT

YAHWEH, THE ETERNAL ONE

"'And it shall come to pass, when you are multiplied and increased in the land (The Eternal Promised Land of Israel), in those days' says the Lord, 'They shall say no more, the Ark of the Covenant of the Lord, neither shall it come to mind, neither shall they remember it, neither shall they visit it, neither shall that be done any more. At that time, they shall call Jerusalem, 'The Throne of the Lord.' And all nations shall gather unto it, to the name of the Lord, to Jerusalem. In those days, the House of Judah shall walk with the House of Israel, and they shall come together out of the land of the north to the land that I have given for an inheritance unto your fathers.'" (Yahweh, the Eternal One; Jeremiah 3:16-18)

"Lord, remember David, and all his afflictions. How David swore unto the mighty God of Jacob, Surely, I will not come into comfort of my house, nor go up into my bed, or give sleep to my eyes, or slumber to my eyelids, until I have found a place for the Lord God of Israel, a Habitation (The Millennial Temple; Zechariah 6:12, 13) for the mighty God of Jacob (Israel)." (David; Psalm 132:1-5)

"And David gathered all Israel together to Jerusalem, to bring up the Ark of the Lord God of Israel (The Ark of the Covenant) unto his place (The

Christ's Triumphant Appearance

Holy of Holies in the Millennial Temple) which David had prepared for it." (I Chronicles 15:3)

"And the priests (The Tribe of Levi) brought the Ark of the Covenant of the Lord God of Israel unto his place into the oracle of the House (The Millennial Temple) to the Most Holy Place (The Holy of Holies), even under the wings of the two Cherubim. And it came to pass, when the priests were come out of the Holy Place, that the cloud (The Shekinah Glory and Presence of Yahweh, the Eternal One) filled the House of the Lord God of Israel, so that the priests could not stand to minister because of the cloud. For the power and glory of the Lord God of Israel had filled the House of the Lord." (I Kings 8:1, 6, 7, 10, 11; II Chronicles 6:10, 11; II Chronicles 7:1, 2)

"Hear, O Israel, the Lord our God (The Heavenly Father and Jesus Christ) is one Lord. And you shall love the Lord your God with all your heart, and with all your mind, and with all your soul, and with all your strength." (Deuteronomy 6:4, 5; I John 5:7)

"You will keep him in perfect peace, whose mind is stayed on you." (Isaiah 26:3; Isaiah, the Prophet, referring to Yahweh, the Eternal One blessing his people with everlasting peace of mind)

"A word fitly spoken is like apples of gold in pictures of silver." (Proverbs 25:11)

Jesus Christ was sent by God, the Father, to restore the lost sheep of the House of Israel. Jesus is the Good Shepherd.
(John 10:11, 14)

"Israel was not created in order to disappear. Israel will endure and flourish. Israel is the child of hope and the home of the brave. Israel can neither be broken by adversity nor demoralized by success. Israel carries the shield of democracy, and Israel honors the sword of freedom." (United States President John F. Kennedy)

"Blessed are the eyes which see the things that you see. For I tell you, that many prophets and kings have desired to see those things which you see and have not seen them. And to hear those things which you hear and have not heard them." (Jesus Christ, the Israeli Messiah; Luke 10:23, 24)

"And the peace of God, which passes all understanding, shall keep your hearts and minds through Jesus Christ. Finally, whatsoever things are true, whatsoever things are honest, whatsoever things are just, whatsoever things are pure, whatsoever things are lovely, whatsoever things are of a good report, if there be any virtue, and if there be any praise, think on these things. And the God of peace shall be with you." (Philippians 4:7-9)

Shekinah is the manifested presence of God, indicative of everlasting peace. The glory of God being restored upon the mercy seat of the Ark of the Covenant in the House of God confirms the Lord's perpetual victory for all of his people. The presence of God, Shekinah, emanates the peace that passes all understanding (Shalom; Philippians 4:7; I Kings 8:1-11).

"My peace (everlasting peace) I give unto you. Let not your heart be troubled, neither let it be afraid." (Jesus, the Israeli Messiah; John 14:27)

"These things I have spoken unto you so that in me you might have peace (everlasting peace). In the world, you shall have tribulation. But be of good cheer. For I have overcome the world." (Jesus Christ; John 16:33)

"Greater love has no man than this, that a man lay down his life for his friends." (Jesus Christ; John 15:13)

"And I have restored unto you the years that the locust has eaten, the cankerworm, and the caterpillar, and the palmerworm by my great army which I have sent among you. And you shall eat in plenty, and be satisfied, and praise the name of the Lord, your God, who has dealt wondrously with you. And you shall know that I am in the midst of Israel forever. For in Mount Zion and in Jerusalem there is now deliverance, and in the Remnant (The Twelve Tribes of Israel) whom the Lord has called." (The God of Israel; Joel 2:25-27, 32)

"And I saw a New Heaven and a New Earth. For the first Heaven and the first Earth passed away. And I saw the Holy City, New Jerusalem, come down from God out of Heaven, prepared as a Bride (The Church of Jesus

Christ's Triumphant Appearance

Christ) adorned for her husband (Jesus Christ, the Bridegroom). I heard a great voice out of Heaven saying, 'Behold, the Temple is with men, and God will dwell with them, and they shall be his people, and he will be their God.' God wiped away all tears from their eyes. And there shall be no more death, neither sorrow, nor crying, neither shall there be any more pain. For the former things are passed away. Jesus Christ, who sat upon the Throne, said, 'Behold, I make all things new (II Corinthians 5:17). There was a pure river of water of life, clear as crystal, proceeding out of the Throne of God and the Lamb, Jesus Christ. Centered on the street of gold, there was the Tree of Life, which bare twelve various fruits. The leaves of the Tree of Life were for the healing of the nations." (Revelation 21:1-5; 22:1, 2)

"Therefore, all those who are in Christ are new creations. Old things are passed away. Behold, all things have become new." (II Corinthians 5:17)

"The Lord God of Israel is in his holy Temple. The Lord's Throne is in Heaven." (Psalm 11:4)

The God of Israel looked down at the Earth from his Throne in Heaven, and said, "I've witnessed just about enough of this!!!" And he took action.

Life is not measured by the number of breaths we take. Life is measured by the number of moments that take our breath away.

"Wherefore, the God of Israel has highly exalted Jesus Christ, and given him a name which is above every name. That at the name of Jesus every knee should bow, of things in Heaven, and things in Earth, and things under the Earth. And that every tongue should confess that Jesus Christ is Lord, to the glory of God, the Father." (Philippians 2:9-11)

In the end, only kindness matters.

Be safe, Israel,

Soaring Eagle out

ABOUT THE AUTHOR

Bruce Davidson's story, "Christ's Triumphant Appearance," initiated from his most recent pilgrimage to his heritage of Israel. In producing his epic novel, Bruce has drawn from the feel of being in the country of Israel and his understanding of the Hebrew Bible and the New Testament of the Holy Bible. He chose to write "Christ's Triumphant Appearance" in a fashion that borders on metaphorical possibilities and concrete reality.

Bruce grew up in the United States, graduating from one of the twentieth top-ranking universities in the United States, and became very closely involved with F-4 Phantom Fighter Jets in Europe while serving in the United States Air Force. It would be from Europe and the United States, all through the years, that Bruce visited Israel to be refreshed and updated firsthand of Israel's current status, that is, culturally, militarily, and diplomatically speaking. And ever since he was a boy, he has been active as an actor in the theater and on movie sets.

Bruce went to a Catholic Church, St. Dominic Catholic Church, located two blocks away from the home where he had lived in Mobile, Alabama (USA), since he was twelve years old. He feels that his exposure to the Gospel of Jesus Christ balanced and impowered his own perspective of Judaism. While he does not have an affinity for the popular label of being a Messianic Jew, Bruce firmly carries a strong, heartfelt belief that Jesus Christ is the Israeli Messiah who the Jews have been looking for so long. The life of Christ in and of itself, in Bruce's own personal opinion, exclusively, is proof enough to amply qualify, verify, and validate the evidence that demands a verdict, where the genuine Israeli Messiah is concerned.

As the author of "Christ's Triumphant Appearance," Bruce Davidson provides the reader with the very Spirit and essence of all the facets and dimensions of the Nation of Israel. This Spirit is very much embodied by the two main protagonists of the plot. The modern-day David and Bathsheba portrayed in this story are an Israeli item who would do anything for each other. There are no weak links in the chain connecting David and Bathsheba to each other and to their devotion to Israel.

At the Valley of Megiddo, the good king of Israel, Josiah, lost his life in 609 B.C. at the hands of Pharaoh Necho II of Egypt in a ferocious battle (The Battle of Megiddo), which resulted in the Israeli king forfeiting his kingdom (II Kings 23:28-30). By stark contrast, there will come a day when there would be a battle at Megiddo in the foreseeable future (The Battle of Armageddon) that will serve to result in ultimate victory for the Israelis, rather than utter defeat.

This will be the war that causes Israel's new borders to extend well beyond the boundaries of its current dimensions to spiritually embrace the entire world. This would be the war in hope of ending all wars, with the

Christ's Triumphant Appearance

intention of ushering everlasting peace into the world. The Israeli Messiah and the Millennial Temple will serve to make that peace a reality to all concerned.

"'The Lord (Jesus Christ), whom you seek, shall suddenly come to his Temple, even the Messenger of the Covenant, whom you delight in. Behold, he shall come,' says the Lord of hosts. 'But who may abide on the day of his coming? And who shall stand when he appears?'" (Malachi 3:1, 2)

Jesus Christ's Triumphant Coming (Matthew 24:27) in modern days, with a host of angels and saints right behind him, will be the special occurrence that finally compensates for all the injustice and hurt that has ever taken place in the world. Christ's swift appearance will come during the Battle of Armageddon, toward the end of the Seven Year Tribulation, on the Great and Terrible Day of the Lord, taking everyone on Earth by surprise. Only this timeless, pivotal event will guarantee that the Millennial Temple will be built on the Temple Mount in the City of David, Jerusalem, Israel. And there will not be a single person on the planet who won't be left in utter awe and wonder of Jesus coming to establish his Millennial Kingdom and government on Earth.

Make the determination for yourself of whether the story represented in "Christ's Triumphant Appearance" is completely metaphorical or an absolute reality. And ascertain if you would conclude that Camelot has a chance of being restored or is doomed to remain lost forever.

Christ's Triumphant Appearance

Christ's Triumphant Appearance

Christ's Triumphant Appearance

Made in the USA
Columbia, SC
18 November 2023